JUSTICE

First Edition December 2021 in paperback

Cover designed by Gregory Davies

ISBN: 978-0-620-97664-0

JUSTICE

Vengeance Is Mine

JACK BRUCE

Right from the first page the story involves the reader through its vivid description of the landscape and its people. The intrigue involving current international events is intertwined in the plot. Once you start the book you will not be able to put it down until the last chapter. To my mind the book would be ideally suited for a film – Gerald Hagemann, Meihuizen International

A riveting read, fast paced with an interesting take on current world events. I'm sure that anyone who keeps abreast of what is happening in the world, will share my view – Mark Nowitz, Advocate

The author weaves a complex narrative where current politics are linked into a wide array of popular conspiracy theories. A wealth of detail regarding military and intelligence matter colors the story. A highly entertaining book in the tradition of Fleming's James Bond but without the obvious and dominating hero – Martin Hess, International Executive

A page turner, chilling, topical, violent, sexy. More for a male but many women will not want to put it down until the last page – Ruth Stott, Author: *Black Mamba under my bed*

CHAPTER 1

The cold wormed its way out of the ground amidst the patches of dirty white frost and implacably forced its way through his camouflaged battledress and insulated clothing. It seeped into his torso, arms and legs until his fingers and toes went numb and he couldn't feel the tip of his nose. The cold was compounded by a slight breeze that floated rather than swept in off the arid desert. But discipline and safety ranked over comfort so he controlled the urge to shiver and glanced occasionally at his three comrades who though they did not show it, must have been as unhappy as he was. But the cold and the stillness gave him time to ruminate. His mind drifted back to the briefing in Hereford, and the arrival of the international contingent. His concentration shut out the cold and hearkened back to what had brought them to this point. And how important was it, really?

"Good day gentlemen and welcome to Operation Lockstep. I cannot emphasise enough how important the successful execution of your mission is to the Service, to the Anglo-American Special Relationship and indeed the world", his commanding officer had told him. On the screen in the spartan briefing room flashed the image of a good looking square set bearded face in a well pressed Iranian general's uniform. "Meet the man we shall call the general. He is carrying items with him which will turn life on Earth on its head. Take him down and you become the unsung heroes of the 21st Century. Fail and watch the horror unfold. "Your mission is…..". Nigel cast his mind over the briefing. Infiltrate, execute and exfiltrate. A totally deniable operation. At the end of it and the question time he had done something Nigel had never seen before. The colonel walked over, stared at him with those implacable blue eyes, the eyes that the Arabs who had known him described as burning into a man's soul, and then he curtly shook hands, with a dismissive "Good luck, they don't know it Nigel, but the world is relying on you."

The words had kept running through Major Nigel Herrington's mind like a catchy tune as they crawled forward through the scrub and over the sand onto the ridge overlooking the distant lights of the airport. Peering through the slit covers on the lenses of the night vision binoculars he could clearly read the main exit road signs marked Baghdad International Airport. The walk in from where they had left the Land Rovers had done little to warm them up. Being early morning there was no traffic on the airport road. In the distance he could hear dogs barking at one of the remote villages they had passed earlier, and nearby a cricket irritatingly chirped. "They're here, they're here." It seemed to be saying.

He wondered how the other four were coping with the tense wait as they guarded the Land Rovers anticipating their return and risked a quick glance over at the other three soldiers. Two Americans from the Seals and a South African former special forces Reconnaissance commando. They appeared to be as uncomfortable as he was. This was a really unusual short notice operation. It had been carefully pulled together with a truly international team of hand-picked professionals. Each one was a proven and experienced specialist in his field.

Lieutenant Atkinson returned Nigel's glance and gradually shifted his six foot aching body slowly away from the thorn bush. He rested his dark handsome features on his hands, adjusted the earphones in his ears and wiped some of the black camouflage cream from his chin. He hailed from Michigan, the son of a maritime mechanical engineering professor in Ann Arbor and a mother who had been a Christian Jordanian refugee. He was himself a distinguished Wolverine graduate of the Michigan University languages department before joining the US Navy. No surprise then that he was an Arabic linguist of note with a contrasting passion for the sea. By his side were two items of radio equipment. One locked onto the airport control tower frequency and the other linked to the team frequency. His ear piece on the Air Traffic Control tower frequency crackled and he nodded at Nigel.

By contrast, Lieutenant John Price hailed from New York where his wealthy family had made their fortunes in high tech and could afford to send their offspring to the best international schools. Although a technical wizard in his own right he loved the outdoors. He had attended an expensive East Coast private school and surprisingly spent an exchange term with an equally costly British public school where his quiet friendliness and willingness to adapt had earned him many friends and much respect. On graduation back in the States he had applied to Ohio State University to study law but had been attracted to the U of M law school ROTC USN Officer Training Corps by a friend at Michigan, OSU's mortal enemy. Michael Atkinson always prided himself on having attracted his buddy to "the other side" as they like to call it. After a semester at OSU he transferred to Michigan to join his friend, signed up to the ROTC and discovered that he too had a flair for languages. He sailed through the university with distinctions in both the legal arena and the language school. A smart officer in the Pentagon began to follow the career of John Price with close interest but there was competition from an unexpected source.

His family were satisfied that a combination of linguistic skills and legal training meant that he was destined for a brilliant career in their company. To their dismay he contemptuously dismissed a desk job in the family firm, to which his doting parents reckoned he was entitled, in favour of a life of adventure with the US military. His legal background and linguistic talents were nicely complemented by his explosives expertise and technology skills. They had become legendary in the Seals and a heavy burden rested on his shoulders in this operation. Whilst the others all carried their favourite weapons, a silenced M-16 or Heckler & Koch machine pistol, his kit comprised a curious instrument much like a condensed telescope with its own laser projector sight and independent power pack mounted on a small collapsible tripod. Every so often he would put his eye to the sight overlooking the deserted road and check the alignment. His only 'insurance policy', as he termed it, was a 9mm Browning automatic on his hip with one up the spout, 12 rounds to spare and two additional magazines. His rifle was back in the vehicle.

Captain Nico Bezuidenhout, the privileged son of an Afrikaans wine farming father and a British mother, born and bred in the spectacular mountainous scenery of South Africa's Cape winelands, ruminated on the curious circumstances that had brought him into the SAS. He was the oldest member of the team in his late thirties and a doctor by training. Having performed national service before graduation from the prestigious University of Stellenbosch Medical School during South Africa's counter insurgency operations against Russian, Cuban and East German forces, he had used his mother's British connections to emigrate from South Africa and join the British army, where his medical and military training had been highly valued and well employed across the world. He could have opted to stay with the vehicles but Herrington had reckoned that another pair of eyes and ears might prove handy. So here they were waiting for the target, and what he wondered was the target thinking at this exact time.

Major General Qasem Sadr gazed unseeingly out the oval window as he swallowed repeatedly to equalise the pressure in his ears. The aircraft was descending rapidly. He always grew apprehensive before landing whether at home or abroad. Even in this day and age the pressurized cabin only really took effect from about 4000 feet upwards. It made a huge difference to his ears, sinuses and peace of mind. There had been many missions in the past akin to this one which had led to the deaths of many infidels. Indeed, the roadside bomb or what the leaders of the Great Satan called the IED, had been his brainchild. And it had proven to be devastatingly effective.

But this project made the IED look like a kindergarten party by comparison. The aircraft bounced in the hot air updraft shimmering off the desert. Even in winter the warm sand acted as a latent heat generator from the previous day's sunlight. He squirmed in his seat against the reassuring tug of the seat belt and appeared to be watching the approaching lights of Baghdad with casual disinterest. In reality his mind was miles away.

Sadr could not help wondering what had brought him to this point. The meetings in Beijing and Wuhan had gone so smoothly. Almost as slick as the Chinese plans for the great new so called Silk road project or what they called the Belt Road Initiative, stretching across half the world. It crossed from Asia to Europe and North Africa taking in the Middle East and linking the whole to the PRC. When completed it would tie three continents together roping in over 50% of the world's peoples. That new highway in Pakistan had been phenomenal, and then there had been the impressive new rail terminal in Kazakhstan, plus the innovative sea port in Sri Lanka and the heavy duty bridges in Laos – all of these combining to create an interconnecting communications and trade web for the new Chinese economic empire which would inevitably contribute to the destruction of the Great Satan and its collaborative fools in Washington DC. The only fly in the ointment was the current leader of the American Great Satan but this trifling issue would soon be dealt with in a most unexpected way.

Those interminable meetings in Beijing and Shanghai had been focused on subjects as far away from his military experience as if he was walking on the moon. As a commander of the Quds special-forces in the Iranian Islamic Revolutionary Guard Corps he had been responsible for what was euphemistically termed extra-territorial and clandestine operations. For years he had been regarded by his friends, of whom he had few, and his enemies, of which he had many, to be the second most powerful man in Iran after the Ayatollah Khamenei. He was generally and rightly regarded as his right hand man and in some ways he was vastly more powerful than his nominal leader.

They had come a very long way together. In the heady days of the revolution against the Shah, he had been a young cadet in the Revolutionary Guards from a middle class family in the construction industry. His colleagues had mocked him both to his face and behind his back. At commissioning they had thrown great parties and celebrations. Not for him these frivolities. Life was as much a serious business as death. And after the revolution there had been an enormous amount of death.

His leadership qualities had soon vindicated his chosen career. In the war with Iraq he had led a company of men, rising rapidly through the ranks due to his innate ruthlessness, courageous focus and iron clad ambition. By the late 1990s he was the leader of the elite Quds. It was his persuasive arguments which had convinced the Supreme Leader, Ayatollah Ali Khamenei, to violently suppress the student rebellion before the students could organise a coup. It had been his information which the Americans had used to launch devastating attacks on the Taliban in Afghanistan. It had been his initiatives which had solidified the links between the Quds and Hezbollah in southern Lebanon. And it had been his crowning achievement to be promoted to full General by the same Supreme Leader, a post which had led to him being described by one senior CIA official as "the single most powerful operative in the Middle East today". He had become the primary leading strategist and tactician supervising Iran's determination to erode Western influence and promote Iranian power across the Middle East, and other parts of the world too. Bosnia had been a case in point.

His reverie was interrupted by the unmistakeable whine of the descending undercarriage and its reassuring thump as the wheels locked into place. In a few minutes, once safely on the ground, he would be met by his Iraqi counterparts and the first part of the plot would begin to take shape. He cast a wary glance at the luggage bin above him and thought of the velvet lined suitcase with the red and blue vials. This new operation was so brilliant and far reaching that it boggled the mind. It even overawed his mind. He had never in his wildest dreams ever dared to contemplate doing anything on such a grand scale before. And it was ingenious in its simplicity.

The time spent with his Chinese intelligence liaison officer in the BSL Level 4 biological warfare research establishment in Wuhan had been shocking and daunting, but rewarding. His hosts had shown him several men and women sentenced to death and thus regarded as acceptable to be used as guinea pigs for the Coronavirus infection. He had dispassionately observed the condemned men and women drowning in their own body fluids as the alveoli of their lungs irretrievably filled with discharges and they began to die, kicking and belting out the unmistakeable machine gun like staccato death rattle.

His hosts had explained to him that the first virus had been purchased from the US Army Medical Command installation at Fort Detrick courtesy of the Obama administration at the behest of none other than the US Secretary of State. The second had been filched from the Canadian BSL Level 4 facility in Winnipeg courtesy of a cooperative and greedy Harvard professor. Even New Zealand, Australia and France had been involved in the original research but they had all backed off. How ironic was it that the original R&D had been conducted at the University of North Carolina. But now the PRC had taken the process light years beyond the initial programs.

Both strains had been horrifically weaponized in the Chinese facility which had ironically been established with the able assistance of the World Health Organization. He was still perplexed by the strange details of some of the information they had shared with him. Contributions for the R&D had allegedly come from the US National Institute of Health, no less, and even from one of the wealthiest private individuals in the world. Why? It still slightly troubled him, this weird American connection. He fleetingly wondered if he was being used as the tool in something bigger but dismissed the thought with contempt when he contemplated the size of the operation.

In Wuhan PRC scientists had injected the virus with an HIV transmission spike and two SARS insertions. The red one was absolutely lethal and the blue one was only slightly less so. Once released he had been warned that both strains could function in tandem and mutate. The Chinese had used the enigmatic term "Gain of Function" in describing what they had done to the virus. It seemed to mean that the bug would intensify its lethality with constant mutation making a vaccine all but impossible and confounding western scientists seeking a cure. Once in Baghdad Sadr would arrange for the Iraqi intelligence services to infiltrate the infection into refugees heading for Europe. He was confident that the pliant EU and guilt riddled German leader, Angela Merkel, would not hesitate to let them in, and once in, it was only a matter of time before the contagion would spread across Europe to central America and into the South American refugees heading for the Great Satan. The time of reckoning was not far off now, and miracle of miracles, he was to be the instrument of retribution.

And there was one other matter which had been troubling him since his return from the PRC. When he had been waiting outside the conference room to see his intelligence counterpart at his palatial offices in Beijing, he had been astonished to watch a small delegation of well-known powerful international merchant bankers leaving just before he was ushered into the esteemed presence. Curious but cautious he reckoned discretion was the better option but it continued to perplex him as he could not help but overhear the dialogue when they were being ushered down the corridor. His impression had been that they knew what was coming. Not only that they knew what was coming but that they had been intimately involved in the planning. There had been references to 911, to monstrous market volatility, to electronic cashless societies, DNA nano trackers and population reduction – all matters that his Chinese colleague had touched on. He had not dared to enquire further but he couldn't help wondering if something very much bigger than even his determination to take down the Great Satan and teach those dogs in Washington a lesson they would never forget, went very much further than even he had contemplated.

The aircraft touched down with a gentle almost imperceptible bump and taxied towards the terminal building. It looked very cold and unwelcoming. In the distance by the dim lights of the terminal building he could see a convoy of cars approaching across the airfield which was shrouded in a light mist.

His musing was interrupted by the steward. "They are ready for you. Sir," he said respectfully with a slight incline of the head. The steward pressed the release catch on the luggage bin above Sadr and reached up for the velvet lined briefcase but his wrist was stopped half way into the bin with a vice like grip. Startled he looked at the Iranian general in fear.

"Leave it," Sadr snapped at him. "I can take that one myself." He released the anxious steward and gently removed his hand luggage. Even at night the pilot was taking no chances and had parked well away from the terminal buildings. Outside the small line of cars awaited him with their engines running in the subdued lighting at the bottom of the stairs. The delegation wasted no time on pleasantries in the cold. He was ushered into the heated interior of the Toyota Land Cruiser without ceremony and the convoy swept towards the gates.

CHAPTER 2

Nigel Herrington had seen the gesture by Lieutenant Atkinson signifying that the aircraft was coming in to land. All four men watched the distant lights descend towards the ground. A slight ground mist had begun to swirl over the city and the airfield. It worried Herrington. Could such a simple unexpected atmospheric innovation ruin a crucial mission? Atkinson followed the cryptic dialogue between the pilot and the Air Traffic Control tower. Assured that the aircraft had landed he pushed a scanner switch on the radio monitor and changed frequency to the cars in the convoy. The initial laconic dialogue involved confirming contact and the air went silent for a few minutes.

John Price was watching him intently. "Ready for predation, Mike?" he muttered laconically.

"Ok, John," Atkinson muttered. His colleague glanced through the laser beam range finder and nodded. He then checked the transmitter to the large drones circling invisibly and silently some 30 000 feet above the sleeping city. A green light responded showing that the main attack drone was locked onto the laser. He leaned over to Herrington and smiled. "Nigel, it's not a US Predator tonight. You might be proud to know she's one of yours, a brand spanking new British MQ-9B Sky Guardian Protector out of the RAF base at Akrotiri in Cyprus. Trust your boys are on the ball tonight, eh!"

Herrington resisted the urge to laugh. So that's why he was here.

As the convoy moved out of the airport precincts the drivers of the three vehicles checked with each other that all was in order. From where they lay the team could now see the headlights emerging in the swirling mist through the gates. Price pressed the release switch and locked the laser onto the middle vehicle. The range finder fired a radio signal to the drone providing instant satellite co-ordinates, velocity and direction of the car and a Sensor Operator sitting comfortably before a massive console of television screens and computers at RAF Waddington in England cross-checked the data link with the computer controlled guided missile on board the Protector. He glanced at the Mission Intelligence Co-ordinators who also checked the data read outs and nodded curtly. The pilot said in a loud voice audible to all at the console. "Target coordinates locked in. Green for Go, Permission to Fire, Sir?" He almost added the "Sir" bit as an afterthought but nobody noticed.

The Senior Mission Intelligence Co-ordinator nodded imperceptibly as if to convince himself of what he was about to approve and said in a no nonsense clipped upper class British accent, "Green for Go. Permission to fire, Launch one. "Fire."

With a touch of nervousness the pilot repeated, "Permission to fire, firing one." The firing signal took 1,2 seconds to travel to the relay satellite in low Earth orbit above the Middle East and back again to the receiver on board the Protector. The AGM-114 air to ground missile streaked out of its wing pod mounting at 30 000 feet above the city. As it released the weapon the Protector, accompanied by its duplicate backup shadow, and both controlled from the HQ thousands of miles away in England, well within its 42 hour flying limits, lazily swung away from the target and obediently headed for its RAF base in Cyprus.

The AGM-114 Hellfire air to ground missile was originally designed by Lockheed Martin, Boeing and later Northrup Grumman in an anti-armour role. More recent models had been carefully modified for precision drone strikes against other target types. In its earlier versions the Hellfire was intended as a fire and forget missile which had culminated in the emergence of the colloquial name – Hellfire. This particular Hellfire was an extremely sophisticated version being both radar and laser guided which meant that the odds on missing the moving target were effectively zero and it was well within its 11 km range. Had it been snowing with total whiteout and gale force winds, the missile, weighing roughly 47 kg including a 9 kg explosive warhead and moving faster than a supersonic rifle bullet, would still have identified and hit its target with the same unerring accuracy.

The only controversial aspect of this missile might have been its thermobaric charge, euphemistically described by the British Ministry of Defence as an "enhanced blast weapon". These weapons had been criticized in the corridors of power in the United Nations and certain other non-governmental human rights organizations associated with the advancement and protection of human rights. They were considered inhuman. They contained a substantial charge of fuel designed to ignite and mix with oxygen in the ambient atmosphere thereby producing a prolonged explosion of greatly enhanced intensity. The US design was ironically the refinement of an earlier Soviet invention. It had been employed with devastating effect in the massive labyrinth cave systems of Afghanistan against the Taliban after the events of 911. Those not killed by the concussion from the blast were literally asphyxiated when the clouds of powdered fuel ignited generating successive waves of heat and pressure throughout the caverns and adjacent tunnels using up the oxygen inside. It was known that part of Soviet warfighting doctrine included the use of thermobaric artillery against enemy missile sites prior to armoured tank attacks and the term itself was derived from the Russian word "termobaricheskiy".

The only confirmation to the men on the ground that the lethal "package" was actually on its way was when the slight beeping noise on the laser range finder changed to a high pitched whine and the green light started flashing indicating the cameras were running. Price looked at Nigel and nodded, but still no one moved. The eyes of the two men flickered from the flashing green light to the slight dust trail of the departing convoy of vehicles. The ground mist seemed to be thickening and swirled over the land snaking between the buildings in the background as the convoy was accelerating.

Snug in his car and feeling secure in the accelerating motorcade al-Sadr sank back into the seat and clutched the briefcase firmly in his hands on his lap. This was the part of travelling that he loathed the most when he was at his greatest risk from dissident elements on the ground. Still it had not been a bad flight and he had used the time to reflect on his mission. The weather outside looked miserable. There were no stars to be seen and the ground fog was thickening, it would make for a safer drive he reassured himself and that was the last thought that ever went through his mind.

The Hellfire missile arrived silently and invisibly ahead of the noise of its trajectory and slammed into the roof of the car with a spectacular explosion immolating the occupants in a fireball that leaped 60 feet into the air and converted what had been a luxury 4x4 into little more than molten nuts and bolts. The driver of the front escort vehicle felt his car kicked up through the air and catapulted nose and tail down the road like a toy. The rear escort vehicle was too close behind the target and drove through the wreckage of the car in front. The heat of the incinerated remnants burst all four tyres before the petrol tank exploded in the searing fireball killing all the occupants and adding to the inferno already spewing its detritus across the Baghdad highway.

The entire episode was caught on film and transmitted instantaneously to the team at RAF Waddington. The pilot of the drone saw the message flash up on the console confirming the destruction of the target. He nodded to the Mission Control officer who showed a rare degree of emotion by patting him on the shoulder and muttering softly, "Well done. Thank you."

So saying he picked up the direct phone link to the Pentagon but before he could report anything his American colleague was overheard to say with a broad Texan drawl, "I owe you a drink at the Rag for this one, buddy. Great work. You Brits sure do things in grand style. Now if you don't mind I must tell the boss, Good night." But the boss already knew all about it.

CHAPTER 3

Deep in the bowels of the White House western wing lies the Situation Room, a five and a half thousand square foot Intelligence Management Centre run by National Security Council staff on a 24/7 basis. It was the room from which the president's predecessor had watched the May 1st 2011 US Special Forces raid on Osama bin Laden's compound via a live feed from a drone flying above the scene of the action. Although termed the Situation Room the complex actually comprises several rooms including a conference centre, a small theatre like room for watching live feeds and presentations and arguably one of the, if not the, most sophisticated and advanced communications centre on the planet.

It was to this room that the president had been ushered half an hour before al-Sadr's aircraft had been scheduled to touch down. Dressed in casual slacks and an open necked shirt with a cashmere sweater draped over his shoulders and clutching a cup of coffee in one hand with a sheaf of documents in the other, he had left his second floor bedroom for the operations centre to watch the action live, as had his predecessor. Sitting with him was the vice president, the Director of Central Intelligence, the Secretary of State, the Secretary of Defence and the Brigadier General serving as the Deputy Commander of the Special Forces.

Sitting in an adjacent room watching on a separate monitor was the Deputy National Security Adviser, the chairman of the Joint Chiefs of Staff, and a motley collection of security and intelligence personnel. The screen they had been watching was a split image from the circling Global Hawk above and the cameras on the ground superintended by the international Special Forces team.

It had been explained to the president many times that the sanctioning of assassinations was a unique tool of foreign policy only to be considered in the direst of circumstances, when all other options were off the table. The sheaf of papers in the president's hand more than justified the drastic measures in the opinions of all the people in the two rooms. Al-Sadr had been tracked for years by various counter intelligence teams from a variety of countries. It was reckoned they knew more about him and his movements than he did himself. The body count for which he was personally accountable dwarfed the imagination. But the lights had only begun to burn in the corridors of power after his visit to Beijing and Wuhan against the background of the knowledge that he had been endowed with a biological warfare weapon that would change the world and fundamentally alter the balance of global economic power. Although the jury was still out on who exactly was behind the ploy there was no doubt that international relations had entered a new and spectacularly dangerous phase following Al-Sadr's China meetings and his return to Iran.

His decision to visit Baghdad and distribute the infections had sealed his death warrant and so there was a sigh of eminent if grim satisfaction across the Situation Room as his car was reduced to a hulk of molten smoking metal. Unlike the operation against Osama bin Laden, there were no cheers or celebrations.

The president sat quietly for a moment looking at the floor as if lost in thought. He then slowly stood up and glancing round the room said in an uncharacteristically soft commanding voice, "Well done to all concerned, thank you very much, but I have a strange feeling this is not the end." So saying he left the group at the table and, thanking certain individual members of his team, motioned to the Director of Central Intelligence. They walked slowly back to his own private quarters. It was his impression that the powers behind this operation had many strings to their bows. Already there were rumours that a serious infection had escaped or been leaked from the bio-warfare labs complex in Wuhan but the World Health Organization seemed to be down playing the threat.

The DCIA walked alongside her boss but knew better than to say anything. The time for discussion would come when it suited the president. Sure enough half way down the corridor he stopped. Looking the DCIA straight in the eye the president said softly, "It's a multipronged attack. One head of the Hydra has been cut off but there is more to come. Check out this New Year's report from Wuhan and keep me posted. We thought that HIV was bad and SARS and MERS were portents of things to come but something tells me intuitively this thing now is in a league of its own. I don't trust WHO, and I'm not sure that I can even trust some of our own so called medical experts on this. As we discussed before, I have to work with the human resources I've inherited and it's a challenge, believe me, it's a real challenge. That was impressive tonight but this is not the end. Those Brits are really good men." Glancing up at a painting from 1776 he said softly, "Glad they're on our side this time." He ran his fingers through the thick shock of blond hair and repeated, "Trust me, no way is this the end. Machiavelli would have had a field day with what's coming, I think. Make sure the ground team are extracted safely and thank our cousins across the water. Keep me and the vice president up to speed. PRC trade deal, failed impeachment and an election round the corner. No, there is much more to this," he almost seemed to be speaking to himself as he walked away from the Director of the CIA.

The men on the ground in the desert had no idea what was happening across the other side of the world in the White House but they were elated if not a little stunned at the results of their handiwork. No sooner was the car and its contents converted into a small version of Dante's inferno than they had switched off their radios and tracker, packed up their gear and trekked back across the scrub desert in a staggered leap frog jog ensuring that there were no tails following them to the waiting Land Rovers. In the distant houses all hell broke loose with barking dogs and lights coming on in several cottages, but the denizens of Baghdad had long ago learned that loud noises were best met with feigned ignorance and real insouciance. They had learned the very hard way that curiosity killed much more than the cat.

Once at the RV point the special forces team found that their colleagues had already removed the camouflage netting and the engines were running to warm them up and make a rapid exit. The assassination team clambered aboard without any discussions and strapped down the equipment. Using NVGs the vehicles pulled on to a secondary road and headed for the overnight Lie Up Point

(LUP) before proceeding to the nearby pick up point with the Hercules transport aircraft

As they drove a number of MREs were removed, opened up and hungrily consumed with bottled mineral water boosted by electrolytes. Meals Ready to eat were an ingenious American invention which provided hot food on a chemical reaction triggered by the removal of the cover. This was not merely a nice-to-have but an essential measure. The immediate after shock of an operation such as the dramatic scene they had just witnessed, was instant hunger and intense thirst.

Although there had been no actual shooting and no 'contact' as such, the high stress of the deployment, wait and execution took an enormous toll on the human body. Nourishment was the order of the day coupled with stimulants to maintain alertness and awareness. The refreshment was particularly welcome as the weather had turned even colder with the approach of first light and what had been a pesky ground mist turned into a gentle rain and then into a freezing sleet. Although unpleasant conditions in which to drive, the change in the weather was a welcome addition to their concealment. If light snow fell later in the day it would cover their tracks on the mud roads.

Operational discipline dictated silence involving what had just happened. Nobody spoke about it but Captain Stewart McKenzie, the driver of the lead vehicle, kept referring to the encrypted live down time satellite image on his hand held computer. Constantly tracking their progress and showing vehicle movement in their vicinity within a 5 km to 10 km radius. Nonetheless, everyone kept a constant all round lookout for signs of unwelcome life in the form of stray animals, vehicles or people. The same SATNAV tracker kept British Forces Cyprus and the SAS HQ in Hereford, England, abreast of their progress without requiring direct dialogue or communication.

McKenzie was a taciturn, tough and highly intelligent Scot from Edinburgh with a genius for anything mechanical who had gravitated from the Guards regiment to the SAS like a duck to water. A graduate in history from the Heriot Watt University within the shadow of Edinburgh Castle he had been attracted to the army by the famous week long Edinburgh military tattoo with its glitz and glamour. His recruitment had almost been unique in the annals of British military history. After the final show on the Edinburgh Castle forecourt one year he had walked up to the Regt HQ and asked to speak with the Castle commander. The duty sentry was about to send him off with a flea in his ear but as luck would have it the Castle Commanding Officer was walking past at the time and heard the exchange.

He stopped and asked what exactly McKenzie wanted. On being told he wished to join the army he carefully looked him up and down and decided that he liked what he saw. A few minutes later McKenzie was unbelievably in the commander's quarters overlooking the lights of Edinburgh with an unsolicited but very welcome sherry thrust into his hand. Colonel Roderick McIntyre was a shrewd judge of character. Having sized McKenzie up and elicited all the relevant information he required on his background, schooling, university and extra mural mountain climbing activities. McIntyre gave him a name and phone number. In three months McKenzie was not only in the British army but enjoying the almost unparalleled benefit of a powerful and well connected mentor and ally.

Next to McKenzie sat his co-driver Sergeant Julian Gough. As McKenzie was passionate about cars and climbing so Gough was passionate about diving, canoeing and all types of naval equipment and hardware. Starting as a schoolboy in Canada and learning the silhouettes of British and German ships and aircraft from WWII he had gravitated to more modern kit and equipment. Born of British parents in Windsor, Ontario, he had sought to emulate his father and join the Royal Navy. From the basic training he had gravitated to a keen interest in Special Forces and it was only a matter of time before he had been recommended for the Special Boat Service. The training had been tough and the legendary selection process even tougher but he had excelled at every challenge placed before him. He had been "volunteered" for the mission as he had never been to Iraq and he spoke passable Arabic thanks to the British army's Defence Centre for Languages and Culture at the Shrivenham Defence Academy. His job was to monitor Iraqi security forces radio channels and report any relevant transmissions to the team. He also assisted McKenzie with the satellite map reading and kept a plot of where they were on a laminated map.

The first part of the journey took them smoothly through built up areas and onto a deserted main highway heading away from Baghdad towards a remote LUP for the day not far from the intended landing zone. There were thankfully no curious onlookers or at least none that they had seen and once out into the country the risk of traffic was slight. At one stage they saw the lights of an approaching bus but pulled off the road into the shadows and allowed it to pass.

CHAPTER 4

As had been carefully planned they reached their first and only LUP well before the sun's first pale rays spread across the empty cold horizon. It was a deserted farm house or so they thought, and had been recommended by Hereford based on satellite and ground intelligence. The standard operating procedure was for the little convoy to pull off well before reaching the objective so that a fighting reconnaissance patrol could move forward on foot to explore the site and check out the local terrain. One vehicle would also make a broad sweeping circle of the fake LUP and the real LUP. In the process fields of fire would be established, probable axes of enemy advance pinpointed, avenues of fighting withdrawal and silent retreat worked out and interlocking fields of fire established.

Nigel Herrington detailed Gough and Atkinson from the second vehicle to make the reconnaissance. Whilst the reconnaissance was underway the team in the waiting Land Rovers constructed the false LUP. This was standard practice but under certain conditions of high risk it was a sensible precaution. They were away for 20 minutes. Once the all clear was given with the completion of the preliminary preparations they moved into the courtyard and took shelter in the abandoned cottage after securing the camouflage netting over the vehicles. With LUPs there was no room for error and every aspect had to be thoroughly and efficiently covered.

A priority was the first tea brew up. The Americans were slightly bewildered by the apparently sacred importance of the first cup of tea on which the Brits always insisted but it soon dawned on them that this was as much a critical standard operating procedure as the science that went into the creation of the LUP. They would have preferred coffee but for the moment tea it had to be. After more MREs had been produced and the first tea round consumed they got down to the customary procedure of cleaning and checking weapons, studying maps, listening out for local radio traffic, rotating the sentries and scrutinizing the SATNAV comms. In this regard fresh satellite photographs transmitted to them from the US via the UK gave detailed 24 hour impressions of the immediate terrain in their vicinity and was more grist to the intelligence mill for the day and night ahead.

Sergeant David Jenkins, a young Royal Marine Commando from London, who had been driving the second vehicle and who had been brought on the mission because of his knowledge of the Middle East and Iraq in particular, took the first watch. His listening post was complemented by RSM Landon Davies, a former member of the RAF regiment seconded to the team for the essential liaison with the Hercules C-130 collecting them the following night. Davies was also fluent in Arabic but he carried an extra asset. He not only spoke Farsi and Persian but could dress, act and conduct himself exactly like an Arab. Born of British parents in the Oman with Arab ancestry, during the heady days of the Dhofari rebellion which had brought the recently deceased Sultan Quaboos to the throne after deposing his tyrannical father, he had been named after the British officer responsible for the coup which had engineered the change.

The day passed peacefully enough. Because of the temperatures they switched sentries every hour. In colder conditions they would have rotated sentries every 20 minutes. Every two hours they would run the vehicles for 5 minutes. There had been times during the day when a wandering goat-herder looked as though he might venture closer but nothing had happened. The goats had approached the cottage and then swerved away across the hillside. They took the watches in silent relays and learned from the BBC World Service that the US president was immensely grateful for what they had accomplished. They were a bit miffed that the mission had been portrayed as an all American operation but then Uncle Sam had been footing the entire bill and they were not yet out of harm's way. If they could hear the BBC so could the enemy.

At about midnight they moved silently out and dismantled the fake LUP. Herrington, Price, Davies and Bezuidenhout took the lead vehicle with Herrington driving. Gough, Atkinson, Jenkins and McKenzie took the second vehicle with Gough driving. They pulled out onto the main road at 23h00 rightly assuming there would be minimal traffic. The RV point was two hours away although the thin covering of the snow slowed them down slightly. No matter, the Hercules would know exactly where they were as would their officers in Akrotiri and Hereford.

The airstrip was a little known old disused dirt runway built by the British during WWII as an emergency landing zone for flights between the Gulf and Baghdad. In the liberation war against Saddam Hussein the Americans had been briefed on it and resuscitated the place for similar emergencies. It lay in a shallow wadi or valley on the top of a ridge well away from the main road. They were about an hour from their objective when the lead vehicle slowed to a stop. There was a long pause while Herrington used his binocular night vision equipment to stare intently at something lying in the road. Herrington pulled to the left and waved Gough to pull up beside him. The men in the second vehicle could hear McKenzie cocking the 7.62 GPMG mounted on the back of the Land Rover followed by the unmistakeable double click of Price and Bezuidenhout's weapons. Herrington silently pointed. Gough stared through his NVGs and spotted an object lying in the road. It looked like a bundle of abandoned clothing. While Herrington's men concentrated on the bundle the others adopted a 360' defensive attitude and Jenkins could be heard cocking his GPMG as well.

Herrington looked inquisitively at his colleagues, "Dead animal? No, but seems to be clothing. Dead body, maybe? Ambush? What do you make of it," he signalled to Gough.

Gough reckoned it was a body. "Only one way to find out and the clock's a ticking." Herrington waved him forward and ordered Price to follow behind.

The two men ran forward then crouched covering each other as they leapfrogged towards the bundle. The others watched the perimeter. Herrington was heard to mutter, "I don't bloody like this." A minute or two ticked by and Gough came back at a run.

"It's a woman boss, and she's very badly injured. She seems to have been hit by a car. Lots of blood and unconscious. We need the doc," Herrington beckoned to Bezuidenhout who ran forward. He bent over the bundle and pulled his emergency medical kit from the webbing on his back. After a tense three minutes he was back.

"It's a woman all right, and she's in shocking shape. Seems to have been hit by something. If we leave her here she'll die. Don't know what the bloody hell she'd be doing out here." He looked at Herrington for guidance. Herrington looked very worried. There was a brief and awkward silence. Then he added, "Three choices boss, Leave her to die, kill her now or take her with us, what's it gonna be?"

"Nick this is bollocks. It's bizarre. I say we leave her here and get moving, it's none of our business."

Price had left her and returned. He looked distressed at Herrington's decision. "Sir, I think you should take a look at her, just a minute Sir, that's all and then we can go." Herrington nodded reluctantly and ran forward. The delay was seriously worrying him. He ran up to the body and stared at her face. What he saw horrified him. She had been an extremely beautiful girl before the truck or car or whatever had hit her. It shocked him, that even through the blood on her face and from the cuts on her skull he could see that this was an exceptional young woman, probably in her twenties. She might have made the cover on Vogue if she had been a continental. Her breathing was laboured. There was a slight groaning from her chest. He put his head down and listened as she rasped on the inhalation. None of this really added up. He sensed rather than heard Bezuidenhout next to him.

He stared at Bezuidenhout inquisitively. "Your call Nick. Can you perhaps save her if we load her up and take her along? Frankly I still think its madness but your expert opinion as a doc please?" Bezuidenhout chewed the knuckle of his right hand.

"If we take her with us I can work on her on the plane. They will have a full emergency medical kit on board. If we leave her she's a goner. Then they can use her for propaganda purposes against us. Boss, it's a tough one but I reckon we should load her and get the hell out of here. Had a similar situation in Angola once with a Portuguese farmer's daughter, we managed to save her, then. And now, well Sir, I reckon history might repeat itself. We can also find out whom, why and when."

Herrington glared at him, hesitated a second and then waved Price back. Price looked stressed. He coughed nervously and said in a low voice, "Sir, Akrotiri want to know why we have stopped. They warn us that Heron is on schedule. We still have to lay out the infrared lights."

Herrington took a snap decision. "OK. You and Julian load her onto the stretcher in the second car and move." Price ran back to the vehicles which had moved in closer and retrieved a collapsible canvas stretcher. The girl should have been a feather weight given her build and size but she seemed slightly heavier. No one paid much attention. She groaned as they picked her up and gently placed her on the stretcher. Every nerve and fibre in Herrington's body told him this was wrong but if she died and he knew she would die, it would haunt him for the rest of his life, short or long.

Bezuidenhout stayed in the second vehicle with her but dared not try any procedures until they were safely in the aircraft. Atkinson joined the lead vehicle. He could hear Davies now talking to the Hercules. "Heron, Heron, Heron – Green, Green, Green". The pilot of the Hercules sent back a double click. There was a brief silence and then another double click.

They made a cautious approach to the airfield but the satellite had shown them it was all clear. Price and Atkinson laid out the infra-red lights on the landing strip whilst Davies gave wind speed, direction and QNH. Heron acknowledged and almost before they knew it the massive dark shape swooped almost silently onto the old runway touching down in a monstrous cloud of flying snow and dust. No sooner was she on the ground and turning than the ramp whined down and without a word of command the second Land Rover with the stretcher swept up into the aircraft. Herrington was driving down the runway collecting the infrared strobes. Only four were needed to guide the pilot for the take off.

He swung the car round and headed at speed back towards the Hercules. He could already hear the pilots starting to increase the engine power preparatory to the take-off run. He could barely make out the subdued RAF roundels on the stealth radar absorbing paint when there was a crackle of transmission static followed by the doc's urgent voice on the emergency net. At the same time he was puzzled to notice a peculiar red glow through the cockpit windows from the rear of the aircraft.

On board, Dr Bezuidenhout was already cutting away the injured girl's garments. He had checked her upper torso and thought he could identify several broken ribs, which might explain the possible lung damage. Now he sliced through her burka with a pair of razor surgical scissors and peeled it right back. For a split second he stared transfixed at the apparatus hanging between the girl's legs. Time seemed to stand still. Then realization dawned and he overcame his paralysis, grabbing the hand held emergency radio which transmitted to the other vehicle and the pilots, he stabbed the transmit button. He shouted, "There's an IED. IED, she has an IED on her."

CHAPTER 5

Herrington watched the red glow supplanted by a brilliant white flash and the aircraft blew up before his very eyes in a gigantic fireball climbing 100 feet into the air. There was an awesome dull booming noise and all that was left appeared to be a gigantic bonfire in the desert. Price and Atkinson were as stunned as Herrington, but Davies, whose job it was to collect the infra- red strobes, was the first to recover. He leaned over and clapping Herrington on the back, shouted, "Go Sir, go like the clappers. Nick said something about an IED. The girl was booby trapped. Maybe for us, maybe someone else. But we must get out of here and fast, Sir. Akrotiri can arrange an alternative pick up."

Herrington knew Davies was right. He had never seen a situation change so swiftly. One moment they were preparing to be airborne off to Cyprus and then home to the UK and the next moment more than half of their team were dead, their transport gone and isolated in the middle of a hostile desert. But he still wanted to drive up to the inferno to see if he could help.

Davies could see the awful expression on his face. With an effort Herrington pulled himself together. "Sir, they're all dead. They are dead. Nothing to do here, Sir. New ball game now, Sir. We must leave. They will be swarming over this place in less than an hour. Take them several hours to know that one of the cars got away."

Herrington wanted to vomit. He looked at Davies, Price and Atkinson in abject despair. Price leaned forward and patted him on the back. "Davies is right Sir, they are all gone. We must get away from here pronto. Give me the wheel, Atkinson can manage the GPMG, and Davies will contact Akrotiri. It's not your fault Sir. It's no one's fault. These things just happen, I guess." He sounded as though he was trying to reassure himself.

Herrington swapped seats with Price and grabbed the SatNav set. Leaning over he said to Price. "Stick to the road for at least forty five minutes. It will take Baghdad some time to work out what's actually happened and while they do we can avoid leaving tracks and head at speed along the road." Without taking his eyes off the road Price nodded. Then adding as an afterthought, "Give it, oh, say 40 minutes, then swing hard southwards away from the road we will find a place to make an LUP."

They swung the Land Rover in a generally Western direction towards the Jordanian border and away from the inferno. As they did so there was a crackle of static on the SatNav/radio coms set. Akrotiri were asking what had just happened. Davies described the trend of events to them. On Cyprus there was a degree of shock and dismay but the details were discussed with Hereford and Northwood. They advised a course for the next LSRV with an LUP somewhere in between which would put them 200 clicks from their present position and within 300 clicks of the Jordanian border as Herrington had expected. The best plan was for a Chinook helicopter to pick them up. Their optimal bet was to parallel Highway 1 between Baghdad and Amman but avoiding the main road. There were secondary trails aplenty and with the aid of the SatNav they could make for an RV in the vicinity of the town of Al Rutbah.

Once Herrington had recovered from the initial shock his training kicked in. Checking that they were all physically unharmed he leaned over took the SatNav from Davies and started to chart a path parallel to but not within sight of the highway to the Jordanian border. For the first twenty minutes all went well. They made good speed without the need for NVGs. The road was a well illuminated dual carriageway with what amounted to a massive ditch and a chain link fence separating the highway from the surrounding countryside. Traffic obviously moved at speed along this highway and the fence would prevent wandering animals from straying onto the highway whilst the ditch ensured rapid drainage after heavy rainfalls or melting snow. But these factors meant that if they encountered a road block ahead they would be effectively trapped. The ditch would have to be shovelled in and Price would need to usefully employ his explosive expertise to quickly blow a hole in the fence.

Herrington reckoned it might be better to deviate from the highway sooner rather than later and kept a close eye on the ditch and the fence until they encountered a maintenance depot with a bridge over the ditch and a gate in the fence.

"Pull off here," he said peremptorily to Price. "Sooner we are off here the better. Don't fancy being caught like rats in a trap. Mike, grab the cutters and cut open that padlocked gate. Shut them behind us."

Price swung the Land Rover off the road and pulled up in

front of the gate. Atkinson was already off the back and looking for the bolt cutters. It took him a minute to cut the padlocked gate and open them. The move was none too soon as they saw oncoming headlights in the distance. They drove through and Price slipped on his Night Vision Goggles. Progress was now painfully slow. The desert stretched out ahead of them but comprised scrub shrubs and occasional bushes. They drove like this for over an hour.

Price was using NVGs for the driving and found it a challenge to concentrate. The green glowing light gave little depth perception and seemed to be drilling into his brain. It was bad enough driving under these conditions at the best of times. When super stressed the impact was intensified. Usually when this happened drivers were rotated but such was the demand for speed and distance from the site of the earlier LSRV they reckoned Price should keep going as long as he could. After two hours Price called for a stop. They reluctantly agreed, and after a five minute delay to ease springs and allow Price to get his eyesight adjusted from the NVGs to normal night vision, they pressed on. Atkinson took the wheel. Herrington used a single lens scope to watch the road ahead and they continued to move slowly across the desert.

Eventually one and a half hours before sunrise it was decided to find a small wadi or a sandy depression where they could construct a reasonably concealed LUP and obtain some badly needed rest throughout the daylight hours. There was a marked scarcity of such formations. Herrington pulled a tarpaulin over his head and with the assistance of a torch carefully studied the maps and the SatNav with the greatest precision. The only places that he could find all looked as if they contained water or had rural habitation nearby, none of which were suitable for concealment and cover.

Eventually he spotted exactly what he had in mind. A miniature canyon or wadi which showed no water and appeared to be at least 5 km from the nearest habitation. There was one challenge. It would give them half an hour to set up the LUP before sunrise which was cutting it a bit fine.

Fields of fire would have to be identified, infiltration and exfiltration routes established, the vehicle thoroughly checked mechanically and then camouflaged but in such a way that the netting could be instantly discarded and they could drive out within seconds if need be, Satellite burst signals communications with Akrotiri had to be created and a comprehensive report on the disastrous air extraction from the disused WWII British airstrip would be required. In return they would be provided with the latest information on Iraqi air and ground forces locations and the latest troop movements. It was also imperative that they eat and find a suitable place to defecate. If the ground was soft enough the latter would be inconspicuously shovelled away and concealed. But if they were on rocky soil even their own physical detritus had to be taken with them. Disgusting as it sounded there were ways and means of providing analytical trackers on human detritus which could lead to serious consequences if they were apprehended and had killed enemy personnel into the bargain.

They pressed on slowly towards the designated LUP point until the SatNav confirmed that they were virtually on top of it. The journey had been marked by a tardy progression across the desert with a break every 500 m or so where they could stop and listen checking out the surrounding terrain and then moving on again. All of them took turns at driving except Herrington who constantly checked the SatNav and the maps whilst occasionally munching on a Mars bar. Smoking was out of the question. A drag on a fag could be seen 4 km away. The worst part of it was the never ending cold although they had brought Arctic gear with them for just such an exigency. In an enclosed vehicle without heating it would have been bad enough, but in an open vehicle with a wind chill factor it was dreadful.

Even with the NVGs and four pairs of eyes peering round them they could not see the wadi. Herrington suggested they spread out 100 m from the vehicle walking slowly outwards. His concern was twofold – either the wadi had been washed away or filled in or it was so well concealed they might fall into it. It was Davies who found it, not 40 m from where they had stopped and he very nearly fulfilled Herrington's second anxiety. There was a line of scrub across the top of the wadi which concealed a 12 foot drop down almost sheer sides into the trench. It was perfect concealment for the occasion but with two disadvantages which not been apparent on the SatNav – there was only one point where the vehicle could enter if they moved some rocks, which meant that there was no back door and there appeared to be a small spring but not a water supply of any significance which is why it had not been calibrated on the maps. Having no backdoor was a serious defect but the presence of water was even more worrying. Water meant animals and animals could mean humans and humans meant compromise and trouble.

Atkinson stayed with the vehicle and the three of them studied the wadi. It was Price who articulated their concerns. "Not the most perfect LUP Sir, but we don't have time to look for another one. Sun will be brightening the horizon in 20 minutes. So….. I guess this had better be it."

Herrington looked inquisitively at Price. "What do you think John? We've run out of time and options. Bad planning on my part."

Price replaced the worried frown on his face with a grim smile. "Sir, you did your best and frankly this is about as good as it gets round here. I mean, hell, we had trouble finding it ourselves, admittedly at night and it seems well concealed. I can hear water trickling down there which is a curse and a boon. We always need water. Let's go for it. As you say, Sir, we are out of options."

They returned to the vehicle and Davies drove them down into the wadi which they were able to enter after rolling a number of rocks out of the way. They now had ten minutes of darkness before first light which was patently not enough. Whilst Herrington and Price kept watch Atkinson and Davies prepared the LUP but the first streaks of a cold grey dawn were already sneaking into the night sky when they had finished. Still the setting seemed suitably desolate and isolated and once they had allocated sentry duties, had a good meal, checked over the vehicle and the kit, replenished their water supply and contacted Akrotiri there was time for some very welcome sleep. There was just one item which concerned Herrington so he called Davies over before turning in.

"Landon, be a good chap and check the rear of the vehicle for a spray bottle about the size of a small fire extinguisher. It is clearly labelled Skunk and was loaned to me by an Israeli friend. Check its all clear and then walk out about 500 yards from our position. I want you to spray small doses of the canister in a circle round the LUP. It will take you about fifteen minutes. Then bring the canister back and replace it in the Land Rover. Make absolutely certain you are in no way contaminated by the stuff because it will cling to you for days and reeks to high heaven. But no one in their right minds will come near the wadi for water."

Herrington received a satellite burst transmission from Akrotiri confirming their position but warning them that there were at least two Iraqi vehicle columns, one of them with armour, in their general vicinity and heading roughly in their direction. The rising sun warmed the ground and the favourite place for kip was by the two front wheels of the Land Rover but not under the vehicle. In Germany on exercises once three soldiers had slept under a 55 ton Chieftain tank but the ground was soggy and during the night the tank had slowly shifted lower and lower into the ground. It was a terrible warning and a costly lesson.

When it came time for Herrington to sleep he took one of the places in the sun by the front of the Land Rover and tried to rest. But sleep was an elusive pursuit. He could still see the transport aircraft exploding in front of him and no matter how hard he tried he could not banish the pleas from his colleagues to take the injured girl. He kept running through the options in his mind. Eventually the sunshine warmed him and sleep came, but not for long.

CHAPTER 6

Herrington felt rather than heard the vibration. He had his head flat on the ground having scooped the sand into a small pillow and laid his shemagh over the sand. He had been asleep for about three hours, which on missions such as this, was about as good as it gets. As he rolled over, Price came scrambling down the side of the wadi, binoculars in his left hand and his rifle in the right. "There's what looks like an Iraqi armoured column heading roughly in our general direction. Looks like they have tanks, Sir. From the East heading at a tangent our way roughly 7 clicks. Too soon to tell if they are for us. Could be on an exercise by the looks of it. Come have a look."

Herrington was not the type to wake instantaneously. It was always an effort for him and he had been in a deep sleep. But this sort of news was enough to galvanise the most inveterate and exhausted sleeping soldier. He slid out of the sleeping bag and checked his Rolex watch under its canvas cover. The sun was already moving across the afternoon sky but it would be a while before darkness. He checked the sky for aircraft and glanced round the LUP subconsciously noticing that all four of them were awake and conscious of the incoming danger.

"Anyone or anything else other than the armour?" He looked apprehensively at Price. "They warned us this might happen."

"No Sir, but it's a large column with trucks and APCs as well as the tanks. They're not in extended battle formation so it could be training but they are heading this way. No infantry in sight but they are probably in the APCs and the trucks."

He pointed to the top of the wadi and Herrington scrambled up the steep sides. He crawled to the rim disturbing a small scorpion which raised its lethal tail defensively only to scuttle away as he started to peer through the scrub. It was a large column all right. He raised the binoculars and studied the approaching formation. At least ten or more tanks plus the supporting armour making up a column of twenty vehicles or perhaps slightly more. Hard to tell at such a distance in a straight line rather than line abreast. He saw only two options at this stage. Pull out and risk being caught or hunker down, hope for the best and bluff it out. Withdrawal was a compelling option but not the wiser choice. A single Land Rover heading away from the column would arouse instant suspicion. Better to watch and wait. He glanced at Price who was patiently observing him in anticipation of the decision.

He bit his knuckle, glanced at the sky and again noted the time on his watch. "We have to tough it out and hold fast. Keep an eye on them. I must brief the others." Price nodded and fixed his binoculars on the column. Herrington turned and slid backwards down into the wadi. He collected the maps and the SATNAV out of the car and gestured to the others to close in on him.

"Ok, here's the deal. An Iraqi armoured formation of about

10 tanks and support vehicles is heading roughly in this direction from the south east." He gestured on the map. Can't make out any infantry but they are probably in the trucks, which is a good sign. They give no indication of being aware of us and to keep it that way we are not going to move. This wadi is hard enough to locate even when the SATNAV says we are on top of it. They may know about it and then look for water here. In that case we have a problem or they may move on past us. This is marked as a non-water point probably because the spring is too minimal and even then, it's quite possibly only seasonal, to justify its cartographic calibration. Get ready to move out fast if we have to. Hopefully they will just drive by." He said the last sentence trying to convince himself that this was the most logical and rational thing for them to do but his tone of voice conveyed less confidence than he actually felt.

Atkinson wiped his face and raised an eyebrow. "And if they look like they're coming into the wadi then we break out before they get here?" Herrington nodded grimly. "And then what. Sir? Which way do we go? It's pretty much a dead end game. This is a deniable mission so we are expendable and there will be no air cover so no extraction."

Herrington had thought this one through already. "If they start to come in on foot, then you," he said pointing at Atkinson, "You, my dear chap, will confidently stride out to them conspicuously grasping your AK-74 and address them in your finest Arabic, and tell them that there has been an incident in the last 24 hours and we are Iraqi Special Forces looking for possible saboteurs and they must leave us alone with complete radio silence on pain of death. Then you will turn your back on them and stride back with all the superiority and confidence which you must genuinely feel and we will watch them. If they look like sending in a larger delegation then we drive out slowly and wave at them as we go. Hopefully there will be no need for shooting. Got it?"

They nodded dubiously. Davies handed Herrington a welcome mug of hot chocolate. He took it gratefully muttering quietly, "Thanks Landon, pity it's not something stronger. Damn shame we lost all the radio monitoring kit on the aircraft. Love to hear what they're saying to each other now."

He dismissed them with a wave and went back to studying the maps. A burst transmission to Hereford and Akrotiri. "They might be setting up a roadblock further down the highway or it could simply be a training exercise. Hello, what's this?" The lead elements of the column were closing to within three kilometres of the open mouth of the LUP when Davies came scrambling up the gully to them, He looked very concerned.

"Boss, there is another column approaching on the north side. Could be an encircling movement. I think you ought to check it out." Herrington patted Price on the back and with a cynical smile said in anglicized Afrikaans to him, "As our late South African colleague, the good Dr Bezuidenhout, bless him, might have said in his native Afrikaans, 'Hou hulle fyn dop!' Price looked at him quizzically. "It means 'watch them carefully' and its one of the few phrases in Afrikaans he taught me. Let's see the new trouble." He turned and slid back down the gully into the Wadi and ran up the other side.

He scrambled up next to Davies and studied the newcomers for about two minutes. The second column was slightly smaller comprising about ten petrol bowsers and 5 trucks with no escorting armour. But to left and right of the column about 500 metres out in front Herrington noted there were two motorcycles. These were the scouts. One of the trucks was a huge signals and communications vehicle painted in very effective desert camouflage and covered in aerials and antennas. It was grinding along towing an impressive and powerful looking generator behind it. He put the binoculars down and stared at Davies with incredulity. They both instinctively glanced at their watches and stared up at the position of the sinking sun. "Strewth, it's a resupply column and an Electronic Warfare system to back up the armoured column. They could be meeting up near here and bivouacking for the night. And they are covering our exit point. We definitely dare not transmit to Hereford now, but we have to break out of here to make our RV with the Chinook. Thank God we didn't do a burst satellite transmission earlier. Now what?"

He glanced back over his shoulder to check the position of the armour. It was impossible to see them because the south side of the wadi was higher than the northern flank. "Keep your eye on these lads and tell me if they head directly for us. I must check what's happening with the armour." So saying he scrambled down and warned the other two. Price was already coming down to him from the other side.

Herrington glared at him, but was reassured by his report. "It's OK Sir; they are pulling up about 1 km away as you expected, sadly on our exit flank and setting up for the night. No scouts and no outriders."

He turned to go, but Herrington restrained him. "Do me a favour, call the others and that includes Davies. I know

47

exactly what they're doing." The others came round him as he spread the maps out on the ground. Atkinson passed round more mugs of hot chocolate. He could see the strain on the men was beginning to tell. Time to give them hope. "OK, here's the buzz. These guys may or may not be looking for us. Frankly, it's not likely at this stage. But the armour is being replenished and beefed up with a large EW system. Their RV point is about a km from here. We did the right thing to sit tight. Once it's dark we must bluff our way out as if we are part of one of them. Now time for food and rest before we move out at midnight."

Atkinson stared at Herrington thoughtfully. "Sir, what makes you so certain they won't be coming here for water?"

Herrington disarmed him with a smile. Looking at Davies he said, "Do you want to tell him or shall I?" Davies demurred politely. "There are a couple of reasons I am not terribly worried. One is that we had trouble enough finding this place even though we knew it was here. The second is that Davies here took an Israeli secret weapon called Skunk and sprayed it in a 500 m radius of our LUP. Skunk is an atrocious smelling liquid harmless enough to drink, not that you would want to, but lethal enough in its smell to deter anyone incautious enough to move beyond their perimeter. No one in their right minds will penetrate the barrier he established and if they do then we will try to talk our way out of it. Good night gentlemen!" And so saying he resumed his observation of the armoured column.

In the desert, in winter, night time arrives swiftly like a thief in the evening. True to form the sun dipped below the surrounding hills and the impenetrable darkness came on quickly. A short impressive sunset with multi-coloured streaks across the evening sky quickly gave way to what portended to be a decidedly chilly night. Herrington had enviously watched the two columns confidently approach each other with no attempt at concealment of lights or recognition signals but curiously they did not link up. Instead both groups settled down for the night separately with roughly 800 metres between them. A laager of sorts was established by both columns, tents rigged with surprising alacrity and campfires lit up warding off the evening chill but to his amazement the Iraqis appeared to be disinterested in posting sentries. The one serious challenge was that the exit point for the Land Rover 110 had been effectively blocked and to escape meant driving between the two camps.

After an hour and a bit Herrington signalled to Price and asked him to watch the two camps. Their MREs were running low now so they shared meals and some very welcome hot coffee. Then what they had all feared happened. Price came scuttling down the embankment. "There are two of them coming this way Sir. Side arms, but no rifles and moving slowly with torches. It may be a pee or they might know about the wadi." Herrington glanced again at his watch.

"OK, let's have a quick look. They haven't reached the Skunk line yet I take it?"

Price didn't know whether to smile or look serious. "No Sir, but they must be coming up to it. I think they are puzzled by the smell. Far from acting as a deterrent it seems to have served as incentive.

They don't mind flashing their torches round vigorously so I think they might just be exploring."

It was a bit early but maybe the time had come to take the initiative. Herrington ordered the men to get the vehicle ready. He called Atkinson and dashed up the incline. The two men studied the flashing torches and the dark shapes behind them as they approached. The men were getting close to the skunk line. What would happen then? They would have found further exploration repellent. They might call another soldier or a senior officer or others to find out what the awful smell was. There again it could have the desired effect. Most people were so repulsed by the stink they simply backed off. It would be obvious enough when they reached the Skunk line as they would stop for a while and discuss it.

Sure enough the two beams stopped moving about 500 m out. On the still desert air he could just hear their voices. He found the lack of concealment so at odds with his own military training and experience that it left him quite bewildered. They would either return to the laager or try to find a way round the stink. To his dismay, after about three minutes, the torches started moving again. He gripped Atkinson by the shoulder. "If they come within two hundred metres of us I want you to go out there and give them the spiel. Be friendly but deliberately vague about who we are and impress on them the importance of secrecy. Timing is everything now. I will tell the others to man the vehicle. Once you have explained who we are, you can tell them there are some dead animals here which is why we are departing and the place is to be avoided. Explain that we are moving out shortly and radio silence is imperative. Keep it as short and business like as possible then walk back towards us. The vehicle will exit the wadi and pick you up and we will drive between the two laagers as if we belonged here. If anything goes badly wrong shoot them."

Atkinson smiled grimly. "Yes Sir," he muttered, reckoning to himself that his CO was probably as mad as a hatter but he just might pull it off. The urge to light up a cigarillo was almost overwhelming. Atkinson did not smoke much at all but on Fridays he enjoyed a peculiar type of expensive Russian cigarillo made from Cuban tobacco and always kept a small box on him. The torches continued trying to penetrate beyond the skunk line and then suddenly they were through and walking towards him. He scrambled down the embankment to warn the others but encountered Davies on the way. A quick word and Davies told him to proceed. If the ruse worked they stood a good chance and if it failed then the others might get away but his chances of survival were minimal.

Herrington slid into the driver's seat on the Land Rover. The camouflage netting was already packed away, they were ready to go. He told Price what had happened and asked them to be ready to roll out. He just hoped that the Land Rover would start without any trouble. He sent Davies up to watch with Price and to signal for the move out.

Atkinson flicked off the safety catch on the AK-74 automatic rifle and started walking towards the men as they approached the wadi. At first they failed to see him then a movement in the darkness must have alerted one of them. As soon as he reckoned they were aware of him he called out the traditional Arabic greeting of "Salaam Aleikum". "Aleikum" Salaam one of them called back and then inevitably asked "But who are you?" The question was asked less from suspicion than curiosity but as he drew closer and they saw his rifle he noticed that they appeared to be unarmed. On closer inspection he noted a side arm in a very smart canvas holster on the taller man but both men were in uniform and wearing berets. He smiled and pulling up a few feet from them introduced himself as Captain Mohammed al-Maghri, Iraqi Special Forces. The shorter of the two men advanced and introduced himself as Major Abdul Rashid of the 6th Armoured Bgde of 2nd Corps and turned to the taller man and said, "Allow me to introduce you to Colonel Yevgenniy Borisov, our Russian liaison officer."

Down in the wadi Herrington tapped nervously on the steering wheel of the Land Rover. Davies saw Atkinson striding confidently across the scrub up to the two torches. Price watched for any signal from Davies. Davies studied the convergence of the three figures. It had been agreed that running his hand over his face would mean start the car and we move out. A chopping motion to the ground meant a fighting exit with or without Atkinson.

Atkinson thanked God for his Arabic and rudimentary Russian language lessons. He flicked the safety catch back on and transferred the AK to his left hand extending his right to shake hands with the Russian. Borisov noted with approval the deft movement reasserting the safety catch on the rifle and shook hands unsmilingly as he looked Atkinson up and down and then almost reluctantly stood back. Atkinson now noticed that the canvas cover on the holster was unbuttoned and the shining butt of a Makarov pistol dully gleamed in the torchlight. In a few crisp Arabic sentences the American explained that there had been an incident and they were a recce unit of Special Forces on a classified operation. It would be appreciated if they would please respect the implicit radio silence but render any assistance possible if so required. And could they please move away from this dreadful smell. He casually reached into his breast pocket and produced the cigarillos. The Russian's eyes narrowed as Atkinson moved his free hand up to the battledress pocket and he watched the movement with ill-concealed suspicion. Would the colonel care to join him in a good Russian cigarette?

Rashid seemed satisfied but the colonel was wary. Atkinson sensed the blue eyes sweeping over his battledress as he opened the little cigar box and offered it round. Rashid accepted without demur. The colonel's face reflected his surprise as he recognized the Russian brand and then a cautious smile crossed his face. He reached forward and took one. Atkinson reached in his pocket for his lighter and as he did so he realised with a sinking heart that he was using a silver coloured Household Cavalry Zippo lighter given to him by an English friend. The colonel moved his hand closer to the unbuttoned holster. Trying to cover the crest on the lighter he lit Rashid's cigarillo and cupped his hands to light up Borisov's. But Borisov's eyes missed nothing. He thanked Atkinson, drew on the cigarillo and then asked to see the lighter.

"What the hell are they doing?" Herrington was growing agitated and seemed to be speaking to himself. Price jumped out of the car and ran up the slope.

"Shhh," Davies whispered. "He just offered them a cigarette and lit it. They are walking this way."

"What the hell is his game? He should lead them away from us, not into the bloody wadi." Price was staring at Davies who in turn was staring into the binoculars. "And now....?"

Davies eased into a more comfortable position. "He's just

handed something to the taller man. They are moving away from the skunk line about 100 metres inside the perimeter. So far, so good."

Atkinson had no choice. He handed Borisov the lighter. Borisov shone his torch on the unmistakeable Household Cavalry crest with its little red crown. "Very nice," he said admiringly in passable Arabic. "May I ask where did you get this?"

Atkinson had to physically resist the urge to involuntarily shake.

"Off a British officer after the occupation," he said trying to sound casual. Borisov flicked the lighter on and off. After another glance he handed the lighter back to Atkinson. He moved his right hand towards the holster but then ducked it into his pocket as Atkinson stiffened. But it was the pocket not the holster he was after and withdrawing his hand he passed a black Zippo lighter to the American. It contained a mauve crest in the form of a compass rose. Feeling like he had been punched in the gut Atkinson recognized it as the same lighter Dr Bezuidenhout had used from his days in the South African reconnaissance commandos. Trying to give himself time to recover he flicked it on and off and then laughed as he returned it to Borisov. "I see it works too. And yours….?" His mind in a whirl he looked at Borisov as he handed it back.

But Borisov who had been watching him intently, almost too closely, laughed and seemed more relaxed. "A South African Special Forces officer we invited to Russia as part of an exchange agreement after the end of the Angolan war gave it to me. You do not recognise the crest, eh?"

"It's a very nice memento," said Atkinson trying to pull himself together. "Now if you will excuse me gentlemen we are about to move out. Would you please just warn your men that we will drive past them. I would hate for an accident to happen," and so saying he perfunctorily saluted them and turning on his heel walked back towards the wadi. He could feel their eyes boring into him and was prepared for a shout which he would meet with gun fire but nothing happened.

"He is coming back," said Davies to no one in particular. Price felt his eyes watering. He dropped the binoculars round his neck and picked up the NVGs. He said that the two men had turned and walked back briskly through the skunk line towards the Iraqi armour bivouac.

Atkinson had to resist the urge to check on them by looking back and even more so the urge to run to the wadi. He came striding up to Davies and Price. "Well?" said Davies. "Consorting with the enemy is a crime you know. Did they buy it?"

Atkinson nodded curtly and all three men slid down the ridge to the Land Rover. Herrington looked at him curiously. "So…," he said brusquely.

"I think they've bought it Sir, but we must move out now. Just slowly not too fast. I asked them to warn their men that we are leaving and told them we don't want any accidents.

One of them is a Russian liaison officer. I offered him one of my Russian Cuban jobs and he was taken aback. Then bloody forgot I had my Zippo Household Cavalry lighter which he noticed and he then produced a South African Zippo Recce lighter like the one Bezuidenhout used to carry with him. Crazy thought went through my mind how the hell did he get Bezuidenhout's lighter, and then I wondered if he was testing me so I feigned ignorance and he told me it had been given to him by a visiting South African exchange group. Weird actually. But I think we have a get out of gaol card thanks to Zippo."

Herrington shrugged his shoulders. "Well done, good man. God bless Zippo. Ok, let's move on out but keep your weapons ready just in case. They might realise in retrospect that this conversation was extremely unsatisfactory and then all hell will break loose!"

CHAPTER 7

Feeling less confidence than he was trying to portray, Herrington started the Land Rover and moved out of the wadi. He glanced over to his left for sight of the Iraqi and the Russian walking back to their bivouac area but it was too dark and he couldn't even see their silhouettes. He cautioned the others to keep their eyes peeled but nobody saw a thing save for the dim shapes of the laagered vehicles and the tents. The campfires glowed in the night and the make shift tents actually looked quite inviting. In the distance Herrington thought he could pick up the throbbing of the diesel electric generator which meant that the Iraqi Army were using the EW van.

The Anglo-American team moved slowly with park lights on. The overwhelming temptation was to move as fast as possible, and nowhere more so than when they crossed the ghastly stinking skunk line. That would have invited unwelcome interest so they just quietly and steadily moved between their adversaries and tried to maintain as low a profile as possible. Atkinson kept going over the short conversation in his mind and the incident of the two Zippo lighters. All of them could smell cooking on the night air. There was no knowing whether the two officers had told the other group about them and if so whether they had used the time to reconsider the entire conversation. It was more than likely that they had indeed bought the story and suggested to the other group that they must ignore any vehicles moving through the two tented areas.

After half an hour they had cleared the two groups without incident and were angling round on a compass heading towards the RV. Herrington was concerned over the EW van and its massive generator. Normally he would have sent a pulse signal to the Chinook team giving them the OK. That would have to wait. The cold coupled with the wind chill factor of the moving vehicle made them all extremely uncomfortable. The good news was that the ruse had worked but the bad news was the uncertainty of ensuring that they were indeed going to be picked up at the designated RV point.

Each man was absorbed with his own thoughts. But simultaneously they were all on the lookout. The driver wore the NVGs and the rest of the team used their single lens electro optical devices. The NVGs provided phenomenal illumination but the electro optical single lens magnifiers covered the flanks and rear of the vehicle. They had enjoyed a brief pit stop roughly 5 clicks from the two Iraqi columns just to make sure that they were not being followed. Herrington resisted the temptation to use the time for communications due to the proximity of the radio truck but he thought that he could possibly get away with a burst transmission to Hereford about an hour before the Chinook was due to arrive with reasonable safety. The frequency hopping radios worked well and were claimed to be pretty much monitor proof from anything that Baghdad could put into the field. Still there were no guarantees.

Every half hour they stopped to switch drivers, listen out, have a comfort break and then move on, but Price kept thinking about why he had pushed so hard to take the woman on board the C-130. It was beginning to gnaw away at his mind. Perhaps if he had been less aggressive and more restrained they might have left her behind. He tried to dismiss the thoughts from his mind by concentrating on the desert scrub but the thoughts kept crawling back into his head.

In a superhuman effort to get his mind off the awful feeling growing in the pit of his stomach that he was somehow responsible for what had happened to the evacuation aircraft he cast his mind back to his Special Operations Group training which was a division of the Special Activities Centre. The SOG was responsible for all operations that involved US clandestine or covert ops with which the US government had no desire to be associated. These forces were distinct from political action groups. PAGs engaged in even more nefarious activities which involved the over-throw of undesirable regimes and hostile or potentially hostile governments and non-governmental actors. He recalled the original briefing where he had been told that he was one of a hundred hand-picked men and women for deniable operations anywhere in the world within 24 hours and sometimes even less. His colleagues had come from the Rangers, the Green Berets, the Delta Force, Force Reconnaissance, SEALS and other US military forces. All of them had excelled in their basic military training and carried additional qualities in the weapons, linguistics and electronics fields, amongst others. Their motto was Tertia Opta, meaning the Third Option when diplomacy and overt military operations were unavailable. He wondered now whether he might not have been better off in the PAG unit where covert operations involved exercising political influence, psychological warfare, economic warfare and cyber space warfare. Then his mind snapped back to the exploding aircraft and he shook his head as if to shake the images out of his mind.

Davies had taken over the driving from Herrington and was still marvelling at the fact that they had managed to skirt right through the middle of the two Iraqi bivouac areas. He was the youngest of the team and the most impressionable. He had already dismissed the terrible scene of the exploding aircraft from his mind as he studied the road ahead. His job was to ensure that their air transport from Jordan arrived on time and in the right place. He was satisfied that to this point in time he had done everything in his power to ensure that their extraction would now go smoothly. From Jordan they would be flown either to Akrotiri and then back to the UK or directly to the UK. He had no idea and didn't really concern him just as long as he managed to get the remainder of the team back in one piece.

Atkinson was still ruminating on his conversation with the Iraqi and Russian officers. How weird was it that two military men from different countries on covert operations in a third country used Zippo lighters with military associations which had been given to them by other members of the military from other countries. On reflection he reckoned Borisov had been quite wary of him until he lit the cigarette. Had either of them noticed his uniform in the darkness without rank or any form of identification, he pondered. But then special forces across the world are a pretty nondescript lot and they tend to wear pretty much what they choose to wear. The AK74 was a common enough weapon and his Arabic had been honed to the point where no one could challenge him on local dialect and fluency. And yet, he wondered, and yet, just a few radio calls would confirm or deny the reality of who he actually was. Perhaps better not to go there.

Davies checked his watch and reckoned it was time to hand over to Atkinson. He started slowing down before a slight ridge crested with bushes and reckoned he would stop just short of the ridge for the handover. Neither of them had checked the SATNAV for about five minutes but there were no signs of any unusual landmarks. He pulled up, peeled off the heavy NVGs which were giving him a slight headache and left the engine running. Atkinson nodded in agreement and as he dismounted muttered to Davies, "Must have a pee. Will check the ridge at the same time and then we can go." He had picked up his rifle but then had second thoughts and left it on the seat next to Davies. He stretched and started to walk slowly up to the bush line of the ridge. He had not gone five metres when there was a shout and a thud, followed by the sound of falling rocks and another shout, then a further thud and a cascade of smaller stones.

Davies grabbed Atkinson's rifle and walked carefully to the top of the ridge line with Price. There was total darkness ahead of him which seemed to be concealing a large hole, surrounded by gravel and an awful smell. Herrington resisted the urge to join the other two and stayed in the vehicle scanning round their position with his image magnifier but he spotted nothing untoward. Davies and Price stared into the hole in front of them. Aside from the fact that they could not see anything there was a terrible smell wafting out of the chasm. Price looked at Davies intently. "Was this marked on the SATNAV?" he asked brusquely.

Davies was as perplexed as he was. "Nothing, just shows desert. You can check it yourself. I need the NVGs." He retraced his steps to the Land Rover and collected the NVGs.

Herrington was still scanning. "What happened to Atkinson?" he asked, preparing to dismount.

Davies explained that it appeared as if he had fallen into some sort of very large evil smelling dark hole. Herrington grabbed his rifle and unhitched a long rope from the back of the car. The two men joined Price on the edge of the crater. They could hear Atkinson groaning down below. Herrington fastened the rope round his waist and gave the loop to Price. "I'm going down after him. Strewth but this place stinks…what on earth is it?"

"No idea, Sir, but the sooner we extract him the better. I think we've driven into a chemical weapons bomb test site, Sir. That's why it's not calibrated on the SATNAV. We should be wearing NBC face masks. The smell is of rotting animal carcases. Sooner we are out of here the better." Herrington nodded and waited for the masks. Davies produced them from the back of the car and all three men donned their special protection gear. Atkinson was trying to crawl back up the slope. He appeared a bit dazed and shaken, blood oozing from several bad cuts on his face. Every movement elicited a severe groan.

Herrington scrambled down the slippery slope, checked Atkinson over cursorily and then told Price and Davies to help pull them up the scree. Atkinson was in bad shape, clutching his side and hobbling in great pain from his ankle.

Herrington looked him over at the top and said to the other two, "He seems to have a bad ankle sprain, several broken ribs and multiple facial lacerations so his driving days are over for the moment. Thank Heaven you stopped when you did or we would have driven into the bomb crater. John, you bind him up, gently, and Landon can check the Chemical Warfare strips in the car."

Every SAS Land Rover operating in Iraq carried CW strips sensitive to chemical weapon contamination. Herrington feared what he might find but none of the strips gave any indications. If they had been exposed to the left overs of a chemical weapons site for a very short time, it was possible they had escaped unscathed.

They helped Atkinson into the Land Rover and Price reluctantly gave him a shot of morphine, which meant that they were now a three man team with one walking or hobbling casualty. Price reversed back down the gentle slope and they made a wide detour round the crater. They had lost about 25 minutes but having departed the LUP early they were still provisionally on time for the RV.

Two uneventful hours later they arrived at the extraction point. This was a small valley within a slightly larger depression. It was not ideal but it was not entirely without its compensations. The floor of the valley was clear which made a helicopter landing much easier. Price and Herrington helped Atkinson out of the Land Rover and laid him on the ground. They then carefully extracted the essential kit, cameras, SATNAV and one or two other items before wiring the car for a remote detonation if need be. This was not the primary aim as it was hoped they could drive the car up the ramp into the Chinook which would then take them all back to Jordan. Davies meanwhile risked sending a frequency hopping burst transmission via satellite to Hereford confirming that they were ready to be collected. Hereford notified Akrotiri and Akrotiri notified the Chinook.

The Boeing MH-47G is a special operations version of the CH-47 Chinook multipurpose, heavy lift helicopter which has long been the primary work horse for the US Army Special Forces Operations Aviation Command and for its British counterpart. The machine is equipped with long range fuel tanks as well as an extendable refuelling probe which gives it an even longer range. The airframe includes a ramp for loading supplies and vehicles. The flying crew of pilot and co-pilot is supplemented by space for a load master and two aerial gunners armed with M240 7.62mm belt fed machine guns mounted either side of the fuselage. A missile warning system, an integrated radio frequency counter measures suite, a laser warning system and XM216 dark flares add fangs to the teeth of two M134 7.62 mm electrically fired air cooled mini guns.

Davies did not have to wait long for confirmation. The pick-up was right on time. Having made Atkinson as comfortable as they could, and leaving Price to keep an eye on him, the Brits did what they always do best and produced four cups of tea with generous lashings of rum into the bargain. The grateful Americans mumbled something about drinking on the job and teaching the British to make better coffee but they nonetheless accepted the tea with good grace.

Herrington checked Atkinson over again and satisfied himself that at the very worst three ribs had gone. They also checked the CW strips again but were hugely relieved to find nothing indicating the presence of chemical agents.

They had just finished their second cup of tea when Davies thought he heard the first glimmerings of the muffled thwack thwack of the two Honeywell T55-GA-714A engines each churning out three and half thousand kilowatts power. Davies grabbed the NVGs and stared to the north but the Chinook was barely visible as it hugged the ground in a wide precautionary sweep before approaching from the south looking more like a vehicle than an airborne machine. It was not a silent approach. The muffled pounding noise grew to a crescendo. All three of the Special Forces team other than the crippled Atkinson cringed at the terrible racket. Herrington would not have been surprised if even the denizens of distant Baghdad might wake up. As the Chinook approached Herrington and Atkinson removed the precautionary explosive booby traps from the 110 Land Rover and the vital kit was trundled back on board the car.

The American Chinook MH-47 came in so low it could have passed for another armoured fighting vehicle but for the excruciating noise. Capable of excellent performance at altitude and designed to manage both heat and cold, the machine was flown by pilots from the highly secret 160th Special Operations Aviation Regiment known as the "Night Stalkers". For helicopter crews on special missions the most dangerous times are the landings and lift offs. The aircraft is flying low and slow. It makes for an almost irresistible target. Hence the reconnaissance before touch down. The pilot's faces were briefly illuminated in the green glow of the cockpit lights and then she was down. The wheels had no sooner sunk into the earth than the rear ramp was lowered and Herrington drove the Land Rover up into the body of the helicopter under the expert supervision of the load master using a small red torch. He was not surprised to see the pilots and the loadmaster all wearing NBC suits given Iraq's history with chemical weapons. Within four minutes everyone was on board and with a banshee like howl the helicopter lifted off, tilted forward and thundered low between the hills for the distant Jordanian border.

CHAPTER 8

About eight hours after the Chinook lifted off from the RV in Iraq another seemingly unrelated event was occurring in central London. An attractive woman exited the Oxford Circus underground station and headed for Selfridges, a short ten minute walk away. She was in her early forties but looked to be in her mid-thirties. Five foot eight, brunette, dressed in a sophisticated style. Her shoulder length dark hair cascaded down round her light high cheeked West Indian features. She was impeccably dressed in a figure-hugging green skirt and jacket. The expensive tweed coat and silk scarf only enhanced her natural good looks in a face that had borne its fair share of pain. Round her neck close to her heart hung a small golden locket with a treasured picture of her late husband.

Stefanie Westbrooke had arrived in Britain as a baby with her parents from Jamaica in the late 1970s. She had never known her native land. Her English midlands middle class accent was as real as the small diamond ring on her finger from her deceased husband. Philip Westbrooke, a cell phone technician and electronics wizard had conducted extensive research on the new 5G communications system. The results had not been good.

Five years of constant and intense exposure to 5G had taken a terrible toll on his immune system and cancer was the inevitable result. He had always suspected that there were serious risks attached to his work and had wisely taken out an extensive insurance policy for his wife and daughter in the event of the unthinkable becoming the reality. The substantial sum left for his wife and beautiful child were no substitutes for the man himself.

It was not surprising that the two women had grown enormously close. Two hours earlier a young nineteen year old girl filled with excitement swiftly exited Oxford Circus Station turned left and started to stroll down Regent Street. Emma, loved the 'buzz' of London and was camped out on the old cliché "if you are tired of London you are tired of life". Emma, was a younger more westernized clone of her mother The same good looks with a slightly lighter complexion and stunning figure but younger, a touch more dynamic and ever keen to learn. Her youthful visage bore none of the pain her mother had experienced. Potential boyfriends there were aplenty but she had yet to find a young man who lived up to the image and standards established by her deceased father. She had attended a good grammar school and finished with a distinction in drama having appeared in several amateur dramatics as a maturing school girl. She found that acting successfully dragged her mind away from the painful loss of her father and gave her strength through role playing the lives of others. In a sense the family tragedy made her a better actress. By chance she had met the head of BAFTA at one such production and on the strength of her good looks, charm and natural acting ability, been encouraged to seek a scholarship to the Royal Academy of Dramatic Arts or RADA. To her mother's surprise and her joy, the prestigious acting academy had auditioned her and endorsed the application.

The work was hard and demanding. But the rewards and the contacts she was making were tangible evidence of her perseverance, resolution and determination. Long periods of intense study and onstage exposure which involved being drilled over and over again were mixed with meeting famous stars. Many were RADA graduates themselves. Everyone needs that first lucky break, Harrison Ford, had been hand-picked by a director when on site. Ford was a carpenter working on a film set when he was asked to play a small role. It was the path to Star Wars, Indiana Jones, President Jack Ryan and many other roles. First stop for Emma was a quick look around Liberty a posh department store, then cross the road into her favourite area the labyrinth of little streets around Carnaby Street. Actress and fashion go hand in hand and Emma was no exception. At school she had picked the 'Swinging Sixties' as a project, the explosion of colour and style of clothing, music, flower power had all interested her, so, so much in that one decade. Standing looking at an outfit in a shop window the young mind was thinking I would look great in that as the lead actress in a James Bond Film. A inward chuckle then it was off to meet mum, thinking if Mick Jagger from that era can still strut his stuff in his seventies I can do anything.

To be able to escape from the hard work, even if only for a few hours each week, meant the world to young Emma. On this sunny but cold winter morning

She was looking forward to a salt beef sandwich at the Brass Rail in Selfridges with her mother in Oxford Street. But fate has a strange way of playing games with people's lives.

As Emma sat quietly in a corner of the Selfridges restaurant checking messages on her phone, waiting for her mother, she failed to notice an expensively dressed heavy set man with drooping jowls on the far side of the restaurant. Even sitting down the sheer physical size of Igor Strelnikov would have made an impression on the most casual observer. His craggy features and pig like eyes conveyed a ruthless hunting animal rather than a sensitive human being. The costly gold watch dangling from his wrist, the smart almost flamboyant clothes and the highly polished tailor-made leather shoes from Jermyn Street, did little to conceal a dangerous man with an unpleasant aura. Strelnikov was a huge player in the Russian underground mafia, the Organizatsiya.

The origins of Strelnikov's extraordinary criminal organisation can be traced as far back as Tsarist times before the 1917 communist revolution. These ruthless syndicates had helped to finance Lenin's revolutionary gangs in brutal bank heists and associated robberies. It was a challenge to draw a distinction between the organized criminal elite and the Bolshevik ideologues. Their operations were indistinguishable from each other. After the 1917 revolution the Soviet government seemed to absorb the mafia. For all intents and purposes they became one and the same. But after the collapse of the USSR and the breaching of the Berlin Wall, the Russian mafia or Organizatsiya, emerged to capitalise on the ensuing chaos, murder and mayhem characterising Gorbachev's, and later Yeltsin's, disintegrating Russia. As the economy and society collapsed, the mafia moved in. They sustained a rotten and corrupt system with even more underhand and filthy practices. Without the Organizatsiya the USSR would have crashed much more swiftly.

It also became internationalised. Links were opened up with its East European, American and Sicilian counterparts.

Thanks to their intimate involvement with the black market and the Russian body politic, valuable and rewarding intelligence connections were established with the Mossad, the CIA and MI6. These links meant that the operators enjoyed a remarkable degree of protection and immunity when conducting their criminal affairs in these countries, even whilst engaged in contractual murder, racketeering, human trafficking, white slavery, drug running, prostitution and pornography. Western intelligence services found the information flows so important that they were prepared to turn a blind eye to the bulk of these 'black' activities.

The gangs gradually transplanted themselves from Russia to the US, the UK and Israel. In the US they were helped by Senator Henry 'Scoop' Jackson's famous bill, the Jackson-Vanick law, which allowed mass emigration of certain sections of Russian society to the US, predominantly Miami and New York. The KGB capitalised on this big time. Whilst conservative Americans naively cheered at having trumped another score against Moscow, the KGB ensured that the most brutal, ruthless and hardened criminals were the ones permitted to leave the USSR for the capitalist delights of the USA.

In the UK they were helped by the decision of both Labour and Tory governments to open London as a post British Imperial world financial centre offering special tax incentives to the uberwealthy who were willing to invest in, and through, the channels offered by the City of London global financial elite. Where such massive sums of money were concerned, which might contribute to growing the British economy, Her Majesty's Government could afford to be conveniently versatile in their approach to local and international crime fighting. Moreover, allowing certain Russian Mafiosi to operate in the UK facilitated easy monitoring of their activities and surveillance of their communications. The ensuing intelligence treasure trove was incredibly rewarding. The human cost was something else.

Israel placed a high premium on these international intelligence and economic connections too. The Israeli government does not recognize drug dealing, child porn and white slave trading as a crime and does not extradite its nationals to other countries so Israel also became a favoured haven. The one exceptional Israeli leader who sought to clean up the criminal elements in his country was Yitzhak Rabin. Fearing the destabilizing impact of these mega powerful criminal figures he met with Mossad and Shin Bet to devise a counter strategy. He was assassinated within days.

But where did Strelnikov fit into this matrix? No boot-legging criminal operation indulged in by the Organizatsiya was small scale. With the passage of time they formed a thin veneer of conventional but hardly respectable businesses and industrial activities. They took over the entire armaments industry in Hungary. In the US they formed their own banks and even their own courts whose devastating versions of 'justice' proved far more effective than the established courts. They formed their own transnational multinational banks and even took over part of the world's oil extraction and distribution businesses with their own massive tanker fleet, trucking empires and petrol station chains. It was the latter oil industry to which Strelnikov had gravitated. He was Mr Oil and his influence stretched from Saudi Arabia to Angola, from Venezuela to offshore Vietnam. His word was law and his rule beyond the wildest dreams of any Sheikh, Sultan or Indian Mogul.

And then, about the turn of the century things began to change. It was slow and barely imperceptible, at first beginning in Russia where a former KGB colonel became the modern democratic Tsar. Vladimir Putin brought the clampdown on the Organizatsiya as never before. Nikolai Khodorkovsky, one of the biggest oligarchs. Was arrested, tried on corruption and summarily gaoled. The Organizatsiya mobilised its western connections and media contacts unprecedentedly, all crying foul play and bad form, but it didn't help. Khodorkovsky got to know the inside of a Siberian prison. He was soon followed by a host of other recalcitrants. Plans were made to assassinate Putin. Inevitably the new Tsar learned about it. Within a month the planners and their families and even their pets, were summarily obliterated, their homes burnt to the ground, all traces of their existence eviscerated. It was the only language the Organizatsiya understood. And it worked.

Even before that Strelnikov had seen the writing on the wall and evacuated his family and operations to New York. There, under the ironic protection of the CIA and the FBI, and with a readymade network of operatives, he arrogantly continued his criminal operations and involved himself with a CIA recommended contact, a multi-millionaire paedophile human trafficker and white slaver called Jeffrey Epstein. Epstein had his own island, his own ranches and his apartments in Miami, New York, London and elsewhere. Like Strelnikov, he enjoyed the protection of the Mossad, the FBI and a host of other law and order organisations whilst running the largest compromise and racketeering operation in the world. He even ran his own Panama based asset Management Company on dubious earnings paid by 'grateful' clients who were blackmailed into investing with him at the risk of their sordid assignments with underage boys and girls leaked to the collaborative media. It was alleged that Epstein's contacts ranged from the dregs of society like Strelnikov to the dizzy heights of the White House and Buckingham Palace. But even Epstein's days were numbered.

In 2016 the net began to come down on the Organizatsiya in the USA with the election of a maverick, rank outsider to the White House. The liberal days of Bill Clinton and his mysterious Manchurian candidate type successor, Barrack Hussein Obama was replaced by a property tycoon from New York. Within two years Donald Trump had wrapped up 1 200 paedophile rings, arrested, charged, convicted and locked up over 11 000 paedophiles and closed in on the white slavery traffic sneaking over the Mexican border. Over 4 000 so called MS13 murderous Mexican terrorists, working hand in glove with the Organizatsiya in the US, were either shot, arrested or detained. Criminal elements at the top in the Department of Justice, the CIA and the FBI, to name but a few, were summarily identified, shamed, fired and moved.

These were the same elements protecting scum like Epstein and Strelnikov. As massive criminal scamming and racketeering operations in both the private sector and the government were curtailed amidst screaming protests from the Democrats, the US economy lifted off like a Saturn V rocket into space. But this was not good news for Strelnikov. Yet again he saw the writing on the wall and departed, this time for London.

It might well be asked how Strelnikov always seemed to know how to get out when the going was good. The answer was simple. Igor Strelnikov ran his own informal and highly effective intelligence and counter intelligence operation. The man sitting opposite him in Selfridges was his own personal chief of intelligence, and the news that former KGB colonel, Mikhail Swerdlov, had for Strelnikov, was not good.

They had been deep in earnest conversation for some time when she had entered the room. His predator like eyes followed Emma across the restaurant, mentally stripping her, as a waitress showed her a window table. Swerdlov saw Igor's eyes shift which was odd because what he was sharing with Strelnikov ought to have had him sitting on the edge of his chair. It could only have been an underage girl or a very pretty young woman. "Very nice, very nice indeed," Strelnikov muttered.

The distraction was very irritating to Swerdlov. "Igor, do you know why Marilyn Monroe was murdered?"

"Didn't know she was murdered." The other Russian said, puzzled by the sudden change of tack.

"She was killed because she refused to take heed of vital information which might have saved her life. An affair with Jack Kennedy and his brother, Robert, provided her with critical information on a par with the sort of information I am trying to share with you. Once jilted by both men she threatened to go public. Despite warnings not to, she persisted. Her phone was tapped and in the interests of national security she was, as our American friends put it, terminated with extreme prejudice. Please get your mind off your dick and listen to me carefully."

Strelnikov's bodyguard seated at the next table shifted

uneasily in his chair. He could not monitor the entire conversation but the comment was loud enough for him to hear it. Not many people dared to address his paymaster like that and lived to tell the tale. He detested public meetings like this. Protecting his boss in private was tough enough but in a public setting it was loaded with risk. This man appeared to have known Strelnikov a long time. Perhaps familiarity bred contempt after all, he mused.

With an effort Strelnikov dragged his attention back to Swerdlov. "I pay your handsome salary, you prick." Then he smiled and seemed to relax. The two men had known each other for years and insofar as there was any loyalty in the Organizatsiya this was the case between Swerdlov and Strelnikov. "So what you are saying is that there has been a dramatic shift in the global coalition of forces since the Trump election. The PRC has been forced to accept an unacceptable trade deal and lost serious international face to the property tycoon whilst trying to stabilise an inherently unstable situation in Hong Kong. And they believe the Americans and the British are behind the Hong Kong troubles too? I don't see what this has to do with the international oil business?"

So he had been listening after all, thought Swerdlov. It was time to deliver the really bad news. "Igor, the Chinese will not take this supinely on the chin. If there is one over-riding characteristic of the Chinese it is that they hate to lose face. It is the greatest humiliation and insult. The Dragon will fight back."

Igor laughed derisively. "Oh yes, fight back with what?"

Swerdlov reckoned the time had come to give him the platinum information. "Igor, we have a major problem looming on the horizon. This latest American president has stirred up a real nest of hornets, as you well know. Not just in the US but all over the world. He's sort of settled North Korea, bringing the troops home from the Middle East and Afghanistan, persuading NATO members to pay their fair share of their defence burden, and rejigged the North American and PRC trade agreements to America's advantage while partially cleaning up what he calls the swamp inside the US, which means mostly our friends. Your buddy Epstein has either been murdered or spirited away somewhere and our networks all across the world are in serious jeopardy.

Strelnikov held up his hand. "Spare me; spare me... you almost sound as if you approve of the bastard!" He wasn't smiling now.

Swerdlov shook his head. "No, of course I don't. But hear me out carefully. You said a moment ago that you pay me well, and you do, and the information I give you isn't just solid gold. Its platinum grade. At least twice haven't I saved your life...your family and your career? Just hear me out on this. Anyway, have I ever let you down?"

Igor smiled grimly. "Well, there's always a first time but go on." Then he interrupted himself. "I will say this; although we do not meet very often you always seem to have very good information. What's the story this time?" Then he leaned over to the bodyguard and nodding in the direction of the girl, now busy on her cell phone, and who had earlier caught his attention, quietly said in Russian, "Find out who she is."

Emma, sitting with her head buried in a fashion magazine at her table across the room was unaware of Strelnikov's attention and only looked up when the waitress clearing the tables approached her. They spoke briefly and leaving her coat and magazine she approached the self-service counter. The message from mum had said be with you in 5 min. Looking up at the menu board she ordered her favourite salt beef sarnie on rye for herself and her mother and returned to the magazine. Having finished with a quick glance at the magazine Emma picked up a discarded newspaper from the next table hoping to catch up on some celebrity gossip. The front page would have been flipped over by most nineteen year olds but Emma was intrigued by it. The headline story concerned the apparent death of a prominent Iraqi general who seemed to have been murdered in a car bomb explosion in Baghdad. It held little interest for her. She had learnt from her mum that it was important for your own survival to keep up to speed with what was happening in the country and the world at large. Her real interest lay in the lives of the stars, like Angelina Jolie adopting umpteen refugee children and breaking up with her husband Brad Pitt or Leonardo di Caprio on his experiences of Africa when filming Blood Diamonds. This was the glitzy life that she aspired to but without the social trauma. It was all so very different from their utterly conventional life style in Harefield, a typical little rural village nestling in the English countryside. She glanced round her glad that she had arrived relatively early as the ground floor restaurant was rapidly filling up. Selfridges counter service was good even under pressure but it was better to arrive early. She tossed the paper aside and pulled out her notes from the last RADA lecture to review them. Her phone was on silent but she felt the buzz of an SMS "hi darling delay on the tube see you in 20 min love mum." Emma thought lucky mum just a sarnie and not a hot meal on our table.

Swerdlov sipped his coffee slowly before trying to engage Igor's attention again. "Igor, as usual you are not going to like what I tell you nor want to believe it but rest assured my sources are as good as they come. Because of the unhappy humiliating trade deal with the US plus the troubles in Hong Kong, for which they blame the Americans and the British, and a host of other irritating items, the highest levels of the CCP leadership have decided to do a deal with the deep state cabal in the US to remove the president. This will be a very risky and dangerously painful operation. It means effectively paralysing and sabotaging the entire world economy and especially the US economy which has been the shining corner stone of the president's success. Not just for the US, perhaps, for the entire world." He paused for a sip of tea.

Before he could resume Strelnikov cocked a sceptical eye at him. "And how do they propose to accomplish this?"

Irritated by the interruption the former KGB man continued. "This is an election year so the ensuing chaos will be laid at the feet of the president. They tried the Russian connection, the Ukrainian deal, the failed impeachment towards the end of last year and they have all failed. You ask how they will do it. Approval has been given for the release of some sort of highly contagious deliberately engineered viral bug based on the SARS and MERS viruses. Ironically it originated in the R&D labs at the University of South Carolina but the Department of Homeland Security said it was too dangerous even for their R&D labs if it escaped so Obama arranged for it to be sold to the PRC. Funding for its refinement came from a prominent US cyber billionaire. There is allegedly neither no cure nor any vaccine at the moment. The owners of the patent for the bug resort in a British firm owned by the same cyber billionaire. They may, or may not, already have a vaccine but only available for the insiders so once the bug starts to spread there will be no stopping it. The consequences and the collateral damage will be epic and horrific. Millions will die. "The world economy will grind to a halt and....."

Igor was so stunned he even managed to momentarily get his mind off the girl. He held up his hand. Swerdlov stopped. The older man rubbed his hands over his chin. There was a long silence while he stirred his cold coffee deep in thought. "Hold it there, just a moment. This is a lot to take in. How sure are you that this scenario will in fact actually play out? How does it affect me?" Then he gestured for the bodyguard to fetch him another coffee from the self-service counter.

Swerdlov took a sip of his own cold coffee and carefully placed the cup back in the saucer. "I am one hundred per cent sure of the accuracy of this because the first play has just occurred and apparently been neutralised, probably by the Americans." He handed the morning paper over to Strelnikov. Igor glanced at the headlines on al-Sadr and fixed his piercing eyes on Swerdlov. "Good God, you mean this is the first shot, literally. So it's already started." There was another long silence while Igor tried to get his head round what he was being told. Swerdlov waited patiently. The bodyguard returned with two hot coffees. Eventually Strelnikov spoke. "Seems to me, Mikhail, that you are running late with your intelligence?" Another uncomfortable pause then he added, "Or did you want confirmation, before telling me?"

Swerdlov nodded. "Yes, you might say that the first shots

have indeed been fired. The odds are that the president has just neutralised the first PRC step. But with Beijing there are always others. My sources tell me that the bug in its less virulent form has already been round for some time. There are at least two strains of it, the S Strain which is akin to an intense influenza and the engineered hunter killer version known as the L Strain. Both of these strains mutate and the mutations could go either way – diluted to extinction or intensified into a catastrophe." He had Igor's undivided attention now.

"Go on," he said.

"To answer your second question. When the world economy is forced to a shut down thanks to the isolation steps required to fight the contagion, there will be no more demand for certain commodities, most notably your commodity. The international oil price will plummet through the floor and you literally won't be able to give the stuff away. In fact you may actually have to pay consumers to take the oil off your hands and even then you can rest assured that there will be nowhere to store it."

Strelnikov nearly choked on his coffee. "For how long?" he said softly, thinking of the destruction of his life's work.

"By my estimate three to six months." Strelnikov did choke on his coffee.

"Six months," he almost croaked. "Six months is a lifetime in our industry." There was another long silence. He studied the coffee in the cup as it swirled round the spoon. "Why six months?"

"Isolation will mean lockdown, no international travel and little commerce or industry other than the supply of vital items such as food and medical supplies. There will be a historically un-precedented glut of oil on the world markets and even more seriously for you, a glut of surplus oil tankers full of the stuff along with it."

Igor muttered a Russian oath peculiar to low level street thugs in Moscow. Swerdlov admired and loathed the man at the same time. He found him personally repulsive but he had achieved the pinnacle of his career. Admittedly over a fair number of bodies in the process but success always came at a price. He also paid magnificently and tended to devote more attention than most which was rewarding for Swerdlov's ego.

Igor took up the idea. "So what you are saying, my dear Mikhail, is that the world's economies will melt down, the stock markets will crash, the vaccine if there is one, will be for the elite and then our cyber billionaire will own the rights to that, once it is revealed to the public. And then in collaboration with the new president, who replaces the incumbent at the next election, he will once again be the wealthiest man in the world as he becomes the giver of life and the chance of survival to the doomed. So, I must dispose now of our oil reserves as quickly as possible, rent out the tankers, withdraw from the equities markets into cash and gold and reinvest once the markets show signs of recovery as the vaccination programme takes off and confidence is restored. A very neat little plandemic or should I say scamdemic, I must say."

"That is not all." Swerdlov continued, fingering his empty coffee cup nervously. "At some stage as the US economy looks to be recovering from the pandemic there will be a staged white on black racial incident. I do not know what form it will take but the effects will be spectacular. An economy already tottering will be dealt a death blow as over 200 cities across the US erupt. Rioting, mayhem and chaos will explode across the nation. Businesses, factories, homes and entire suburbs will be incinerated by angry mobs calling for racial justice. Some cities will even be occupied with the collaboration of complicit State and local governments. Liberated zones will emerge. There will be demands for the police to be shut down and the National Guard to be disarmed. The contender for the presidency will be held up as the saviour."

The girl in the far corner was all but forgotten. Money, power and wealth were the drugs on which Strelnikov thrived. His other weakness was sex with young girls and children. His mind was a little overwhelmed.

The bodyguard had been busy during this exchange. After handing the waitress two £50 notes and having a quiet discussion with her he leaned over and passed his boss a piece of paper. In the childish handwriting of the waitress it read, "Emma Westbrooke, RADA student. Here most Saturdays for tea and sandwiches with her mother. Have a good day." As he read it and glanced up, Stefanie entered the restaurant and joined her daughter. The sight of two such beautiful women was too much even for Strelnikov. He motioned for the guard to pay the bill, thanked Swerdlov and brusquely demanded another meeting in two weeks. There was clearly much to be done but at this point he needed to get his mind off the enormity of what he had just learned.

CHAPTER 9

The Chinook flight back into the relative safety of Jordan was shorter than they had anticipated. The warmth of the helicopter after the bitter cold coupled with the psychological comfort of the comparative security had allowed the men to doze but real sleep was out of the question.

Once on the ground they were immediately shifted with their surviving Land Rover 110 into an RAF Globe-master C-17 transport aircraft. They would be flying directly to England. To Herrington's amazement the first of many debriefings was awaiting the exhausted men on board. But first there was more to come. It was all frankly disquieting. The aircraft had been sectioned off. A mobile porta-cabin had been installed with showers and decontamination cubicles. The RAF crew were all wearing NBC gear, and a doctor on board took their temperatures whilst they were told to strip off their gear and thoroughly shower. The cast-off operational kit was sealed in large plastic bags which were then sprayed down with some form of decontaminant. They were then placed in isolation chambers which formed part of the porta-cabin system. None of the team had ever seen this before. They were also carefully questioned by the doctor on their general state of health, which was both disquieting and unusual.

Once satisfied that all was well, three men appeared from the front of the aircraft. Conspicuously out of place was the mysteriously soft spoken, tall and good-looking grey haired Englishman with a cleft chin who materialised from the bowels of the aircraft. He was clad in an immaculate tweed jacket and Guards division dark blue and red tie. He was obtusely introduced as "Sir John, from London". Herrington noted that he was wearing khaki cavalry trousers and tailored desert boots but his steel blue eyes were expressionless even when he smiled. He was accompanied by an equally softly spoken uniformed British Army colonel whom Herrington had never met before and a US Special Forces colonel familiar to the Americans. Herrington liked to know who he was dealing with. Missions might be dangerous but the most astute special-forces members knew only too well that debriefings were the most dangerous part of the entire operation. Missions could get you killed, but debriefings could be seriously life changing career limiting actions.

"I'm sorry, I didn't catch your surname," he said to the man in the tweed jacket.

With a facile smile that seemed more of something between a wince and a grimace, the tall Englishman said just loudly enough to be heard above the noise of the aircraft, "That's correct."

OK, I get it, thought Herrington. I know what you are even if I am not meant to know who you exactly are. We must go out there into the field, blow things up, kill people and not even know who we really work for. Fair enough. That's why they pay us, I suppose.

After perfunctory introductions they took Herrington aside. In-dividual questioning began over an astonishingly delectable hot meal prepared in an efficient but compact galley. Whilst both officers took notes and recorded the answers to their questions Tweed Jacket just listened intently. It was soon clear that he spoke fluent Arabic and Hebrew. He seemed to have an intimate knowledge of the Middle East and his questioning was more conversational than interrogatory. Whereas the two colonels asked detailed and pointed questions Herrington had the impression that in his approach 'Tweed Jacket' was more penetrating and thereby potentially dangerous. His tone and line of conversation almost led one to believe that he was on your side until a sneaky little observation would turn the argument on its head. At one stage Tweed Jacket stopped a particular line of military questioning and both uniformed officers deferred to him with respect. Herrington noted wryly that as soon as they had finished with him he had been assigned to a separate part of the aircraft and the next man had been interrogated, Obviously the actual loss of the aircraft and its crew was a source of major concern but to his surprise the bulk of the enquiry seemed to focus on the killing of al-Sadr and their experiences with the injured girl afterwards. They were all warned that the full debriefing might take two to four weeks and the Americans would not be returning home for the duration. They would also be subject to sporadic medical check-ups. It was going to be a long month.

In the restaurant Emma embraced her mother and welcomed her more like a sister than a mum. She admired, respected and adored Stefanie more than anyone else in her life. And in many respects she subconsciously emulated her mother as a perfect role model.

Stefanie, for her part, had watched her daughter mature

from a frivolous and slightly buck toothed school girl into a more serious young woman blessed with classically beautiful high cheeked features. She was a compulsive student of people, whether emotionally or sartorially. She would have been the first to agree with Shakespeare that the entire world's a stage, and the men and women on it merely players. Her experience in the loss of her dad had impressed on her the desire to go deep within, to learn to recognise and discard the superficialities of life and to come to grips with the real inner core of what she termed 'one's essential being'. She had come to terms with the fact that all people suffer from insecurities – some visible and many invisible, some identified and others latent. Her half English and half West Indian background made her a child of two cultures and she intuitively understood that this could prove a handicap or a tremendous advantage as the years rolled by into later life. It was understanding this and appreciating the opportunities it offered as well as developing the right attitude that had impressed itself on her young and receptive mind.

Her acting ability had already been apparent as a youngster and had led to many practical jokes, not always appreciated by the targets. At school she had demonstrated an open and enquiring mind. Just like her mother she could be critical without being judgemental. As a thirteen year old teenager she had just been learning from both her parents about the dangerous world of men, parties, alcohol and drugs when her father suddenly fell ill and died. The loss of her male role model and the most important man in her life had been completely devastating.

After laying him to rest Stefanie had used part of the funds from his estate to take the two of them to Egypt the following year. It had proved a fascinating trip. They had flown to Cairo and stayed in the Mena House hotel within a stone's throw of the great pyramid of Cheops. The hotel with its vast gardens, rolling golf course and splendid reception facilities was one of those classically famous institutions where Churchill, Montgomery and Roosevelt had stayed during the war, and where President Carter's peace treaty had been negotiated between Israel and Egypt. These luminaries meant little to the young girl from England. For Emma the real joy had been the vast swimming pool in the new part of the hotel and it was here that she had met her first serious male admirer.

Sixteen year old Mohammed el-Noury hailed from a wealthy Dubai family making their first visit to the ancient sites of Egypt. They were scheduled to fly to the Red Sea port of Safaga from where a short drive took them to Hurghada and the lure of Red Sea diving as well as a submarine trip. Emma and her mother were to take a paddle wheeler up the Nile as far as Aswan. His parents had gone to the Egyptian National Museum on the afternoon that he went for a swim in the hotel pool and bumped into the raven-haired bikini clad beauty languidly sunning herself on one of the recliners. He was tall, good looking with square cut features and athletic. She was tanned, of medium height, already sporting a superb figure and classically lovely features. They struck up a conversation and were soon intrigued by each other's contrasting circumstances. But if the whiff of romance was in the air so was the strong smell of disapproval from her mother.

The next day, having talked to her mother with sparkling eyes and a new found zest, which had pleased her mum immensely as it was the first time Emma had shown real excitement since the death of her father. Emma had been whisked off to the incomparably boring Step pyramid in Saqqara and dinner at the famous Gezira Club with a distant uncle who represented the Jamaican government in Egypt. Mohammed had reluctantly said farewell and joined his parents on their Red Sea safari, but fate was to play a strange trick on that holiday. Following the cruise up the Nile, stopping at various exotic temple sites and enchanted by the manner in which the desert in places came right up to the banks of the mighty river, Emma and Stefanie had booked into the Aswan Cataract Hotel.

It is said that hotels with history always seem to carry a mystique of their own. This one was no exception, a mighty rambling comfortably elegant truly colonial remnant of the British Empire with a spectacular view over the first Nile cataracts. Nor had it been exclusively confined to the British. Over a coffee Stefanie had picked up a booklet and read with interest the history of this wonderful building In 1937 the crack Nazi General, Erwin Rommel, had stayed at the Cataract on an ostensible North African safari whilst meticulously noting secret camel routes and communication corridors for possible future use against his British hosts. Here too, Howard Carter, the discoverer of Tutankhamun's elusive tomb had made an arrogant idiot of himself. This was the luxurious retreat in Suite 338 where Agatha Christie allegedly wrote Death on the Nile and where the Aga Khan, King Hussein of Jordan, Prince Philip and even Henry Kissinger had come to relax and unwind to enjoy the almost magical atmosphere at sunset with the feluccas on the river and a string quartet serenading the guests as they sipped their sundowners.

Emma and Stefanie had strolled onto the large terrace for

a pre-dinner drink when a startled exclamation drew their attention to young Mohammed and his family similarly engaged. "Oh, Emma, please do join us," he had begged with childlike simplicity and his father had stood up with all the courtesy that an expatriate English schooling demanded to introduce himself and his wife to Stefanie. It had proven to be an unforgettable evening for both families. The sun sank into a darkening scarlet sky, a warm wind swept in off the desert under the stars, the Nile quietly burbled its enigmatic way towards the distant Mediterranean amongst the dark volcanic rocks and on the terrace, immaculate waiters, in their smart starched whites, served splendid cocktails on glittering silver trays, and Emma felt the first tugs of teenage affection in her heart.

The next day they had driven together for five hours in an air-conditioned bus as part of a long convoy of vehicles under Egyptian military armoured escort from Aswan to visit the imposing Abu Simbel temple site. Heavily armed bandits operating out of nearby Sudan made this journey dangerous necessitating the convoy system. Stefanie also noticed that the tarred road was marked with large poles and on either side towered gigantic sand dunes unlike anything she had ever seen before. So huge were these monstrous undulating dunes looming over the road that she felt quite unsettled, almost threatened but she noted with amusement that Emma and Mohammed had little interest for the wonderland round them or the fact that they were being escorted by armoured cars and troops. The long line of busses, trucks, cars and assorted vehicles passed the turn off to Wadi Halfa, a remote Sudanese town, submerged by the second Russian built Aswan High Dam. This too went un-noticed by the young couple who were only interested in each other, talking about their favourite things in life that affect two young teenagers.

Abu Simbel is perhaps one of the unsung wonders of the ancient and modern world combined, having been rescued from the predatory rising waters of the Aswan dam by the untiring efforts of UNESCO, carved apart and resuscitated in exactly the same position relative to the sun at painstaking astronomical cost. It is not exactly clear why Rameses the Second actually built this extraordinary monument so far from his capital. The local aged tour guide, who looked as though he might himself have dated from the 12th Century BC and known the ancient king personally, explained that Rameses ordered its construction in the thirty fourth year of his reign and that for years it had remained covered and protected by vast quantities of sand before its more recent 'discovery'. It had not meant much to the British girl from London or the native from Dubai but for different reasons they would never forget it either.

Abu Simbel was the first place that a boy took her behind a pillar, or more truthfully into an adjacent chamber in the mighty temple, and gave her a lasting first kiss that would live with her for the rest of her life. Emma had shared her acting ambitions with Mohammed on the bus and he, in turn, had told her of his dream to attend the Harvard School of Business and follow in his father's merchant banking footsteps. The bus had delivered them to the ancient site before lunch and they looked in vain for the temple structure after disembarking in a somewhat disconcerting and sinister circle of armed tourist police, black berets at all angles and un-ironed white uniforms. Emma looked to Mohammed rather than Stefanie for an explanation. He told her that security in this part of Egypt was obviously a major concern after the tourist massacre at the Temple of Queen Hatshepsut some years earlier.

After a lavish luncheon overlooking part of the man-made Lake Nasser that comprises part of the vast Aswan dam, they were driven to a small mountain near the temple site. Stefanie could not help wondering how many ancient temple sites were secluded beneath its blue waters which had not enjoyed the essential UNESCO resources for their preservation and salvation. This approach makes for a memorable experience as the tourist walks round the corner of the artificial mountain and suddenly comes face to face with the four massive figures staring impassively across the lake and its smaller counterpart on the right, the latter devoted to the sun god Ra's partner, Hathor, and to Nefertari, wife of Rameses the Great. Even Emma and Mohammed managed to exhale in unison at the awesome setting and the power conveyed by the massive structures.

Stefanie hung back trying to make out what the ancient tour guide was endeavouring, mostly unsuccessfully, to impart whilst Emma and Mohammed charted their own course through the reconstructed edifice. As the tour group entered the temple they ducked into a small doorway adjacent to the temple. It was marked by a sign paying tribute to the wisdom and foresight of the late President Nasser in having saved the site. Mohammed pointed it out to Emma.

"Ha," he said disdainfully as they entered the gloom. "Little tribute to UNESCO. Lots of homage to Nasser. Yet our taxes and contributions to the UN paid for this lot. Shall we let them go ahead and explore in here."

So saying he opened the small door and they stepped

through into the darkness. She took his hand as if it was the most natural thing in the world and as their eyes adjusted to the gloom they stared in amazement. It was a long cement lined hallway leading into an enormous cavern topped by a huge dome, the whole supported by massive steel girders. As they stared upwards in amazement they could discern gantry walks and access systems with steps and ladders. Emma held her free hand up to her mouth. "It's all unreal. The entire mountain is a fake… it's been manufactured. Imagine the genius that went thinking this all out!" She spoke with an artist's eye.

Mohammed gripped her hand tighter. "I don't know about the design but the cost must have been spectacular," he said looking round him non-plussed. There was a long silence as they took the awe inspiring sight in and then he added. "Nasser could never have done this without the help of the UN and the international community. It's so incredible it's all a bit overwhelming….like meeting you." So saying he took her in his arms and squeezed her unresisting body against his. Their lips met and magic enshrined them. Time stood still. Rameses the Second would have a whole new different meaning for them for the rest of their lives. Then it was over and back outside into the blinding sunshine and rest of the entourage.

The two of them spent the evening at the Seti Abu Simbel lake resort. Stefanie knew with a woman's intuition that her daughter had started to make the change from little girl to young woman. Mohammed's parents also sensed that something was different about their son. He was more quiet, slightly reserved and thoughtful. A new world had opened for all of them.

The drive back the following day to Aswan through the desert seemed to take five minutes and the dinner that night overlooking the Nile assumed a dreamy sensation all of its own mystical making.

When they boarded the plane back to Cairo and then London Emma and Stefanie both knew that something had changed. The little girl was turning into a woman, although she remained a girl in a woman's body. Stefanie was now more a consort and guiding friend, than a parent. 'Was this the time to start letting go?' The trip had done them both a world of good in that having gone some way to easing the pain of their recent loss it had also helped them to both grow up some more with hints of new prospects, opportunities and a new life beyond death.

So it was on that morning in the confines of the Brass Rail that Stefanie returned her daughter's embrace and the two women discussed the mundane trivialities of everyday life. Emma glanced up introspectively. "Mum, you remember Mohammed from our Egyptian visit?"

Surprised Stefanie nodded. "The young man from Abu Simbal whose parents lived and worked in the UAE? Yes, of course. I could hardly forget him. Why?"

"Well, it's just that he phoned last week. He is graduating and has asked for an entry level position with a bank here in London."

Stefanie smiled. "My darling child, that was five years ago and a lot of water has passed through London bridge since then. How did he track you down?"

Emma was reassured. She hadn't known what to expect from her mother. Boys and young men were apt to be seen as something of a threat by Stefanie. "I asked him that too. He was really thrilled with my surprise and told me that he had his ways and means. I begged him to reveal them to me and he was reluctant but then he relented and said that he had seen a script of my play The Producers, on the Web and noted that I was at RADA. Simple really, when one knows how."

Stefanie studied her salt beef sarnie like a surgeon about to make an incision. "So how is it going at the Academy?" She took a delicate exploratory bite. "Hmm, they always manage to get it just right....so?"

Emma grinned. Her mum was ever the cautious one. No big bites in life and no big bites in food either. "Well, mum. It's all about assimilation, acquiring skills and developing techniques. Rolling out working and research practices and exercises which we touched on last year."

Stefanie was unsurprised although drama was about as far from her field as possible. "So, in a sense you are learning to refine your processes from the first year, yeah?"

Emma laughed so loudly the couple at the next table glanced over at them. "Mum, you are ever the clinical psychologist, aren't you? It never stops. But yes, you read it right. This is the final preparation for speeches, plays and possibly castings for our end run next year. We look at things like the role of the professional actor in the industry." She brightened up. "And that means, workshops with actors, directors, producers and script writers which are the really stimulating part. You know the real joy of RADA is that they actually go the extra mile to help one land castings and roles before you leave. And it's a horrendously crowded market out there. But enough of me, how is it going at Wrexham?"

Stefanie swallowed her sandwich. She hated talking about her work, even to her daughter, perhaps particularly to her daughter. Wexham Park Hospital ran a serious unit for those afflicted with severe mental problems and as the Chief Clinical Psychologist at the department she saw the full gamut of human frailty. Perhaps she was over protective of her child but she saw no reason to involve Emma in her line of work.

"Oh, so so,....... you know darling there will always be the unfortunates out there who are not equipped to cope with the rubbish life hurls at them. Frankly, I sometimes wonder if we can't do more to help them and I think to myself, maybe, just maybe in fifty years people will look back and condemn us for being back in the stone age, a bit like we look at the cruel and barbaric practices of a hundred years ago no I reckon we have still only scratched the surface of what really goes on in the human mind and how the brain actually works. I suppose the saving grace is that humans are apparently infinitely versatile and adjustable entities. Humanity might not have survived this far if they weren't."

Emma felt proud to have drawn her mother out this far. Perhaps she could just go a tad further. "There seems to be a lot of talk these days about AI, artificial intelligence," but she saw her mother start frowning. "Do you think that AI might help or exacerbate the sort of problems you see? That rocket scientist guy in the States thinks it's all up to maggots. He reckons it's dangerous."

Stefanie resumed eating which gave her time for a considered answer. "Emma, my darling, you know I hate talking about my work. I will give you an answer and then I want to talk about you. In my opinion AI is possibly the most dangerous thing in the world since they split the atom at the end of the war. It is a form of transhumanism which deprives mankind of our essential humanity. Take away the compassion, the emotions, the ability to be attracted to one another, even the ability, dare I say it, to hate one another and what are you left with – an empty mechanistic shell. The idea is nothing new. Rudolf Steiner always claimed that we would eliminate the soul via medicine. He suggested a vaccine would eventually be produced which would be administered directly at birth."

Emma looked up incredulously at her mother. "You can't be serious. A vaccine… for the entire world? What absolute nonsense."

Stefanie did not smile. "Yes, for the entire world resulting from some terribly lethal epidemic or even a pandemic, doubtless. You can rest assured that it's not such a bizarre idea. Trust me, I'm a doctor!" She laughed now. "This vaccine, administered for other ostensible reasons would obliterate the very thought of the existence of the soul and spirit. It would conveniently destroy the human conscience – the ultimate human obstacle to the materialists. So this would detach the etheric body making the relationship between the universe and the etheric body tenuous at best. Humanity would have a materialistic constitution and cease to aspire to the spiritual. Might as well have a world of robots!" She stared long and hard at Emma. "Which brings me back to what we were discussing a moment ago. Mohammed and his call to you. Would you like to see him again?"

"Oh gosh yes, it would be great. He might be here in two weeks for interviews. He seemed surprised that I had no one in my life but I explained that the main focus of my life is building a career."

"And that is precisely what you should be concentrating on," Stefanie said approvingly. But then mellowed and added, "Though it would be nice to resume contact with him. More coffee?"

Emma nodded and glanced over Stefanie's right shoulder. A large burly well-dressed man was walking out of the restaurant followed by a younger man who could have been a heavy weight boxer. Their departure had been preceded by a nondescript fellow who had not caught Emma's attention when she was talking about Mohammed. The burly man glanced in Emma's direction in such a way that it made her skin crawl but she did not know why. "They get some weird types in here," she said vaguely.

Stefanie hadn't heard her. She was thinking of Mohammed and gazing pensively out the window. "You know it's strange that Mohammed should call like that."

"Why?" Emma always followed up her mother's comments.

"Well, do you remember the old man we met on the paddle wheeler, Empress of the Nile? What was his name....Sendero, Juan Sendero from Bolivia or was it Peru. Yes, Lima. He used to sit every evening in the corner on the upper deck across from the bar overlooking the pool, drinking a whiskey and smoking a cigar. "Remember him? Always smartly dressed in an open necked shirt and blazer."

Emma was not inclined to remember old men but this one with his respectable attire and old world manners had made a profound impression. One evening at dinner he had sat alone at a table next to them. It was after the visit to the

Temple of Philae, another site salvaged from the rising Aswan dam. They had placed the same dinner orders and started talking about the trip. He was a font of knowledge of ancient Egypt and he made it sound exciting and alive. He had invited them to join him for coffee and his customary cigar on the upper deck as the ship slowly steamed up the river to Aswan passing ancient floodlit temple sites and huge sand dunes magnificently silhouetted against the setting sun in the night sky.

They had shown him their digital photographs on the new Canon camera bought at the duty free in Heathrow. They had splendid shots of Luxor and Karnak and they expressed their bemusement at the multiple coloured orbs which had somehow infiltrated their night shots of the Karnak complex. He had studied the pictures for some time in silence before exhaling a large cloud of smoke from his cigar. Were the two women aware of the spiritual energy of ancient Egypt? It was then that he had confessed to being something of a psychic. Emma was intrigued. Could he see into the future? Well, yes, he could, and surprisingly into the past as well, but it was sometimes capable of serving up, in the words of a former US vice president, an inconvenient truth or two.

Stefanie was wary of such people and had said so. She was familiar with voodoo practices from the West Indies and tended to shy away from such nonsense. But she could not deny the plethora of orbs on her camera. Meanwhile Emma begged the old man to give her proof of the psychic powers he claimed. The old man had demurred and made to retire for the night but Emma was insistent. A pretty girl, her attractive mother, a lovely balmy evening, and perhaps a chance for another cigar.

He sat back down again and reaching inside his jacket removed the second cigar. With a deft motion he extracted a small gold clip from his left hand jacket pocket and snipped the end of it. Taking a heavy gold Dunhill lighter from his right hand pocket and a splint, he ignited the splint and lit the cigar to his satisfaction. Returning the lighter to his pocket he looked up at the two women almost wistfully. After a moment's thought he called for Emma's empty coffee cup. He swirled the remaining coffee round and then tossed the remnant liquid into a saucer. Emma was fascinated. He had stared at the bottom of the empty cup for a long time, a much longer time than she reckoned was polite. The only noise was the swishing of the paddles of the steamer and a warm evening breeze on their faces. The smoke from the cigar wafted across the deck and disappeared in the breeze from the movement of the vessel. He glanced up at the two women.

"I do this reluctantly but you have asked and it shall be given. You have both suffered a grievous loss recently. The one you loved is safe and secure on the other side. He returns your love. Know that wherever you are in the world he remains with you. The finances are ok and this holiday has done you both good." He gestured at Emma with his cigar. "You my dear, have met somebody whom you shall meet again before the vacation is over. And then you may in fact meet yet again but not here in Egypt, and not any time soon." The two women had glanced nervously at each other.

"That first part is correct," Emma had said in a whisper. She had tears in her eyes. Stefanie was pensively fiddling with her scarf.

The old man looked up sharply. "I do not need, nor do I

seek, confirmation." Then he relaxed and smiled. "What is given, is given. What you do with it is up to you. I am merely the conduit and not necessarily a willing one." He lapsed into silence and stared out across the deck to the darkening bank of the river. On the far bank a peasant could just be made out leading a camel past a ruined building in the darkness. He turned his attention back to the cup and stared at it morosely shaking his head.

Several minutes went by. The night grew darker and the steamer seemed to pick up speed. She was over taking another paddle wheeler and people were waving to each other from the passing decks. The old man sighed and put the cup down. Emma leaned forward. Stefanie wrapped her shawl tightly round her shoulders.

"You, young lady, must be deeply wary of men from the East. And as for you," he said, pointing his cigar at Stefanie, "You must take very special care of her. Your troubles are not yet over." He put the cup down, and resolutely stood up. "I bid you ladies a good night." So saying he turned and walked away without so much as a hint of a smile on his face. They never saw him again.

Stefanie and Emma looked at one another across the table in Selfridges. They had almost forgotten, five years down the line, that bizarre encounter. It was unsettling to be reminded of what had happened. Both women suddenly felt the urge to go out into the street and get away from the weird thoughts now rekindled in their minds.

Emma noticed that her mother had finished her coffee. "Why don't we take the underground to Green Park and walk up to Fortnum's? I need some air and I think you do too. We can window shop at the Ritz and browse in

Hatchards, if that suits you. I could even buy you a proper lunch," she said sweetly.

"That's a very good proposition," Stefanie said. "Anyway, this place is really filling up and I hate crowds."

They gathered their coats and handbags and made for the door. The walk to the relative warmth of the Oxford Circus Underground was ten minutes followed by a short train ride and out into the cold sunlight of Green Park opposite the Barings branch. The Ritz had its usual gaggle of expensive luxury cars outside and costly jewellery displays in the windows. Hopeful black cabs lined up outside and a number of journalists appeared to be awaiting the arrival or departure of some celebrity. They waited for the lights to change and crossed St James Street, passing Vodafone on the way.

Emma loved these excursions with her mother. Stefanie offered more than just security. She was a rock of stability in an unpredictable and uncertain world. By contrast the men and women in Emma's chosen career were hard to fathom. One always had the feeling that they were playing a role, even playing themselves sometimes as parodies of themselves. It was difficult to dig down through the cosmetic personalities and diaphanous characters to find the real people with real feelings. She cherished their moments together like she had cherished the Egyptian trip for she knew that these shared experiences could not last forever. Life was like that. Indeed, the only certainty in life was death. But hopefully for her that would be a long way off.

Neither Stefanie nor Emma had spotted the man who had left Selfridges before them and impatiently waited outside for their appearance. They failed to see him board the train in the adjacent carriage at Oxford Circus. They were oblivious to his presence whilst he shadowed them past the Ritz maintaining a discrete distance behind them, carefully noting their every move as they entered the distinctive green doors of Fortnum and Mason with its pinstripe suited staff.

CHAPTER 10

The aircraft touched down on the single operational runway at RAF Northolt outside Uxbridge, an airfield that manages civil aircraft as well as military. Northolt air base actually predates the founding of the Royal Air Force by three years having been established in 1915. Northolt had become famous in WWII as the most critical airfield closest to inner London and had become famous for housing the ill-disciplined if deadly Polish fighter squadron No 303 equipped with the legendary Spitfire. Most RAF stations in those days were named after the nearest railway junction, so Northolt took its name from Northolt Halt which is today better known as South Ruislip station. Davies was explaining all this to Atkinson and Price as they had come in to land as well as a mention of the large memorial to those brave fighter pilots.

Herrington was relieved that they had flown back to the UK. In his debrief during the flight on the aircraft he had described the explosion which had killed al-Sadr, their escape, the girl on the road, and the subsequent detonation on the aircraft. He had glossed over their escape to the emergency RV although it appeared that the others had been closely cross examined on the armoured convoys they had encountered and the journey out. The smelly pit which had proved Atkinson's undoing was also discussed in some depth. Three of them had expected to be driven or flown by helicopter to Hereford for a more detailed debriefing but to their surprise they were told they were going to the nearby Northwood Headquarters the multi-national NATO HQ base and permanent tri-service British Ministry of Defence HQ from where all overseas military operations are planned and controlled. Atkinson would be joining them later but was immediately taken off in an unmarked ambulance for medical attention to the ankle and ribs as well as his multiple facial abrasions.

England welcomed them back with its traditional cold and foggy weather. The drive to Northwood was preceded by a chance to strip off their uniforms, shower and generally clean up. To their surprise even their fresh uniforms were placed in decontamination bags for specialised chemical analysis after the Iraqi pit experience and they were kitted out in near perfectly fitting civilian trousers and jackets. Clean shaven and refreshed they were presentable if exhausted and somewhat surprised to find themselves at Britain's overseas operational command HQ. On arrival they were ushered into a comfortable debriefing room and told to wait. Tea for the Brits and coffee for Price complemented the excellent meal they had been served on the aircraft.

It was not long before an immaculate avuncular British vice admiral entered the room accompanied by his American counterpart and the two colonels who had conducted the earlier debriefing on the flight to England. Of Tweed Jacket, Herrington noted with some relief, there was no sign. He had not even said goodbye after their arrival but seemed to have disappeared at speed into an unmarked bullet proof Range Rover heading for London. Good riddance, thought Herrington, feeling more comfortable with his military environment. Vice Admiral Sir Alan Keyes was a tall good looking man with square cut features. He welcomed them and introduced himself as Chief of Joint Operations. Hmmm, Herrington thought to himself. This is serious. He had no idea how right he might be proved. They shook hands all round and he told them to please sit back and relax. He said that even as they were speaking Atkinson was receiving first rate medical attention and would be re-joining them in due course. He told them that in his opinion they were owed an explanation. He had an un-nerving characteristic of slightly cocking his head fractionally forward and looking each man directly in the eye through his bushy eye brows before speaking. Herrington wondered if this was a command characteristic he had picked up earlier in his service career while serving as captain of an RN aircraft carrier for several years.

"I want to start by thanking you and congratulating you on accomplishing your mission. The loss of the aircraft is a serious matter and will be gone into later in the debriefing. I am deeply sorry about the deaths of your colleagues. Sadly, as you will appreciate only too well, this is a deniable operation so there will be no public announcement of their deaths. There is another reason for this. The operation is not over. One arm of the octopus has been excised but it seems that there could well be others arising even as we talk. You may be relieved to know, however", he said with a slight pause and staring at Herrington through his eyebrows, "that your part in this mission is over. By your actions you may have averted a world-wide catastrophe. Unfortunately, the game is not finished. Not by a long shot at this stage, by all accounts."

Herrington raised his hand. The vice admiral nodded. "Sir,

are we permitted to know a bit more about the target. And indeed where this all goes from here."

The vice admiral glanced at his colleagues. "The reason you have been brought here is because of the very special nature of this mission. Al-Sadr was not just a terrorist. He was a super terrorist with extraordinary ambitions. His objective was the contamination of multiple Middle East and North African illegal migrants with an artificially engineered peculiarly contagious and lethal strain of the SARS respiratory virus for infiltration into Western Europe and the United States. A faction of the Chinese Communist Party in the PRC was working with him to facilitate the spread of this deadly concoction. The idea, so far as we can ascertain, was to force the shutdown of the Western economies by virtue of the necessity for isolation to prevent the spread of the disease, collapse their markets, generate massive unemployment and job losses in addition to the multiple ensuing deaths, and then buy up the essential industries and businesses as they crashed. At the same time, taking further advantage of the international chaos, Beijing was planning to launch aggressive strategic maritime moves from their artificial island bases in the South China Sea, on the border with India in Ladakh, through their dependent acolyte in North Korea and massive cyber-attacks on the West kicking off with Australia. In short, it is the sort of ploy that Stalin, Hitler and Mao Tse-tung could only dream of but never had the biological wherewithal to accomplish. By killing al-Sadr, who, by the way was carrying the virus in glass vials in his briefcase at the time of his demise, you have temporarily stopped one phase of the implementation of the plan."

The three men looked stunned. The vice admiral had

stopped smiling. Herrington made a gesture to speak but was cut short.

"I think I know what you are going to ask. If this was the first phase then what lies ahead of us. Truth to tell, we are not certain but the indications are that it cannot be ruled out that the city in the PRC where this bug is manufactured and believe me, engineered it most certainly appears to be, may experience a deliberate "accidental" leak. The PRC authorities will deal with this so called 'accidental leak' quite ruthlessly and will be apparently unable to stop it. It will then spread round the world uncontrollably and unrestricted. "Your mission has just stopped that for the moment."

Davies couldn't contain himself. "Strewth Sir, Surely the World Health Organisation will pick this up and what about their own people?"

The American colonel nodded to the vice admiral. "Allow me to elaborate on this. The PRC is a totalitarian communist state. It comprises 1.4 billion people. It is their most compelling resource. If they lose a thousand, ten thousand or even hundreds of thousands it will make a very small dent in a massive human machine. But if countries in Europe are infected such as Greece at 9 million, Spain at 47 million, Italy at 60 million or even the UK at 66 million, not to mention the US at 328 million then the ramifications are diabolical. As for the WHO it is currently headed by an Ethiopian communist who owes his position to the PRC and will likely collaborate with them to slow down the Western response and discredit those countries that take early prophylactic measures against the virus."

Price looked aghast. "Seems to me, Sir, there are too many

people in the world already?"

A pained look crossed the American colonel's face. "You've touched a raw nerve. There are those in the West who would agree with you and see both financial and other opportunities in the event of this scenario playing out. For instance, the virus originated in the US at the University of North Carolina but research on the bug was considered too dangerous so our Department of Homeland Security shut down all research. Incredible as it may sound, a certain individual in the US government then arranged to sell the bug to the PRC and even arranged funding through a front outfit for further research. That funding amount to over thirty million dollars and weirdly emanated from the Pentagon. In addition, there was involvement from Canada, Australia and even the French were invited to contribute but backed off. The same globalist elements see an unprecedented marketing opportunity for a compulsory global vaccine with an attached DNA tracker. Our intelligence people suspect that there might be potentially lethal consequences attached to this so called vaccine, which is in part, in reality, a form of gene modification. Oddly it existed before the impending disease threat and all the animals it was tested on have died."

There was a stunned silence as they tried to absorb the meaning of what had been shared. Herrington shifted uncomfortably in his chair. "My God, you're suggesting that the disease was invented to pave the way for the vaccine.... Sir?" Having blurted out his thoughts aloud he suddenly felt very lonely and isolated as the others stared at him.

The vice admiral clasped his hands together and looked each of them in the eye as he took a deep breath to carry on. He ignored the question. "So you see, gentlemen, it's even murkier than what I have told you but this is sufficient for the moment. Your crucial role in this matter is over. Well, almost over. However, you have been brought here for extensive debriefings as we need every scrap of intelligence we can lay our hands on to cope with what we suspect is coming. You will also be given constant medical checks and on the basis of those screenings you will be allowed to mingle with the civilian population in between debriefing sessions."

The vice admiral allowed himself a smile. "Colonel Jones has been very direct. This conversation never took place. Now it's time for you to relax and rest as we proceed with the information analysis and acquisition. Thank you again gentlemen and my condolences on your losses."

And so saying he dismissed them.

The de-briefings were tediously exhaustive and endless. Again and again the actual strike had been examined and the ensuing escape and evasion. The girl with the bomb in the road had apparently been identified from internal intelligence. It was strongly suspected that she had nothing to do with their operation but had been the victim of a vicious internal Sunni versus Shiite internecine power struggle. Iraq was known to be riddled with competing factions seeking control over the area through which they had been travelling. It gradually transpired that it had just been, in the words of the vice admiral himself, "a most unfortunate decision" to proceed by taking her along with them. They even included soil samples from the wheels of the Land Rover 110. Some of this had proven to be mildly radioactive to the consternation of the interrogation teams. The old uniforms were cut up and analysed for chemical, nuclear and biological contaminants. Traces of several possible chemical warfare substances were found on Atkinson's kit. Atkinson himself joined them after two weeks. He had been subjected to 14 days isolation or what they termed preventive quarantine plus numerous medical tests and repeated health checks. The severely sprained ankle had been set in a boot like contraption. There was little they could do for him in respect of the broken rib.

The other critical part of the debriefing involved a careful psychological assessment of the men's state of mind. Herrington was appalled by what had happened to the men on the Hercules. Davies also felt a huge sense of loss as he was the RAF liaison officer. Atkinson curiously, although the only one physically wounded, seemed to have emerged psychologically relatively unscathed. But it was Price, the doctors noticed and reported to the de-briefing team, who bore the overwhelming guilt complex for what had happened. And that was natural, because Price had been the one to argue the case for taking the injured girl along with them, who had persuaded Herrington it was in all their best interests to do so and who had encouraged Bezuidenhout to endorse the proposal.

A dark and sinister cloud of overwhelming guilt hung over Price which gnawed at his being, his spirit and even his soul. Price was becoming introverted in the extreme, keeping himself to himself and having little to say to his colleagues. On occasion they noticed him talking to himself. He chewed his finger nails and the cuticles to the point where his fingers cracked and bled. He would often run his hands over his face and through his hair. Often at the dining table he would sit with his right knee bouncing uncontrollably up and down as his foot tapped out a silent staccato on the floor under the table. He became crusty and short tempered. The scenes, not from the explosion of the aircraft, but the wounded girl in the road, went round and round in his head endlessly. Price effortlessly blamed himself for what had happened.

It was late January and nearly four weeks into the debriefing Herrington asked to see the vice admiral.

It was a less amicable meeting than on the first occasion. The American colonel who had been on the returning aircraft to England was present as well. He explained that the team were concerned about Price and suggested they be allowed to spend some time off base. His parents happened to have a home nearby and Davies conveniently had family in the vicinity. A break would do them all a power of good. Davies would be happy to accommodate Atkinson. The medical personnel had given them all a clean physical bill of health. They would be within easy travelling distance of the base but under less rigorous circumstances. A relaxing interlude could only do them all a power of good. The colonel and the vice admiral looked at each other and explained that they had been thinking along the same lines. But there was a serious problem. Price was taking strain. Everyone could see that. If his friends went home for a week what would happen to him?

Herrington explained that it would be his privilege to accommodate Price in his family home. Take him out to a pub for dinner one night or a local restaurant. Try to pull him out of himself, so to speak. The senior officers were sympathetic but insisted that they would have to consult the psychological team first. Herrington said that he fully understood that. In his opinion the sooner they all had a change of scenery the better and the more productively fulfilling the rest of the debriefing process would be. The senior officers were as good as their word. The following morning Herrington was informed that the break had been welcomed and approved. They could leave that afternoon.

Conveniently, Herrington's parents lived in a comfortable typically English home on Monro Gardens, not far from the bus garage, a part of Harrow Weald, close to Northwood. The family welcomed Price as if he were a long last relative. Price seemed to settle in well feeling quite at home in the suburban development with its homes, schools, small shops, supermarkets and pubs. Although the name 'weald' referred to a forest or woodland, not much remained of the original verdant hills responsible for the name. But traces of the ancient woodland could still be found on the border of Middlesex and Hertfordshire which counted amongst the highest ground in the greater London area. It was here that Herrington took Price for long delightful walks into the eastern part of the woods which merged with those of Stanmore and Bentley Priory or striding through the Harrow Weald Common adjoining the Harrow Weald site of Special Scientific Interest. Bentley Priory was where RAF Fighter Command had been headquartered during the war and from where Hugh Dowding had successfully directed the battle of Britain. Price decided that he loved England. Like many Americans he treasured his English ancestry and the compelling atmosphere of history and continuity which seemed to give the British a curious sense of security and confidence lacking in so many other societies.

The foot tapping stopped and the nightmares seemed to fade. John Price was gradually coming back into himself.

One afternoon after a particularly congenial family luncheon they were strolling along the southern edge of the high ground along the Old Redding road to the car park with its panoramic views of London. The weather was cold, crisp and clear. Price suddenly turned to Herrington and said, "You know Nigel, this is an amazing and enchanting country for an American whose ancestors hailed from here. I almost feel as if I could settle down and live here. Very comfortable and satisfying it would be too. And you have been incredibly kind to me since the disaster in Iraq. The last few weeks have been kind of stressful but this break has been wonderful. Can't I take all the lads out to dinner somewhere nearby?"

Herrington was very touched. "By all means, if you would like to. It's a great idea. Instead of dinner we could make it a luncheon. There is the Namaste Lounge that was the Northwood Hills Hotel nearby and a reasonably civilized place. It's just across the road from the Metropolitan line. Why not aim for tomorrow? I can contact the others and arrange transport." Satisfied with their plans, both men turned and walked back the way they had come.

Herrington was giving Price some verbal info on his choice of lunch venue "There is a plaque on the wall that states George Hill the landlord gave Sir Elton John his first gig. Back then he was Reginald Dwight and as Reggie he worked Thursday to Sunday nights for twenty five pounds plus tips. On the piano he played songs by Jim Reeves and Ray Charles".

Price laughed. "Whoa, that must have been a long way back in time."

"1962, and he was fifteen years old," Herrington observed ruefully.

In London three weeks earlier after his climactic luncheon with Swerdlov, Igor Strelnikov had detailed his bodyguard to follow Emma and Stefanie whilst he hastened back to his offices in his armoured Mercedes limousine. Once there he called his PA, Viktor Kapitsa, to come back to work. Then he had made a series of phone calls to confirm the astonishing information provided by his spy. It was hard to verify but the reports emanating from the PRC indicated that they had notified the World Health Organisation on 31 December of an impending problem with a contagious infection. To his chagrin his well-paid contact at the WHO would not confirm nor deny the rumours that the bug was highly contagious. Igor thought his female friend in Switzerland was being just a little too coy. He put the phone down on her and turned back to the computer. He was keen to know how the incumbent head of the WHO had achieved his position. It was astonishing how fast one could learn simple facts by simply studying data in the public domain on a computer. His eyes widened as he learned that the WHO chief was not a doctor, had actively campaigned for the position with the backing of the PRC and that he himself was a former high ranking Communist cabinet minister in the Ethiopian regime responsible for covering up a massive cholera infection to the detriment of his countrymen. He had also been involved in some shady deals with a very well connected political family in America. In short, he owed the PRC big time and might well order a cover up.

Strelnikov sat back and stared at the ceiling. His office was ultra-modern, all glass and steel with some contemporary art on the walls which was allegedly both highly thought of and expensive. A large model of one of his oil tankers took up one side of the room and a bookcase filled with books mostly on the Russian energy industry took up the other wall. A few plants, assiduously cared for by his PA, gave a bit of life to what would have otherwise been a depressingly austere setting.

He reached over and pulled the gold cigar box across the desk to within reach, removed a cigar and a gold clip and walked over to the model of the tanker. He carefully clipped the cigar, lit it and then stood for a long time staring at the model deep in thought. This was one of the more critical decisions of his life. If his informant had got it wrong he would be ruined as would many others in the criminal underworld who depended on him for a living. That would be the end of him in more ways than one. If he got it right, he could double or treble his fortune. What also perplexed him was that a number of American CEOs were suddenly handing in their resignations and collecting their massive pay packets. It didn't make sense. Well, he thought, it certainly did make sense if they knew what he knew. The rumour was that this man in the White House was directing enquiries into paedophilia with links to some of these CEOs in the light of the Epstein so called suicide but that might be a cover for something much bigger. He puffed on his cigar and walked over to the window. The sun had disappeared behind a cloud bank and it was gently raining again. He stood there a long time wreathed in smoke and then strode back to the desk. Punching the intercom he summoned Kapitsa.

Half an hour later Kapitsa exited Strelnikov's office wondering if the boss had gone stark raving mad. It was going to be a long night. Effectively, the firm was entering a state of suspended animation. All tankers were to off load their stocks and offer their vessels for storage at a price. Wells were to be shut down with immediate effect; employees put on half pay or summarily retrenched. Existing storage tanks were to be emptied and offered for rental as temporary oil storage facilities at a ridiculously high price. He couldn't help wondering if his boss thought the world was going to end. The only aspect that had given him hope was an enquiry to be directed to one of the body guards involving a young woman he had spotted in a restaurant at Selfridges. Before he did anything else, the PA picked up the phone and called his broker. "Hello Juergen, this is Viktor at the Firm. Yes, Juergen, listen to me carefully. I want you to sell all my equities now. I don't care what the market is doing or what you think it is going to do. Cash in now. No, I cannot explain. Just do as I say."

If he had told Juergen to jump off a cliff, he couldn't have elicited a more volatile reaction. Having looked after himself it was time to look after the boss. The phone calls and confirmatory emails began to go out. Howls of protest were met with stone walling and then threats. The threats met with counter threats and so it went, but gradually Igor Strelnikov stripped himself and his company of his exposure and his liabilities. And the details on Emma began to come in too. It seemed there might be life after death, after all.

They arrived at the Northwood Hill Hotel and congregated in the bar for a drink before entering the Namaste dining room with its long neon lights, wide screen HD television and tables and chairs on the raised Dias. The plan was to enjoy a really congenial luncheon under the most pleasant and relaxed circumstances imaginable. As with all soldiers the conversation focused on military matters. True to form nothing was mentioned of the circumstances surrounding their mission but they did note that all hell seemed to be breaking loose in a remote Chinese city called Wuhan. Places were being locked down, people were being detained and what the American president was referring to as the China Virus appeared to be taking off. They all looked wryly at one another and drank a toast to the special forces. Atkinson complained that his ankle was still giving him more discomfort than he had been led to expect and the curious boot affair he was forced to don didn't make it any easier.

Before they knew it the time had advanced to four pm and in a jolly mood they piled out of the hotel with Atkinson in tow. A distinguished elderly gentleman wearing a Cavalry and Guards tie clad in an expensive cashmere coat followed them down the steps outside and allowed them to pass. He stopped in the car park to light his exquisite Dunhill pipe.

Herrington hung back to phone for their car. He handed the half full glass bottle of spring water to Price and was still punching the buttons on his mobile when loud voices made him look up. Across the road heading for the station he spied a scruffy group of young men, clad in jeans, sneakers and anoraks. They looked as if they were heading up to London for an entertaining Friday evening. Price and Atkinson were slightly ahead of Davies. At this point the military driver answered the call. Herrington apologised for the late request but asked for a pick up. The driver agreed but before Herrington had finished the call he saw the youths cross the road exchanging insults with the two Americans. "No fancy dance moves there mate," one of them taunted.

Atkinson ignored him, but Price took offence. All the good work accomplished by the walks, the counselling and the dinner bonhomie evaporated in a flash. Price said something in reply and one of the youths gave Atkinson a shove unwittingly on the broken rib. Atkinson gave a startled cry. He went down like a sack of potatoes. Before Davies or Herrington could intervene Price stepped forward and punched the assailant hard in his face. Blood spurted from a broken nose, several teeth fell out and the yob went down squealing.

A larger yob colleague stupidly stepped forward dancing on his toes. "Goddamn Yanks, overpaid, overfed, oversexed and over here. Why don't you eff off to your friggin country, you piece of…." But he never finished the insult. One step too close was enough for Price to whom unarmed combat was second nature. He grabbed his assailant's inner right wrist, pulled him close while blocking the blow from his left hand into which a knuckle duster had magically appeared, and brutally head butted him. He smashed the half full glass water bottle into the thug's knee then swung the groggy thug hard round hurling him to the ground just in time to catch the man in the cashmere coat who had sought to step round the fight and was fumbling for his car keys.

In his day Colonel Garth Cartwright, formerly of the Grenadier Guards, had been quite a pugilist, but that had been many years ago. The lout from Uxbridge slammed into him, with all the force Price could muster. Cartwright, caught unawares, staggered then lost his balance and fell back heavily slamming his head into the kerb. Blood poured from the head wound. He groaned, his eyes fluttered, then turned upwards and he passed out.

"Fook it," shouted a Scottish lad. "That's me outa here afore the coppers come". Leaving their two prone friends the gang took to their heels and fled.

Colonel Cartwright started to go white as the gutter filled with blood from the back of his skull. Davies and Herrington came dashing up. Davies rushed to check on Atkinson who was still rolling on the ground in pain. Herrington whipped off his white scarf and wrapped it tightly round the wound on the old man's head. Once bound he phoned for an ambulance. But with the ambulance came the police summoned by an observer from the hotel. And with the police came major problems for Price, his colleagues, and two governments at perhaps the worst possible time.

CHAPTER 11

By early February Strelnikov had made the final arrangements to rid himself of his exposure to the oil industry.
True, staff and his closest colleagues thought that he might
be having a nervous breakdown but they did as they were
told. The consequences of ignoring Strelnikov did not merit
consideration. Simultaneously, he monitored developments
in China with the closest interest and derived immense
satisfaction from learning that there were vigorous efforts
to ruthlessly suppress any information on the outbreak of
the new virus. When he learned that plans were afoot in
Wuhan to destroy all samples of the virus and to destroy
the laboratory where it might have been developed, he was
delighted. His contemporaries were utterly baffled. The
other item that obsessed him was the girl in the restaurant
at Selfridges. He could have his choice of any young girl but
Emma ticked all his perverted boxes and he had to have her.
Having identified where Emma resided, he arranged for a
member of his underworld entourage to visit the house on
the pretext of checking for gas leakages.

Twenty four year old Melvin Pollitt was good at this sort of
thing. He had been brought up in the back streets of Belfast
and conducted similar reconnaissance operations many
times for the IRA. Emma's house was carefully watched
and her hours were noted. One afternoon when Stefanie

was still at work he made his approach. Dressed in overalls and clutching a clipboard with a fake ID identifying him as Martin Peters he confidently rang the doorbell of the little semi-detached house in Harefield. Emma came to the door to find a young handsome Irishman with an official looking notice from the Council seeking admittance to check for gas leaks.

Melvin's alias knew he was a catch for the girls. Well built, good looking in a cavalier way, blessed with the gift of the gab and a shock of blond hair that refused to swing out of his eyes, he charmed Emma into a cup of tea and a revealing conversation she ought never to have entertained. When he left the house over an hour later, he had impressed even himself with his success.

On reporting back to Strelnikov the Russian himself had difficulty accepting how much information Martin, or rather Melvin, had coaxed out of Emma ranging from her family circumstances, her daily routines, her friends and even her cell phone number.

After listening carefully for fifteen minutes to an account of the dialogue he dismissed Melvin with a generous enhancement to his end of year bonus, and sat back to think of a way to start enticing the girl. She was still just young enough to satisfy his more peculiar sexual aspirations, and indeed when he had finished with her to his satisfaction, to add to the coterie of eastern European young women that he regularly trafficked to a paedophile contact in the US. In fact, on reflection, he reckoned she was tailor made for the experience. A working mother unable to keep a close eye on her, a deceased father unable to warn her of life's more devastating realities and a youthful idealistic enthusiasm for a posh career in the flashy rewarding entertainment business.

Emma was walking back from the bus stop to her home one evening about a week later when she heard her cell phone ringing. It was not a number that she recognised but when she heard Melvin's voice a little thrill coursed up her spine. Would she like to meet an international movie agent who had excellent contacts in Hollywood and was a good personal friend of Melvin's? It might even lead to a small role in an upcoming Hollywood production, although he couldn't make any promises at this stage. Emma fell for it hook, line, sinker and rod. That evening she couldn't wait for Stefanie to get home. Lucky breaks like this came once in a lifetime.

For her part Stefanie was suspicious from the outset. "Why is he doing this for you, are you sure he is not after something else?" Every mother worth her salt has an intuition second to none where her daughter is concerned. In Stefanie's case this intuitive ability to recognise, or rather feel that she was looking into danger, was even more finely honed due to the death of Emma's father. Stefanie listened carefully to the account of how they had met and did not like what she heard one iota. Did Emma appreciate that Hollywood was a cesspit, that opportunities like this were scarcer than hen's teeth and this young Irish lad was probably only too keen to wrap her round his finger for a long time. Had he provided any proof of his so called friend's movie making connections – indeed had he even mentioned a name? She was not surprised when Emma could not supply satisfactory answers to any of her questions. She suggested that Emma decline the invitation to meet the young man again and write off the whole thing to experience.

Daughters tend to take their fathers more seriously than their mothers. Psychologists say that in normal families there is friction between mother and daughter competing for the attention of the father. But in this case the father figure was missing. Stefanie would customarily have appealed to her husband to give Emma some serious man talk but that option was not available. Moreover, she did find Melvin attractive, and the attraction made his offer all the more compelling. So, when the call came, she listened carefully to what he had to say and without telling her mother agreed to a meeting. There was one saving grace. She mentioned the whole thing in passing to a friend at RADA, Victoria Parker, who was studying script writing. They were lunching at a nearby Starbucks when the subject came up. Victoria was a sensible girl with a father. She listened carefully and immediately congratulated Emma but added that under normal circumstances she would discuss it with her dad.

"Emma darling, I think it's an awesome opportunity but just be a bit careful. Don't you have a male relative you can talk to?"

Emma pondered for a moment. They were sitting at a table by the window watching the rain gently pouring down outside and dispassionately observing an unfortunate Starbucks waitress standing in the freezing rain. She was offering free small cardboard cups of coffee to passing pedestrians in a futile attempt to lure them inside. Emma reckoned it was a generous gesture by the Starbucks management and it did occasionally work but in the main the poor girl was either contemptuously dismissed or totally ignored. "Vicky, truth to tell, other than my mother's brother, I have no one like that. And he wouldn't approve it either."

Victoria was taken aback. "Why?"

"Well you see he's a Detective Chief Superintendent in the Thames Valley Division at New Scotland Yard and he is naturally suspicious of everybody and everything. And if it's real it's such a terrific opportunity. If it comes to nothing, I will put it down to 'I gave it my best shot'." And so it was that Emma's fate was sealed.

When the call came it was carefully timed to ensure that Stefanie could be nowhere within ear shot. One of Strelnikov's thugs ascertained that Stefanie was in consultation at the hospital. Yet another was watching Emma on the bus and gave Melvin the thumbs up. The operation nearly failed from the inception because Emma had her phone on silent mode but just as Melvin was about to give up, she felt the vibration in her coat pocket.

"Emma, its Martin, how are you getting on?"

She felt a little knot in her stomach. "Hi, I'm so glad you called. I'm good and you?"

Strelnikov silently nodded approvingly across the desk in his office from Melvin. "I spoke to my friend and he is keen to meet you. Would you like to meet for lunch at Greens restaurant just off Jermyn Street and I can introduce you to him?"

The knot grew tighter. "Yeah, great. When Martin?"

Sticking to the script Melvin stared into Strelnikov's steel eyes and said, "Is tomorrow Friday too soon for you. Say at twelve thirty."

They agreed to meet and she could hardly contain herself. That night not a word was said to Stefanie who sensed that something was afoot. She knew that if she pushed it too far her daughter might do the exact opposite so she bit her tongue and held her peace. In time to come she would bitterly reflect on that.

The lunch was cordial and professional. She wore a green matching skirt and jacket with her hair done up in a bob. She knew she really looked a million dollars. Melvin arrived with Strelnikov in tow. He came across as suave, debonair and sophisticated. His manners were impeccable, standing behind her chair and making sure she was comfy before he sat down and his approach to her as convincing as his line. He was a very successful Russian businessman in London with extensive international connections. That much was certainly true. He had a friend in Hollywood called Harry Waxman who was always on the lookout for talent. Harry was a heavy weight in the entertainment business and also owned a world class modelling agency. Might she be interested in flying over to meet him for an interview and a simple audition? Of course, the flight would be paid for plus all accommodation. Harry always worked that way. It all sounded too good to be true. It was.

When they came out of Greens it was sleeting. Where was Emma going? Ah, to the Piccadilly Underground. Well, here was his Mercedes limousine. Could he gallantly offer the two of them a ride to the Underground? Emma noted the bodyguard in the front passenger seat and laughingly remarked that her mother had always cautioned her against accepting rides with strange men. Melvin agreed with a cynical little laugh and then added.

"Don't worry I'll make sure you are secure!" The turn of phrase caught her attention and was then discarded. It was a promise he was to keep. Mr Strelnikov courteously opened the car door for her while Melvin got in on the other side. Strelnikov squeezed in beside her on the right and locked the door. She thought she faintly recognized a familiar hospital smell over the powerful reek of stale cigar smoke but she couldn't place it. The car moved into the London traffic. Now she noticed that the windows in the rear of the vehicle were totally blacked out. Strelnikov put her at ease pointing to a young woman walking a little dog on the driver's side of the car. Martin leaned forward and removed a plastic zip lock bag from the seat pocket in front of him as she watched the little dog. Too late she remembered the sudden overwhelming stench of chloroform. She tried to reach the door handle as the pad was locked over her face but both men forcibly restrained her and with the next breath she was gone. The nightmare had just begun.

At about the same time a different nightmare was starting for John Price. The British police are proud of the fact that, on average, they can get a car anywhere in an urban setting within four minutes and anywhere in the country within eight to ten minutes. In Uxbridge they excelled themselves. A car surprisingly arrived on the scene in two minutes. It didn't help that the driver was a trainee woman police constable who seemed aghast at the sight of blood and her mentor was a man she intensely disliked. An ambulance arrived in five minutes. The crew took one look at the colonel and administered immediate first aid, carefully loading him onto a stretcher and whisking him away. The two thugs were similarly taken away to another hospital by the second ambulance which arrived shortly after the first. One of Atkinson's assailants had a smashed knee, and severe concussion. The other suffered a broken nose, a dislocated jaw and equally severe concussion.

Recognising the immediate dangers of a security compromise in their situation Herrington sought to take charge of the proceedings. The two young police officers were having none of it. He produced his military ID and tried to persuade them to come into the hotel and sit round a table to discuss what had happened. The WPC did not know what to do but was amenable. She was inclined to start the discussions in a polite amicable way. Her mentor brusquely disregarded her suggestion and having curtly studied his ID card, informed Herrington that this was a civil matter resorting purely under the police unconnected with the military. Herrington was not accustomed to being crossed like this and took immediate offence. Tempers began to flare.

Matters were further complicated when a distant siren announced the arrival of the Royal Military Police in an enormous camouflaged Land Rover 110. They had wisely been summoned by an astute Davies who could smell big trouble a mile away. Unlike the civil police they were all experienced policemen accustomed to managing problems like this. Three astonishingly burly 'Red Caps' piled out of the 110 and strode over to the group standing outside the hotel. One had a video camera and began filming from a distance as the other two introduced themselves. As luck would have it they were all officers who had been planning on some quick evening shopping and they had very little respect for the civil police.

The only independent witness to what had happened was the colonel who now looked dangerously close to succumbing. The manager of the hotel had heard the final stages of the fracas as Herrington shouted to warn the yobs off and called the police with commendable alacrity. The harder Price tried to explain what had happened, endorsed by Herrington, the more difficult the Investigating Officer became. Colonel Cartwright's perilous condition did not help. In the interim the car summoned by Herrington to collect all of them had arrived. The manager gave a brief statement to the police as to what he had witnessed but his account was limited to the final stages of the confrontation.

The two police officers insisted that Price accompany them to the local police station for an extended "interview". Herrington took the two Red Caps aside and after a quiet word the RMPs explained to the local police that Price would travel with them in the Land Rover, the military driver would take Atkinson and Davies and Herrington would travel with the two police officers. Dignity being satisfied all round they set off in convoy for the police station. In the police car on the way Herrington phoned the vice admiral at Northwood and the SAS Commanding officer at Hereford. On arrival at the police station all four men were separately interviewed in the presence of the three Red Caps and the two IOs. Astoundingly for the police, all their stories dovetailed.

Such was the gravity of the situation that it was felt necessary for the Station Commander at Uxbridge to be consulted by the two IOs. It swiftly became clear to all of them that the police were determined to charge Price with assault with grievous bodily harm. Herrington took extreme exception to this as did the three RMPs, who clearly felt that this was matter that fell entirely within their jurisdiction. There is no love lost between the Royal Military Police and the civil authorities. The former reckon that they are a cut above the run of the mill police officer and expect due deference. The Red Caps placed a call to their Commanding Officer. There ensued a protracted discussion between the Station Commander and the Officer Commanding the Royal Military Police which ended with an unsatisfactory compromise for everyone except Price. It was agreed that Price would be charged but released into the custody of the RMPs. Trial was set for 21st February in three weeks. Dignity having been satisfied all-round the meeting adjourned and the four Special Forces men joined their military driver for what should have marked the end of a most pleasant relaxing afternoon.

Back at Northwood there was consternation. What the American president was terming 'The China virus' was now spreading like wildfire across the world, despite the much publicized operation against al-Sadr. The public at large had no idea as to why he had really been eliminated, nor the British involvement in the operation. It had to stay that way. But a public trial of the soldier involved could well leak the depth and extent of strategic and tactical Anglo-American co-operation at a critically sensitive time in world affairs. On 31 January the American president had announced a controversial travel ban on the PRC. Initially heavily criticized by his opponents for imposing the quarantine, he would later be equally vehemently condemned for not imposing the ban soon enough.

It would not be long before travel bans were put in place all over the world in a futile and desperate attempt to stop the plague spreading. The matter was considered so serious that the British Prime Minister was briefed on what had happened in Uxbridge and it would not be long before he himself succumbed to what was now being termed the Covid-19 infection. Later his MI6 advisers would warn him that they could not guarantee that he had himself not been deliberately infected as part of an assassination plot. As it would turn out the PM would be lucky to survive.

Plans were discussed at the highest levels to just secretly repatriate Price and Atkinson but that would create an even bigger civil versus military conflict. In any case it soon became evident that it was unlikely that anyone would be travelling anywhere in the world as borders started to close, airlines shut down, controls were imposed and infected death rates increased. The British Minister of Foreign and Commonwealth Affairs and his American counterpart, the US Secretary of State, discussed the matter on secure telephones. The US Secretary of State told his British colleague in no uncertain terms that his president had made it clear that while he was grateful for the British co-operation in taking out al-Sadr, he wanted his men back. All involved took a keen interest in Colonel Cartwright's medical progress which was not encouraging. Questions were asked by the Americans as to why the two thugs had not been arrested and charged with assault. If their man had to face the music so should they.

The British demurred diplomatically saying that they fully sympathised with the US view but that was sadly not the way the British justice system worked. Well, said the US Secretary of State to his British colleague, in his view, the whole matter reeked to high heaven and he and his president took an extremely dim view of the way it was playing out. It was particularly galling as they had just dealt with a similar matter where a covert female CIA officer on a diplomatic posting in the US London embassy had accidentally collided with, and tragically killed, a young Brit on a motor cycle. Accustomed to driving on the right, she had allegedly been driving on the wrong side of the road. The tragedy had been compounded when the American had fled the UK back to the States. The president had tried to resolve that one by inviting both parties to the White House but the British family would have none of it, leaving the White House frustrated and embarrassed. Do something, do anything, he told him, but sort it out.

One week before the scheduled trial the team at Northwood approached the Crown Prosecutor in the case. The vice admiral accompanied by his two counterparts decided to request a further three weeks delay in bringing the case to trial. This would give them time to design a course of action which might satisfy the demands of British justice and ameliorate the Americans. If the international ramifications of the case and its attendant circumstances were partially explained there might perhaps be a satisfactory outcome. The Crown Prosecution Service listened carefully to the proposal. A delay was inconvenient but might be feasible given the convoluted circumstances.

The Colonel from Hereford then explained the stress that the men had been under without giving away where the action had taken place. Colonel Algy de Montfort hailed from a family that had seen generations of national service. His crisp upper class diction reflected that effortless superiority and confidence which embodied literally hundreds of years of attachment to the land and her people. His ancestors had arrived in England with William the Conqueror in the last successful invasion of the British Isles in 1066. They had settled in the West Country. One ancestor had been a colonial governor-general in the Far East, whilst another had fought at the battle of Trafalgar. He had gravitated from an elite private school, to an elitist college at Oxford University and thence to the crème de la crème of the British Army, the Household Division. His Special Forces track record was a paragon of excellence. He had little need of persuasive tactics. His entire mien carried an awesome air of quiet authority and supreme command. He spoke softly but every word carried force, punch and weight. He said that a relatively large number of their colleagues and indeed friends had perished under appalling conditions. All the men had been under terrible pressure and Price more than the others as he felt personally and directly responsible for what had taken place. The incident was particularly unfortunate given the fact that Price had just started recovering from the awful stress to which he had been subjected. The CPS listened uncritically and courteously. There was a long silence. Eventually the American colonel felt that he had to say something. Colonel Jay Hargreaves was a man's man, himself a former Special Forces operative from the South East Asian war and not without sympathy for Price.

"If I may say so, gentlemen, my British colleague here is giving a very fair and candid assessment of what has happened. It only took a provocation such as the one which took place to put back all the counselling and hard work that has gone into rehabilitating Sergeant Price. A delay in the proceedings will give us time for a considered solution to the matter without causing any further embarrassment to two governments, which, if I may say, so, seem to be contending with a global threat that is vastly more serious than the fracas outside Namaste."

The CPS spokesperson was a stony faced young woman, an Oxbridge whiz kid with a reputation for ruthlessly winning her cases, characterised by toughness, resolution and determination. She had two older lawyers with her who had seen more of the seamier side of humanity than most people will experience in ten lifetimes. She was about to give her considered opinion when one of her colleagues put his hand up. Sir Gerald Trefoyle sniffed and took off his glasses.

"Gentlemen, this is an almost unique case given all the circumstances. I think you deserve a moratorium to work out an approach that addresses the diplomatic niceties and satisfies the requirements of the British judiciary. I would suggest we postpone the trial for a month. My only concern is that the stress of awaiting a decision on his future is unhealthy for Sergeant Price. We should recognise that an outcome sooner rather than later is in the best interests." He paused and looked round the table. "In the best interests of everyone." He glared at the Oxford whiz kid. "Your man is not able to flee the country even if he wanted to under the present circumstances of the world crisis. Let us all put our heads together on this one and work out a mutually satisfactory solution. Would 19th March be a suitable date?"

It was the out that the vice admiral and his team had been hoping for. They shook hands and departed. The Oxford whiz kid made a careful note never ever to invite Sir Gerald to another arbitration meeting. She could feel her prey slipping away already.

CHAPTER 12

Her head throbbed as if she had been hit with a sledge hammer. She was stark naked under a sheet on a single bed. She glanced at her wrist but they had removed the watch. Of her handbag and cell phone there was no sign. The room was more like a prison cell than a bedroom. She lay there trying to recall what had happened. Slowly it all came back to her, the lunch, the car and the chloroform. She could still smell traces of it on her face but they had wiped her down. She went over to the door and tried the handle. It was naturally locked. She looked in the cupboard for her clothes. Nothing. She returned and lay down on the bed. What to do now. Kidnapped, effectively by people she hardly knew. One of them possibly Irish and another Russian. Not a good combination that. Was it morning or evening? She glanced at her empty wrist and then recalled her missing watch. A quick peek out the window and it was dark. Evening. So what now? A conversation she had once had with her uncle in the New Scotland Yard counter terrorism unit about kidnapping five years earlier began to come back to her. She had been about to embark on the trip to Egypt. Egypt at the time had been in turmoil and the possibilities of a kidnapping for any variety of reasons loomed large. At the time the gist of the dialogue had seemed far-fetched when he had sat down with her and her mother.

"Now listen carefully to what I say and never forget it. You are entering a danger zone and although the Egyptians have their tourist police bad things can happen. If you are taken hostage, never confront your kidnappers. No matter how much they may provoke you, keep calm and think through all your actions and words. Remain at all times polite, and insofar as possible, co-operative. Firstly, find out who they are and what they want. If its money they will generally take care of you. If its sex, they will make that apparent soon enough. No one wants sex with damaged goods so violent confrontation is unhelpful. Ask for small concessions – water, regular meals, toilet facilities, decent clothing etc… Try to find out where you are and always check your security arrangements on the off chance that a burglar bar is loose, or a door unlocked. Try to get a message out but be careful of trusting anyone you meet through them. If you can escape get out as fast as you can and notify the police where you are. Even the police may be on the payroll of the kidnappers so be discerning. The most important thing is your situational awareness of the circumstances you are in and the prospects for escape. We call it being jungle sensitive and it can save your life. Talking of your life, the next most important item is your health. Maintain basic hygiene and eat providing what they are giving you is palatable. Keep hydrated. Remember that ultimately, your first duty is to engineer an escape and then to contact the local police."

At the time they thought he was way over the top. Naively she had asked, "But surely we can call for help on our mobile phones?"

He laughed and then a serious expression crossed his face. "My darling girl, the first item to go will be your phone, followed by all sentimental personal items, watch, jewellery, purse, personal photos and so on. This is deliberately done to dehumanise you, to cut you off from your past and to make you feel isolated. But, and this is a big but, providing you can get a message out, or somebody witnesses your abduction and just as importantly, they turn your phone off without removing the battery, we can trace you anywhere in the UK. The same applies to Egypt with the co-operation of the authorities. That's also a useful trick to remember if you don't want to be tracked by a hostile government in a hostile country." He glanced meaningfully at Stefanie.

"But can they actually track us even though the phones are switched off and no longer in our possession?" She sounded slightly incredulous.

"My dear girl, allow me to tell you a story. Our electronic intelligence monitoring capacity is the best in the world. Years ago certain members of the Grimaldi family were allegedly engaged in drug smuggling activities involving using the Monaco principality in the Mediterranean for the importation of heroin, partially processed opium, from Corsica into Europe. They had been rumoured to be doing this for years and the fact that there is no border between France and Monte Carlo made it all the easier. But the late prince became a tad avaricious. He sought greater rewards and began skimming more intensely. Three times he was warned to stop. The warnings went unheeded. Sadly, he underestimated the power and ruthlessness of the criminal cabal with which he was involved. Somebody tampered with the brake fluid chambers of his wife's Rover so that every pressure applied bled the chambers until they spectacularly failed on the most treacherous stretch of road leading into Monte Carlo. The car, driven by her daughter Stephanie, plunged fifty feet over a sheer cliff and the glamorous princess Grace Kelly was brutally killed. Emma, my dear, this at the time was gossip never proven but how does this gossip start?"

There was a sharp intake of breath and Emma swept her hands up to face. "But how do you know all this?

Uncle Peter replied unsmilingly. "A gigantic cover up ensued. The Rover car will never see the light of day. Prince Rainier was inconsolable. Stephanie has never really recovered from the shock. It is suspected that the Committee Monte Carlo and the Lodge P2 were responsible for issuing the orders. But my point is simply this. With a little bit of luck and excellent police intelligence we can pretty much trace you anywhere in the world. So never ever give up hope!"

At the time she had thought the briefing was just her uncle being paranoid from all his years in the police. Now she thanked God. How on earth would her mother cope with this? Could she possibly get a message to Stefanie? What did these people want from her?

For her part Stefanie had returned home that evening and was instantly on guard. All her instincts told her that something had gone terribly wrong. Oddly she had started to get the feeling when in the hospital writing up a report on an incipient alcoholic. For that reason she had left work early. She checked Emma's room and noticed the smart suit was missing. Odd thing for during the week. Her good handbag was also missing. And the smart shoes had gone with her too. She called the cell phone number but it seemed as if the phone had been disconnected. That was a bad sign. She tried all Stefanie's friends. No one knew anything. The grim feeling in the pit of her stomach was growing worse. Stefanie wasted no time. She tried to contact her brother but he was temporarily unavailable conducting an interrogation. He would call back in an hour. She poured herself a stiff drink and sat down to run through the trend of events.

Emma reflected long and hard on what had happened to her. She was battling a throbbing headache and seemed thirsty. A bottle of sealed mineral water lay on the rudimentary table beside the bed. Breaking the seal she drank long and hard then looked for a toilet. A side door gained access to a small bathroom, but the windows were frosted and barred as were the windows in the bedroom. She listened intently for the sounds of traffic but nothing materialised so she reckoned she was in the countryside. The temperature was cold despite the heat from an adjacent radiator so the odds were that she was still in the UK. What to do now? It was already dark so she must have been out for some time. She did not have long to wait.

There was the sound of a key in the lock and a bolt being withdrawn. A young woman of Asian origin dressed in a white service outfit entered the room. She had towels, soaps, and new clothing but no food. In broken English she asked if Emma was feeling no after effects from the chloroform. Emma pointed to her head. The young woman smiled and said it was nothing to worry about but Miss Farmer would be along soon. Would Emma care to dress in the meantime? The jeans, flat heeled shoes and sweaters were a near perfect fit. Emma asked about Miss Farmer but the young woman put her fingers to her lips, and said she would find out soon enough. She left as silently as she had arrived. Emma reckoned she was under CCTV scrutiny and the conversation was being monitored. She asked no more questions and the young Asian lady left the room carefully locking the door behind her. She was still looking in the mirror when she heard a key in the lock.

Another woman entered the room. She was about five feet eight inches in height with short dark hair and high cheekbones. She had a slim and trim figure with an air of authority about her. Her clothing was designer tailored and she spoke with a cultured English accent.

"Good evening Emma, my name is Nikki Farmer and I work for Mr Strelnikov. He would like you to work for him as well. We have brought you to one of his country estates. He likes you very much and would be honoured if you might join him for dinner this evening. He knows a lot about you and your desire to make it big in Hollywood and he reckons it might be possible to arrange something for you along those lines if you could just see your way clear to cooperating with us. I am sure that I do not need to explain what that co-operation entails."

Emma was stunned. There was no pretence. It was all perfectly straightforward. Satisfy Strelnikov's desires and he might open doors for you. Refuse to co-operate and your body might be found in an isolated wood a long way from where she was being held. Recalling her uncle's advice, she assented to dinner and asked if she could be shown round the house. Nikki Farmer demurred but assured her that more information would be forthcoming in due course. Would she care to accompany her to the drawing room?

The house was enormous. She followed Miss Farmer down wood panelled corridors with knights in armour lining the wide passages and into a large room with a small leather topped desk and a roaring log fire. Strelnikov was writing at the desk when she was ushered in. "I am so glad you have come," he said standing up. He made no effort to shake hands, instead offering her a sherry.

"I didn't really have much choice, did I?" Emma said taking the crystal sherry glass and wondering if it too was drugged. She felt sick at the thought of what she was expected to do with this revolting man Frightened of the situation she was in she inwardly thought hold yourself together, play along with what he wants and do not give this pig of a man one bit of satisfaction of knowing how scared I am.

Strelnikov noticed the glance at the glass and shrugged. "I assure you it's not tainted. In fact the finest South African sherry we can obtain in England from our Russian friends. But enough of that. I am looking forward to getting to know you better and maybe, I can assist you in your proposed acting career. But it is very much a two way street. "You help me and I can help you…."

That was how it all began. In return for certain deviant sexual services in which Emma was coached by the ubiquitous Nikki Farmer it soon became apparent that all things were possible. Days became weeks and Emma realised that she was somewhere on a vast English country estate. The acclimation began with massages then gravitated to conventional sex and finally kinky sex, all of it supervised by Nikki Farmer. Occasionally Nikki joined in. It became a sort of group feast. She found satisfying Strelnikov's demands utterly revolting but she kept her calm, fulfilled what was obviously expected of her and taking her uncle's advice to heart learnt as much as she could. She kept saying over in her mind do not panic, however much this man disgusts you play along and soon there may be a chance to get away.

For his part Strelnikov actually found her co-operation and willingness to please him, both perplexing and intensely satisfying. It was a contrast to the frightened, cowed and drug addicted women supplied to him in the past. This girl was pleasantly different. He enjoyed talking to her but never about business. It was always world affairs, global developments and money – large sums of money. Once she made the mistake of asking him if she could just let her mother know that she was alive and well. Strelnikov exploded.

"That is very naïve Emma. Your life has now changed and you are part of the big league. Your mother, your previous friends, they are all things of the past. You actually belong to me, body and soul. But if you really want a taste of the Hollywood good life then rest assured I can arrange this too." And oddly enough he proved as good as his word. But several thousand miles away across the pond things were happening which would play a major role in Emma's life.

The China virus which had exploded in Wuhan in November and December 2019 had now started to spread around the world. In Iran, Britain and Italy the disease was making itself felt with a vengeance. In the corridors of the White House concerns were rapidly growing. Dr Li-Meng Yan, a researcher from the Institute of Public Health in the troubled former British colony of Hong Kong, had defected to the American intelligence services. She feared for her life. She came with information from the China Centre for Disease Control and Prevention which she had obtained at the request of her WHO consultant supervisor, Dr Leo Poon. The news she had brought with her was devastating. By the 28th April Dr Yan would be flown out to the United States from Hong Kong, abandoning her family for her own survival.

The bug, now identified by the WHO as Covid-19, was easily transmitted from humans to humans and could also be contracted via aerosol projection as well as tactile transmission. This contrasted wildly with assurances from the PRC that the virus could not be so transmitted. By mid-January 2020 it was evident that the Wuhan area of the PRC was experiencing a serious and lethal epidemic with possible global ramifications. On 23rd January Wuhan went into lockdown. The situation in the PRC was so serious that the US president himself was given daily briefings on the progress of the disease. By early February the National Security Agency was briefing the president to the effect that 21 million cell phones had gone dead in the Wuhan district. The owners were dead, dying or hospitalised surmised the president's intelligence advisory team. On January 31st the president called an emergency meeting of his national security advisory team. The president demanded the latest medical intelligence on what was happening in China, Iran and Italy. His staff gave him horrific details of what they believed had occurred in the PRC, the attempted cover up of the contagion and its human to human transmission nature. They explained that the WHO had dismally failed to communicate the volatile nature of the infection and its dispersal. The president listened carefully and made some notes. There was a long silence. He read quietly through his notes seemingly oblivious to the others in the room. So long was it that some of the men and women began to shuffle uncomfortably in their chairs.

Then he looked up and met the eyes of each person round

the table. He told them in no uncertain terms that he completely failed to understand why his medical experts had not advised him earlier to shut the border with the PRC, but that as from now all contact with the PRC was to cease forthwith by air, sea and land. Canada and Mexico would be notified immediately. All returning US nationals from the PRC would have to undergo 14 days of isolation and medical scrutiny before being allowed back into the US. He was also considering extending the ban to Western Europe with the exception of the United Kingdom and Ireland although if the deluge of medical intelligence arriving from those areas vindicated such prophylactic measures he would not hesitate to extend them to Ireland and the UK as well. He said that a declaration of a state of emergency would be justified in abrogating the requisite powers the Federal government required to combat the threat. The White House Chief of Staff and his legal, the White House Chief Counsel, both looked distinctly unhappy. The two men were Republican traditionalists and preferred to err on the side of caution. They felt inaction was preferable to action and frequently challenged the presidential initiatives but were just as often over ruled. They glanced meaningfully at each other. The Chief of Staff was about to open his mouth when the president held up his hand.

There was another protracted silence as he glanced through his notes again. Then the bombshell. The president said he was deeply concerned about the patriotism and the loyalty of some of his top scientific medical advisers and that he had it on excellent authority that many of them had been compromised in video and taped blackmail materiel from the homes, the aircraft and the St James Island of the late Jeffery Epstein. There was a sharp intake of breath from several of the men and women round the table. They all knew that the president not only relied on his conventional three letter intelligence sources but that he had his own extraordinarily powerful and well placed intelligence team.

Unlike the three letter agencies this team had no agenda other than the sanctity and accuracy of the data conveyed to the president himself. The president leaned forward on the table and clasped his hands together. His voice softened so that they all leaned forward to hear his next comments.

"If the so called Cold War was World War III then rest assured that we are effectively in World War IV. I very much suspect this medical assault is not just directed at my presidency, or even the United States. It is directed against the entire free world and it is intended to melt down the capitalist economic system on a global basis. It cannot be ruled out that this disease is actually a hoax for something bigger. Whatever it is my guess is that it is being assisted by what can only be described as a fifth column comprising members of various compromised financial circles, cyber firms, the media, compromised intelligence services both in this country and elsewhere, leading compromised scientists and compromised medical experts who will render late, inadequate and or inappropriate so called medical and scientific advice designed to grotesquely exacerbate an already serious situation. Check this out for me but in a sense it seems to be a contrived operation amounting almost to a hoax but nonetheless a deadly one for people in certain older age groups and suffering from predisposed health problems."

The DCIA looked surprised. "We will try to verify this for you Sir. Preliminary intelligence suggests an effort is being made to exaggerate the numbers of infected and to thereby justify shutting down the world economy. The real indicator will be the death rate. Those figures will also need confirmation. If you are right on this Sir, then it is possible that millions will starve to death in the developing world, and millions more will lose their incomes in the developed world. At the same time the PRC may take advantage of the chaos."

The president glanced at his Director of Central Intelligence as she was making her own shorthand notes. "Brief the Five Eyes fully and sharpen up counter cyber measures to be put in place. I also want to know who in our government, academia, business circles and medical scientific fields has been compromised by the Epstein paedophile operations. That will explain a great deal of misinformation and disinformation which is about to hit the headlines. I want Epstein's associates brought in for interrogation and no slip ups this time. We must crack who has been compromised and controlled to feed false medical and pseudo-scientific disinformation and misinformation into the pipeline as well as to the World Health Organisation." He looked at his Treasury Secretary, an old merchant banker friend. "Steve, I am requesting you and your team to work out an emergency financial rescue package for our economy which I can sell to both Houses for approval. By the time of the November elections I want this country on the road to economic recovery from what is about to hit us. That is all for the moment," and so saying he got up and walked out.

Stefanie had eventually heard from her elusive brother in law. After studying all the facts and hearing her out, Peter Westbrooke sat back in the living room and calculated the options. "Stefanie, what about the young chap she met in Egypt who said he would be coming to see her. "You don't think that maybe….," his voice trailed off. Stefanie shook her head vigorously.

"No, absolutely not. She would have told me. We shared just about everything after my husband died. I know something awful has happened, but I cannot put my finger on it. Oh, there was a curious incident, just recently when the Gas Board sent an inspector over. She said he seemed a nice enough young man. Name of Martin. Don't know what he was checking but he seemed pleasant enough and quite good looking."

Westbrooke pulled out his mobile phone and pressed a fast dial number. A curt female voice answered. He asked the voice to check for a Martin Peters on the local Gas Board. Ten minutes elapsed while he flicked an imaginary speck of dust off his trousers with his forefinger and engaged Stefanie with small talk. The voice on the return call confirmed that no such man existed. Westbrooke slid his phone back into his side pocket. "That's our man, I would say. He might be what they call a talent spotter. Somewhere there must be CCTV images of him approaching the house. I will need to talk to her friends at RADA. I can call in a few favours at GCHQ. I need all her relevant cell phone details. Give me three days and I will get back to you. If you need me, don't hesitate to call. Even if it's just to shoot the bull. Call!"

Her brother in law stared into the gas fire for a long time. Should he explain to her about the international paedophile rings or keep quiet. "Stefanie, you recall the Jill Dando murder a number of years ago?"

She recalled only too well. "Oh my God, they shot her on

her front door step! But what has that got to do with my Emma?"

He looked at her long and hard. "Stefanie, the world is full of evil people. They are found in various important fields, politics, the media, science and finance to name but a few. Disraeli wrote years ago that the world is governed by very different personages from those the public might imagine. It is a sordid sleazy world of honey traps, sex crimes, paedophilia, drugs, human trafficking, bizarre armaments deals, bullion transfers, massive cash advances and many forms of unimaginable human deviance, all of it with a view to compromising and controlling people. Dando was likely murdered because she had been investigating paedophile child sex rings in the media and reporting it to the wrong people. It cannot be ruled out that Emma has been taken by such a group being young, beautiful, fatherless and ambitious. I will put the wheels in motion and keep you briefed. A tap will be put on your landline and mobile phones and we will intercept your mail." He paused and then added with a slight smile. "All with your consent of course."

"Of course," she nodded as tears dribbled down her face.

Emma served Strelnikov well, not because she wanted to but because her uncle had briefed her on what to do and what to avoid. For his part Strelnikov had set out to use her like he used all his women but somehow he found her very different. She was co-operative, never argumentative and utterly willing to do his every bidding. He found it all a bit uncanny but also refreshing. Usually there were tears, arguments, attempts to escape, the customary beatings and anger followed by eventual acceptance and submission.

There had been none of that with Emma. She had made it clear from the outset once her initial confusion had settled, that she had a new life and she would make the very best of it. Little did Strelnikov realise that Emma had been briefed by one of the best counter terrorism officers in the British intelligence community. She knew full well deep down that her mother would have contacted him immediately and that the full resources of the powerful world-wide offices he represented would be devoted to tracking her down. Of that she had no doubt whatsoever.

The introduction by Strelnikov and his staff to what was expected of her began slowly and gently. Initially she was taken into his presence for friendly discussions. They had long conversations, He told her about his life as a parentless brat on the streets of Moscow and she told him about her grandparents and mothers early life before the family moved to Britain. They found they had much in common. The brutality of their childhoods coupled with the sanctuary that they had found in totally different ways. Emma explained how, through her family establishing themselves in a civilized English society governed by laws and certain understood social norms, she had developed a new found self-respect. For his part, Igor revealed, that by asserting himself in the ganglands of criminal Moscow, and proving himself though his cunning and ruthlessness, he had learned to work the criminal system to his advantage. It was made clear to Emma that they could help each other.

At first this was all a game for Igor and one that he had played out many times before. For Emma it was a case of survival. Play the game, escape or die. So she played the game and threw herself with all her acting skills into the greatest role of her career that might just save her life.

The discussions turned into massage episodes and the massage episodes turned into sex, at first gentle, then raw and then deviantly rough. But Igor found himself curiously restrained. His urge to resort to sexual violence and sadism was curbed. Emma in some ways was a female version of himself. He began to identify with her hopes, her dreams and her acting aspirations just as he had sought to emulate the master thugs and criminals who had brought him up off the streets of Moscow.

Gradually he came round to the idea of actually trying to help her. One afternoon he placed a call through to his old Hollywood buddy Harry Waxman. Waxman was a Hollywood mogul but he was also more than that. From his massive mansion estate in Ohio he ran a famous line of clothing and cosmetics in addition to his movie making operations. Both pursuits required endless supplies of beautiful ambitious and co-operative young women. His clients ranged from a former US president and leading politicians to a senior executive at NASA, several prominent CEOs and merchant bankers as well as billionaire cyber geeks from Silicon Valley. All the trysts were filmed and recorded. The information was filed with a local intelligence service and two offshore services, one in the Middle East and one in Europe. For this service Harry Waxman was generously rewarded. Although he was married and his 'wife' enjoyed almost as much power as he did, women meant nothing to Waxman because, like Noel Coward, he preferred men. In fact the man he preferred above all others, was none other than Igor Strelnikov. So when Igor phoned him and offered him Emma he was delighted. But Emma was not to be treated like the other girls that Strelnikov supplied so liberally to Waxman. Emma, Igor carefully explained, was special. She was his girl, and she was on loan to Harry. It was up to Harry to try and give Emma the Hollywood break that she so desired. And if anyone could accomplish this, Harry Waxman could. It would be up to him to determine if Emma had real talent, but RADA graduates were world class and so Harry Waxman was not just receiving a piece of solid gold from Igor, he was receiving a special platinum commodity who required special treatment. One thought that went through Harry's mind was, is this girl going to forget everything that has happened to her for one chance to make it big in Hollywood or is Igor going to jail for a long time. He then realised that like many before her this girl in time, would disappear when Igor realised how stupid this situation could become.

There was just one small problem. The man in the White House had started to place the entire country under quarantine. The world was beginning to follow suit. Gradually global communications lines were shutting down. First it was airports, then airlines, and now sea ports and harbours with many ships and international yachts finding themselves virtually marooned at sea. Fortunately for Strelnikov his timely warning of the coming crisis had seen him perfectly positioned in the global oil markets but the new travel constraints were negatively impacting on his other nefarious interests, drugs, bullion, guns, cash and human trafficking. It was the latter issue which was proving the greatest challenge to moving Emma out of the UK. In the past it had been the provision of false documents and fake passports but these were simple matters to solve with a bribed official in the right quarters.

However, the problem was not over whelming. Waxman had his own fleet of private aircraft. After a long discussion on an encrypted line, or so they thought, it was arranged to fly Emma to Canada and drive her across the border at Windsor Ontario across the Ambassador bridge through Detroit to the mansion in Ohio. The arrangements were duly finalised. Emma's life was to take another new turn.

CHAPTER 13

Peter Westbrooke was reckoned to be on a fast track career. He was smart, efficient and remarkably well connected. His working life had started as a naval officer in the Royal Navy, but his affinity for languages and particularly Russian and Arabic had marked him for greater things than command of a ship. In fact, he had volunteered for Britain's nuclear submarine fleet. He would have doubtless survived the dreaded Perisher selection course to ultimately command one. But fate had something else in store. As the world had changed from the Cold War to the multipolar threat of international terrorism involving the IRA and various fanatical Jihadists his scope and range of career opportunities had blossomed second to none. A recommendation by a retired British admiral had seen him transferred to a little known unit operating in Northern Ireland. Det 14 specialised in getting to know the enemy better than the enemy knew themselves. It was a deep cover and deep penetration sabotage and information gathering unit involving exceptional men and women. Peter Westbrooke had excelled beyond all expectations. From Det 14 he had gravitated to the counter espionage section of the British Metropolitan Police Special Branch Counter Terrorism team. It was rumoured in the circles that should know that he knew more secrets than the Chief of MI6 himself, and the assumption was not far wrong.

Emma was a conventional young woman in many respects, especially when her cell phone was concerned. But she was unconventional in that she kept a separate written old fashioned daily journal. That was to prove her saving grace. Within hours of his visit to Stefanie, Westbrooke had compiled a complete list of her friends and contacts. Each individual was quietly approached and closely cross examined.

Emma was a hard girl to pin down. Her friends, such as they were, indicated that she was devoted to her career, studies and cherished her position at RADA. The only serious man in her life was Mohammed from Dubai according to her friends. The diary seemed to prove this. When young Mohammed arrived from the US and tried to contact her, he was, to his chagrin, intercepted at Heathrow airport and taken to a very private interview room. There he was minutely cross examined on his relationship with Emma. Why had he wished to see her again? What had he been doing with his life since he had met her? When had he last been in contact with her? He was warned that in no uncertain terms he must notify a certain telephone number if he heard anything more from her or about her but he was then summarily dismissed as a possible lead.

However, one contact in her diary proved solid gold. Young attractive carefree Victoria Parker agreed to meet Westbrooke over a coffee at the same Starbucks near RADA where she had met Emma. The shop was packed when Westbrooke arrived early but he managed to corner a table by the window as a young couple left. He ordered a cappuccino from a harassed waitress. The well-spoken girl was quick and efficient. He thanked her and enquired if she was a student. No, was the surprising answer. A PhD in nuclear physics unable to find a job. Not encouraging he mused. Then he recognised Victoria coming through the door in a blast of icy air with her classic features and long blond hair almost immediately. She confirmed that Emma had been thrilled to discover a possible Hollywood contact with Melvin the elusive gas man. In fact they had been planning to have lunch together at some stage. But she knew not where and when. It was the first real break that Westbrooke had been looking for.

Back at New Scotland Yard he placed a call to an old buddy at GCHQ in Cheltenham. Could he please call in a favour with dear old Nial Irwin at GCHQ? "But, of course," replied Irwin. How could he help? Irwin was in a position to help. As Deputy Head of GCHQ he was responsible for the monitoring and logging of every single electronic communication in the UK, plus all of Europe, Africa and the Middle East. There were also other peculiar elint signals that GCHQ occasionally picked up which did not seem to come from any terrestrial source. These were automatically logged and transmitted to the US version of GCHQ, the super-secret National Security Agency in the US. Certain top people at GCHQ often wondered who or what the American NSA staff were communicating with off planet but it was considered extremely bad manners, not to mention bad for one's health, to pursue such questions too deeply. GCHQ had started out in WWII as the Government Code and Cypher School at Bletchley Park intercepting and reading all the German and Japanese signals traffic on the Enigma system. After the war Britain had supplied many of her newly independent colonies with 'souped up' versions of Enigma.

All of these systems had built in bugs which conveyed the so called secret traffic directly to Cheltenham. So Britain knew exactly what secrets were being hatched and discussed across a vast swathe of the world and unhesitatingly shared such vital intelligence with the Americans as part of the Five Eyes agreement.

But these were not issues of current concern to Westbrooke. He wanted to track all Emma's phone calls in the week prior to her disappearance. He shared her black book diary containing its annotated numbers with a member of Irwin's team at Cheltenham. Cheltenham is not supposed to monitor British nationals but they have an agreement with the Americans. The US monitors the British and all American domestic nationals targets are listened to and logged on supercomputers by the British. That way no laws are contravened and both sides are delighted. In microseconds all the numbers were identified and legitimized as regular contacts bar one. That was the incoming call from an unknown cell phone number registered to a certain Martin Peters the fake name used by Melvin. Westbrooke asked for a trace on all calls to Mr Peters cell phone. The Irwin team came back within the hour. Mr Peters it transpired was a bad egg. He had worked as a scout for the IRA, involved himself with the lucrative London drug scene, prostitution rings and protection racket gangland and lately associated himself with the Russian mafia. A few hours on the Scotland Yard Counter Terrorism Cyber network and Westbrooke knew more about Martin Peters than Peters knew about himself. The information flow on Peters was impressive and enlightening but not encouraging in respect of the outlook for Emma. Westbrooke knew all about the Organizatsiya and its links to paedophilia, human trafficking, bullion smuggling, illicit armaments deals, racketeering and cash transfers. As a matter of course GCHQ had tried to track Emma's phone but the machine had been either deactivated through the removal of the battery and sim card or more likely destroyed. That was predictable. It is a little known fact to the public but a well-known one to the spooks that all cell phones are trackable even when switched off. Removing the battery complicates the tracking but does not negate it. So that option was closed.

But what GCHQ did discover was that Emma's last call on her phone had been in Jermyn Street which meant that she may have met Martin at a nearby restaurant. Footwork was now the order of the day with investigating officers discretely visiting every restaurant in and off the vicinity of Jermyn Street armed with photographs of Emma and Martin. With a bit of luck they might hit the jackpot. At Greens just off Jermyn Street they did. CCTV cameras were checked in the vicinity of Greens. It took a number of days and then they hit pay dirt. They collected images of a number plate on a large Mercedes Benz which belonged to a very wealthy Russian oligarch resident in the UK called Igor Strelnikov. Mr Strelnikov was placed under close surveillance. Again Irwin at GCHQ was asked to provide some assistance. A record of all Strelnikov's phone calls emerged. Now began the donkey work of identifying and sifting out the wheat from the chaff. After a week there was one number in particular that caught Westhrooke's eye. A certain Mr Waxman in Hollywood who was known to be a highly well connected human trafficker in addition to his legitimate oil interests intrigued Westbrooke. But there was more. Mr Strelnikov had suddenly started offloading his oil interests before there was talk of a possible collapse in the international price of oil. The FBI were alerted to their British colleague's interest in Mr Waxman.

And at this point collaboration between the British and the Americans began to falter. Mr Waxman seemed to have incredible connections at the highest levels of the US law enforcement agencies. He was considered Royal Game, a peculiarly British form of protected untouchability, beyond reproach. Westbrooke grew increasingly frustrated. His immediate superior who had briefly served on the enquiry into Princess Diana's tragic car crash learned of the enquiries being made and called Westbrooke in. The investigation had to stop. Westbrooke was incensed. On a whim he called in another favour. He was great friends with the PA to the Chief of the Secret Intelligence Service. They had worked together in Northern Ireland on a case involving the Irish Republic. He had literally saved Colin Penn's life. A meeting with Penn was arranged not far from the imposing MI6 edifice on Vauxhall Bridge. Could Penn ask his boss to intervene and gain access to a telephone tap on Waxman? Penn was adamant that this would have to be cleared with his boss and then with the Americans. That, explained Westbrooke, was not a viable option. In that case, said Penn apologetically, he could not help.

At Court it was a dismal grim drizzling afternoon on Friday the 21st of February. The accused, Mr John Price looked every bit as uncomfortable as he felt in his ill-fitting suit. His rank had been ignored in favour of the request by the MoD for the matter to be kept as low key as possible. The barrister for the defence had engaged in protracted negotiations with the Crown Prosecution Service and the Judge had been well briefed on the sensitivities of the case.

Colonel Cartwright was still languishing in a coma with neither improvement nor deterioration in his condition. It was obvious from the start that the CPS was out for blood. It was equally conspicuous that the judge was unsympathetic to Mr Price. The Judge clad in his sombre wig and scarlet robes entered the chambers and the court rose in respect. The judge waived the court to their seats with a cursory almost bored nod. The charges were read out and Price was asked to plead. "Not guilty your honour," he said softly but immediately realising he had made a mistake.

The Judge adjusted his glasses and glared at the accused. "In British jurisdictions I am referred to as My Lord. Some prefer the more familiar term Mi Lud. I understand you have a lot on your mind Mr Price but it would be appreciated if we could please adhere to the traditional protocols."

Price shuffled his feet awkwardly and muttered in an even softer tone of voice, "Sorry your Honour, ah, my Lord. It won't happen again. No disrespect meant, my Lord."

The Judge nodded without so much as a hint of a smile and turned his attention to the defence. "I understand that there may be extenuating circumstances attached to this case. I have to say that the CPS are unimpressed with the arguments proposed but in view of the international ramifications of the case and the associated sensitivities which we need not go into here, I am willing to consider extenuating circumstances. The accused has been under considerable stress and pressure in the past two months. After devoting some careful thought to the matter I have decided to have the accused sectioned for examination of his mental state at the moment to ensure that he is not a danger to anyone else in the British public. I am therefore withholding further proceedings pending the outcome of an assessment to be provided by Wexham Hospital. We shall resume on 19th March in four weeks' time." So saying he stood up and gently inclining his head to the upstanding observers swept out of the court room.

The relationship Emma had with Strelnikov was a curious one to say the least. It followed a pre-ordained pattern which few individuals, least of all a young and vulnerable woman, could cope with. Fortunately for Emma her conversation with Westbrooke had left a deep and lasting impression. The truth of what he had told her was reinforced with every passing day. The name of the game was to play along. Not too keenly, and not too reluctantly. And it was the most challenging act she had yet had to play in her short life to date.

The art of coercive persuasion is a long refined and carefully honed application of isolation, fear, degradation, threats and occasional indulgences. These measures are coupled with careful applications of denigrating humiliation and sometimes faint praise for co-operation coupled to dietary and sleep deprivation. If successfully applied it can lead to the complete subjugation and winning over of the subject as occurred with Patti Hearst, the kidnapped American millionaire heiress to the Hearst fortune in California when she was taken by the Symbionese Liberation Army in the 1970s. Hearst, initially a kidnap victim, became a collaborator with the SLA. It was a noose round her neck for many years to come.

In Emma's case she was not subjected to total isolation. Nikki Farmer made sure of that. Emma had to be malleable in bed for Strelnikov so Nikki became the intercessor who trained Emma in what satisfied Igor and what did not. But in the process Emma became dependent on Nikki, an experience which might have gone the way of Patti Hearst had not Nikki also participated in the peculiar sex orgies between Strelnikov and Emma. That shocked Emma into the realisation that she was being forced into a dependency relationship with Nikki which served as a warning. Emma now understood what Westbrooke had meant when he warned her of the impact of social deprivation, false friendships and apparent friendliness. Emma was also acutely aware of the efforts by Nikki and Strelnikov to focus attention on her immediate predicament and the need for absolute co-operation to avoid punishment either through physical abuse, isolation, hunger and/or sleep deprivation. She took the efforts at humiliation and degradation in her stride. She recalled Westbrooke describing in graphic detail North Korean interrogation procedures on their captured service men and women and the horrors of his training and recruitment into Det 14 at the hands of his own British Directing Staff. Exhaustion was her biggest enemy. With exhaustion came mental confusion and then the mental gymnastics to alleviate her plight. Threats there were aplenty but neither Nikki nor Strelnikov reckoned that they needed to apply them too harshly to Emma. The more she co-operated the more indulgences they granted her, better food, longer rest, access to television and so on. For her part she conceded to them that she recognised from word go the futility of resistance. She tacitly if not overtly convinced them that she acknowledged their omnipotence. When they imposed trivial demands on her she invariably responded with suggested trivial rewards and always reminded them of their initial pledge to offer her a career in Hollywood.

Strelnikov had to admit that he had never before enjoyed a relationship so much with such a beautiful and co-operative young woman. She was worth a lot to him and Harry Waxman in the States would know exactly how much. So, with Emma's apparent approval it was arranged for her to meet Waxman and maybe, just maybe, Waxman could find a real role for her after seeing for himself what Strelnikov prided himself on having talent spotted. Strelnikov would tell him a small part for release only in the States and she would be a big asset to him in compromising the idiots who could not help themselves undoing their zips.

While they were still standing watching the judge grandly exit to his chambers Price turned to Herrington, who was sitting behind him, and raised an inquisitive eyebrow. "What does that mean exactly? Am I some kind of nut?"

Herrington resisted the urge to smile. "John, relax. It's the best option possible. We all know the stress and strain we have been under. The judge has brilliantly bought us time to give you a clean bill of health with a proviso that you were under monstrous provocation and that clarifying medical endorsement will clear your name, keep the case under wraps and see you reunited with your unit Stateside. Unless you would like to stay here. We must just hope and pray that the old colonel makes a full recovery. Good luck mate, it's all going to be OK, trust me, I'm not a doc," he said with a dismissive forced laugh.

The police officers in the court wasted no time. Price was escorted into a holding room and from there into a waiting police car. Handcuffs were produced and immediately met the objections of the Red Caps. It might be a civil matter but it was a military man, and a foreign soldier at that so there would be no handcuffs and the Royal Military Police insisted on keeping Price under their observation if not under their jurisdiction. The RMPs insisted on having an escort officer accompany Price in the civil police vehicle and the US Embassy official in attendance followed at a discrete distance in his own car. Within the hour, having changed out of his ill-fitting suit, Price was being processed for admission to the Wexham psychiatric clinic. Stefanie, already worried about Emma, was in no mood for an additional professional burden but as the head of the unit the entire matter resorted under her care.

It was explained to Stefanie by a senior justice official that this could well be a major diplomatic incident unless appropriately and discretely managed. Price was to be courteously and considerately examined but should be regarded as dangerous due to his training and recent enhanced stress levels. The examination was to be impeccably professional, utterly thorough and unimpeachably prosecuted. Inevitably Stefanie demanded an explanation as to what sort of stresses Price had been subjected to. That was a matter which fell under the Defence of the Realm Act and was covered by the Official Secrets Act. Was Stefanie a signatory to the latter and familiar with the former? Well, no not really but she had heard of them. A surprisingly small piece of paper was produced titled OFFICIAL SECRETS ACT comprising three short paragraphs and a threat of a ten year gaol sentence for its violation. Would Stefanie kindly read the document aloud to the official, confirm verbally that she understood what she had read and attach her signature at the bottom?

Was this absolutely necessary she asked. Yes, it most certainly was, the men in the smart suits explained. The matter carried with it enormous international ramifications and a mighty burden now rested on Stefanie's shoulders during the course of which the magnitude of her new responsibilities would soon become evident. Price might share highly confidential and dangerous information with her in the course of her examination which she would be expected to keep to herself. However, the revelations might well prove crucial to her medical assessment on which Price's future career would depend. At all times she was to keep in mind the fact that Price was an expensively and highly trained special forces soldier. HMG could therefore take no responsibility for any danger in which she might find herself during the course of her examination and to this end yet another single sheet of innocent looking typescript was produced for her to sign which indemnified the British and US governments from any legal repercussions arising from physical or mental injury to Stefanie or her staff during the course of her examination.

At this stage of the proceedings Stefanie's sense of self-preservation kicked in and she excused herself briefly to consult privately with a 'colleague'. The colleague was her brother in law at New Scotland Yard and when Peter Westbrooke took her call he was mightily intrigued. He advised her to sign the document but to make a photocopy for his own perusal later. Stefanie returned and demurely signed. An almost audible sigh of relief permeated the room and the assembled throng departed. Stefanie sat back in her office chair and stared at the ceiling. Despite the astonishing nature of the new responsibilities dumped in her lap something somewhere intuitively suggested to her that this could in some bizarre way relate to her missing daughter. She dismissed the thought and prepared to introduce herself to Price.

Emma's arrival in North America was about as unconventional as it is possible to be. She was provided with a real UK passport lifted from an innocent returning passenger to London Gatwick airport. A photo of Emma was then added by a professional forger along with a false name. The private jet which departed from Stanstead arrived in Canada several hours later. Accompanied by the omnipresent Nikki a nondescript American car collected her at a private airfield outside Toronto and drove her through the night to the Ambassador Bridge border post between Canada and the United States. Emma entered the United States on a British Passport in the name of Shirley Cullen, an attractive model visiting her boyfriend in Chicago. Once on the Detroit side of the border she was driven to the Waxman estate in Ohio.

Harry Carter Waxman was described in Who's Who as a self-made billionaire movie mogul and brand entrepreneur who fathered the cosmetic brands Clandestine Couple, Ambient Access and Secret Success. It was a badly kept secret inside and even outside of Hollywood that would be starlets who sought super screen status had to satisfy Waxman's more basic sexual desires. Even more distasteful the male wannabe stars had to engage in much the same more unconventional liaisons. Waxman didn't differentiate. He unashamedly batted on all sexual wickets and his generally grimy unshaven slightly overweight appearance belied a cunning, devious and ruthless mind-set. Even the first sentence in the wiki biography was seriously misleading. Waxman had hardly managed his success on his own. Of Russian origin himself Waxman had been born in the United States but into a family from the rag trade that enjoyed long standing links with the US based Organizatsiya and the Italian American underworld. A keen student of the arts, architecture and the film industry Waxman had graduated from Ohio State University with a distinction in business administration. He had flirted briefly with a law degree at Harvard on the basis of excellent OSU recommendations and hefty family financial backing but soon became bored with the idea and focused on running his family business.

Waxman soon branched out into opening his own clothing operations heavily sponsored and underwritten by various criminal syndicates across the US Mid-West and later California, using the clothing front as cover for cash, drugs, human trafficking involving men, women and children and bullion smuggling. Later guns and even small nuclear weapons came his way, as the USSR plunged into disintegrating chaos. For all his sins, Waxman had one outstanding and astronomically unusual quality which largely contributed to his phenomenal success. In the criminal world it was known that his word was his bond. Persuading him to give his word to an agreement, however crooked it might be, was entirely another story. But the fact of the matter was that once Waxman gave his word on an agreement it was as good as done. Like Al Capone before him, Waxman slipped up in respect of his tax returns. A painfully long IRS investigation proved conclusively that Waxman was as delinquent in his conventional tax returns as he was in his seedier activities. A prosecution was prepared but before arrest warrants could be issued he came to the attention of the three letter intelligence services. They offered him a deal. In return for overlooking his missing taxes he could preoccupy himself in providing political and commercial intelligence on various leading figures in the political, financial and scientific worlds, and assisting in rolling out complicated blackmail operations comprising serious film and audio records of compromising conduct by the rich and famous, Waxman gained access to the leading lights of Hollywood. The profits of his less dissident operations were consequently ploughed into enormously successful Hollywood productions which added to his veneer of successful respectability. Even Fortune 500 accorded him a special status.

It was into this distorted tortuous sick world that young Emma found herself consigned by Strelnikov to 'promote' her acting interests. On her arrival at the massive Waxman rural walled compound in Ohio Emma was consigned to the 21 000 sq, foot estate 'cottage'. Nikki warned her that in order for her to break into the acting industry she would have to satisfy Waxman of her 'adaptable compliance'. It was Nikki who introduced her to Bruno, the estate security officer, a former US Special Forces operator, who explained to her that she was little better than a valued prisoner in a gilded cage. When asked to elaborate Nikki was a bit more reticent. Shortly after her arrival Nikki explained one evening over a superb meal that no Hollywood star really made it big time in the industry without sexual and or criminal cooperation in one form or another. She explained that Emma could consider herself privileged because she had found a 'soft' spot in Strelnikov's steel make up which meant that she was on 'loan' to Waxman and if she co-operated in satisfactorily entertaining Waxman as well as some of his more important guests, her acting career would be assured. But there was also an ominous quid pro quo. Emma was warned never to leave the cottage without permission from the main mansion which resembled a palace. She was told that there were sharp shooters with orders to shoot to kill, and a pack of Doberman pinchers rambling across the estate capable of tearing any living creature, human or animal, to pieces.

It took only three days for the truth of Nikki's warning to be realised. Emma had tried to raise the main house mid-morning in order to arrange a meeting with Waxman himself. After ringing innumerable occasions with no answer she opened the main door and started to cross the sculptured gardens towards the main house. Across the lawns she spied a pack of salivating animals that might have doubled for the Hound of the Baskervilles hurtling in her direction. Stunned she stared at the approaching cacophony and then wisely rushed back into the cottage. As she slammed the door behind her the pack smashed into the large door howling and growling until the chief of security arrived on his Quad and called them off. A few minutes later the phone rang. Predictably Nikki with a warning that if Emma ever tried to do that again she would either be shot or torn to pieces.

But it was also Nikki who provided Emma with a selection of film scripts and possible film parts. It was Nikki who also supervised the transit of a seemingly endless bevy of beautiful young women who appeared and disappeared as mysteriously as the occasional immaculately attired businessmen and politicians who spent time with them in the spa, swimming pool, tennis courts and 9 hole golf course facilities offered by the estate. All of them came and went in the strictest confidence by air, either on the estate landing strip or by helicopter. The girls were forbidden to speak to Emma or the mainly Mexican staff who couldn't speak English anyway. Some of the girls emerged from their experiences in absolute terror, others in tears and others mumbling hysterically.

One morning Nikki summoned Emma to the main house. She was warned that Waxman wished to see her and she needed to look really sharp. The encounter was nothing like she had expected. Emma was ushered into a vast room that resembled an enormous version of the Oval office in the White House. Waxman appeared through a side door typically unshaven but almost unctuously friendly. After the introductions Nikki was dismissed, He explained to Emma that Strelnikov was a good and trusted friend. He had spoken highly of Emma. Had she studied the scripts supplied by Nikki? Emma nodded hopefully. Any one of those scripts might well have a role for Emma but Waxman required some assistance from her to facilitate the first audition. This was almost too good to be true. He then dampened her obvious put on excitement by explaining that the first audition might take the form of a film advertisement for one of his new products.

A very important person would be visiting that afternoon. No, he couldn't tell her who it was at this stage, but she would find out in due course. Would Emma entertain him? Her mouth went dry. She stared at Waxman for a long time. He smiled and took her hand. It would really be appreciated and after all, there were those tantalizing scripts. Moreover, he was trusting her because he had yet to tell even Nikki who would be coming. Emma returned the smile and nodded. Waxman stood up, and approached her. She thought he was going to shake hands but instead he hugged her. It was she thought, much like being hugged by a gigantic spider. He escorted her to the door and asked her to wait while he had a few words with Nikki. Emma sat in the gigantic hallway her mind racing. Was this how the world really worked?

Were these the people who made things happen? Was she now an integral part of this perverted command, control and compromise operation? And where would this end? Would she ever really see Hollywood? Did she even want to go to Hollywood if this was what it took?

Nikki came through the doorway after a few minutes. Emma had never seen her under such stress. "A very important person is coming," she said almost breathlessly. "I must fetch the nubiles, I must get the nubiles," she muttered.

Emma was even more perplexed when Waxman opened the door behind Nikki and in a soft gentle voice said, "No Nikki, not the nubiles this time, Emma will do perfectly."

CHAPTER 14

Stefanie wasted no time. She returned to her office having collected a coffee from the canteen and reviewed the file on the case. Concentration only came with great difficulty. Her brain wanted to go everywhere except where she wanted it to go. Images of Emma kept creeping in at every turn. She dragged her mind back to the job in hand. There were in fact several files. One contained the details of the charges Price was facing. It carried an account of the incident and several patchy eye witness accounts of the fracas. There was attached to this file a report by the senior RMP officer who had been called to assist. She noted that his description was far more professional than the account rendered by the regular police. The regular police were relatively young and new to the job. The RMPs were purposeful and more experienced, she reckoned. This indicated that the RMPs saw the situation in a slightly different light to the regular police who were simply doing a regular job. Why, she wondered, would the RMPs have taken special interest in a case for which they had not been specifically summoned until the last moment? Did they sense that there was more to this than met the eye? She pondered the issue and made a note to herself on an adjacent pad. These notes would prove helpful if she became distracted by other matters. Distraction, came easily she thought to herself so these notes were important.

She picked up the second file provided by the MoD. It was much more interesting. It indicated that Price came from a good school and could have afforded to go into the family business. A top university was a given with his outstanding academic and sporting prowess. Yet once in university a friend had induced him to transfer to a competing university where he had volunteered for the military. He was a highly trained and proficient serving soldier. His performance hitherto had been exceptional. Fitness, mental acuity and swift ability to learn coupled with a single-minded devotion to duty and to his comrades. He had been talent spotted by some clever career supervisor in the Pentagon and allocated to a secret special unit. In the course of his duties he had served in several countries on a number of special missions requiring courage, daring and dedication. There had been no slip ups. That was where the file ended. Stefanie sipped the remains of her now cold coffee and stared out the window at a watery sunshine. These documents were bland and their information anodyne. She had never been put in charge of a case like this. Would the subject be willing to share more information than was to be found in these cursory briefing papers. There was only one way to find out. She reached for the phone.

Nikki knew that this VIP had special requirements from his women. They should be young, extremely good looking, compliant and conversationally intelligent but not too bright, naturally, they were expected to satisfy his every carnal desire. At the end of such satisfaction he had a bad habit of showing his dominance. She thought it better to warn Emma. Many of his women had reportedly been slightly mutilated with what was an act of consummate brutality. This involved a vicious bite on the lower lip leaving a painful reminder of his dominance and power. What she was loath to tell Emma was a detailed litany of the alleged ghastly shenanigans his wife got up to with her friend's and under age teenagers on the Caribbean island now under lockdown and investigation by the new president's revamped and sanitised FBI. The video tapes were allegedly so graphic that the investigating team could only watch the ritual horrific acts for a limited time before being violently ill. All of them had required counselling during the process and some would do so for a long time afterwards. What was worse was that the temple floor on the island had been excavated. A large pipe was uncovered leading through the rock to the sea bed. What slightly concerned Nikki was what the FBI divers had discovered. Down there they had found multiple human bones on the adjacent sea bed floor ranging from adults to underage teenagers. There had also been disturbing talk in the media about the need to obtain adrenochrome from the victims and how it was eagerly sought after by politicians, actors, leading business figures and so on. The public were growing aware of the anti-aging qualities of adrenochrome extracted from the blood of the victims under severe terror and physical duress. Since the advent of the new administration with its focus on inhibiting child and human trafficking it was becoming increasingly difficult to obtain adrenochrome. How far might these investigations go? Nikki was still, remarkably it has to be said, not unduly worried. She had excellent connections in the three letter services and Waxman was still taking good care of her.

For her part, Emma had suspected for some considerable time that she was about to be introduced to someone at the highest end of the international spectrum. The thought flashed through her mind, well, I mean, really, just to think of it in a curious way was both horrifically exciting and terrifying. Was this somebody she could ask for help. It seemed not. He was an integral part of the criminal cartel. She had no idea when or how it would all be played out or even the manner in which he would arrive. But the dread of the encounter was matched by her bizarre curiosity. It was no surprise therefore when Nikki came up to her suite and explained what was about to occur. The VIP would arrive by helicopter and be met by Mr Waxman personally together with the Duty Manager and Security Chief on the estate. He would be entitled to choose the rendezvous with Emma but he normally preferred the main house with its secluded swimming pool, tennis court and entertainment area. Nikki would have a few words with him and escort Emma through the underground tunnel to the entertainment area near the main house from the mansion that passed as "the cottage". She would make the introductions and discretely withdraw. Emma realised she was in the grip of not just an international criminal cartel but what was perhaps "the" international criminal cartel of all cartels, and it took some time for her to understand the enormity of what she had been sucked into. The concept of an underground tunnel slightly frightened her. If the two mansions were connected by some subterranean structure what else was lurking below ground.

CHAPTER15

In Washington DC at this time a conversation was occurring which would have a direct bearing on Emma's future. The incumbent US president looked at his advisers with incredulity.

"I'm still not sure that I fully understand what you are telling me. Let's run this through one more time." He leaned back in his black leather armchair and glanced at the portrait of President Andrew Jackson on his left. In his day Jackson had just taken on the money lenders. It sometimes seemed to the contemporary president that he was taking on the world. He ran his fingers through his thick blond hair and leaned forward on the desk glaring at his three most trusted intelligence chiefs. "You are suggesting that the entire compromise operation was organised by the dark side of the FBI, plus at least nine other intelligence services round the world, and aimed at the entrapment of leading personalities from the international business, scientific, academic, medical, military and political communities using underage boys and girls. That these trysts, for want of a better term, were filmed and taped and distributed to our own renegade intelligence community members and a leading intelligence service in the Middle East. And this was done to extract a so-called anti-aging agent in their blood and to allow pressure to be applied on the targets to execute whatever actions, including murder, were sanctioned by the agencies and or their governments. Now you're confirming to me my earlier suspicions that much of the scientific battle against this spreading pandemic involves so called expert advice by compromised medical practitioners and scientists who will say what they are told to say."

The DCIA sat calmly in her chair opposite his desk and nodded. "Yes, Sir, that is part of it and we have recovered the tapes and video records though by no means all of them. If I may point out my colleague from the NSA has supporting copies of emails, phone calls and social cyber signals confirming all this. The honey-trap is a classic entrapment method ….," but she never got to finish the sentence. The president was on a roll now.

He interrupted her. "Honey-trap? We're not talking bees here Gina? How far does this accepted method go…? Remember I was the guy who first blew Epstein to the FBI when he had a crack at an underage girl during a stay at Mar Del Largo as my guest. I have to say that I was pretty disappointed in their response and the reaction of the entire Justice department. No wonder. How exactly do you define a honey-trap?"

The DCIA recovered herself and continued. "Technically Sir, a honey-trap in intelligence parlance refers to an espionage conspiracy to engage an intelligence asset via sexual entrapment customarily with an adult man or woman to the public detriment of the target ensuring their compliance. The most famous case was the failed effort by the British MI5 counter intelligence operatives to use a call girl, Christine Keeler, to seduce a Russian GRU operative in London in the 1960s. Sergei Ivanov, the Soviet Naval attaché at the Russian embass….," again she wasn't allowed to finish.

The president nodded. "Yes, Gina, I know all about it and it was a dismal failure. It had serious repercussions. Don't we ever learn from our mistakes. The Russians turned the operation against the Brits and revealed to the British media that the British Defence Minister John Profumo was having it off with Keeler just like Ivanov. Profumo lied about it in Parliament, and the British Conservative government was disgraced."

The DCIA saw an opportunity to teach the president something as he paused for breath. "It was actually much more serious than that, Sir."

The president raised an eyebrow. "Oh yeah, Go on…."

"Profumo resigned and the British government later called an election. One of your predecessors nearly got caught up in the scandal….."

"Not Kennedy?" the president interrupted again.

"As a matter of fact, yes it was. When visiting London he was using women provided by the MI5 operative, Dr Stephen Ward, who had supplied Keeler to the Russians. His brother, Bobby Kennedy, as Attorney General managed to hush it all up. But the Russkies then invited the leader of the Labour Party, Hugh Gaitskell, to visit Moscow. One of my predecessors, James Jesus Angleton…"

The president interjected. "My God, what a name, Was that his real name? Sorry, go on…."

The DCIA ignored the question. "Sir, James Angleton was a legend in his life time, one of the best. He learned that Gaitskell was kept waiting at the London Russian Embassy for over an hour while collecting his Russian visa. This was despite the fact they knew he was coming. While waiting they served him tea and biscuits. He died 18 days later. He was replaced by Harold Wilson. We long believed that Wilson was a Soviet asset. Wilson won the 1964 British general elections, made forty visits behind the Iron Curtain as British Prime Minister. On one occasion he disappeared from his own MI6 officers for five days. He withdrew British defence forces from east of Suez, handed the crucial port of Aden to a pro-Russian liberation movement, cancelled the TSR-2 advanced bomber project, initiated the arms embargo against South Africa and the international sanctions campaign against Rhodesia, reduced Britain to a post-industrial society, dismantled the remnants of their empire to socialist or at best, communist governments and shut down Britain's secret space programme. He also…"

Before she could continue the president, who seldom used bad language in front of his staff. muttered, "Jesus", quite audibly.

The DCIA saw her chance. "Sorry, Sir, oh yes, his name was Jesus, as in James Jesus Angleton." The president, who actually enjoyed and respected people who challenged him, managed to smile. The admiral and the head of the NGA had a tough time not laughing. The admiral was secretly quite impressed with what Gina had learned during her stint as station chief in London before becoming DCIA.

The DCIA smiled sweetly. "In 1970 Conservative Prime Minister Edward Heath came to power. He discovered that Wilson had let so many KGB and GRU agents into the UK the British couldn't keep track of them. Heath threw out 105 Soviet spies on coming to power. So, honey-traps are serious affairs Sir…"

"Obviously in more ways than one," the president inter-jected with a sly smile. "But honey-traps are conducted with adults. This abuse of children is outrageous, in fact it is inexcusable. Hunt these barbarians down and hold them accountable for their crimes. Surely you have people on the inside…? I mean assets?" he added with a knowing glance at the admiral. "We need brave men and preferably women who can testify as to what the hell is going on."

The DCIA shifted uncomfortably in her chair. "Working on it, Sir, but we are dealing with ruthless people. Several women have come forward but ex post facto, after the event. One Australian lady has been particularly courageous but it is almost impossible to get active assets on the inside now.

"Just how dangerous is it?" The president had started twirling a gold cross pen in his hand.

"There is another aspect to this. In seeking information on the origins of the Chinese virus one of our agents, Philip Haney, approached a Russian disease expert, "Olesya Krasilova". They met in Cape Verde. On returning to the US Philip was murdered with a bullet in the back of the head. The Russian lady has vanished. She may be in protective custody in a Spanish prison. We don't know what crucial information she shared with our man because he was killed before he could be debriefed."

"I take it Haney wasn't a suicide. So, you are investigating who killed him, yes?" The president looked grim.

"Well, Sir, that's the thing. US attorney Tony Delgado was investigating the assassination but he and his wife Tamara have just been gunned down. We are still working on the real origins of the virus." She said almost apologetically.

The president's eyes widened at the Delgado murder. "You're following that up too I assume?"

She nodded.

"Keep me posted on that. God damn!" He shook his head in disbelief. "Delgado and his wife…. Damn!"

He stopped twirling the pen and put his finger tips together, a sign that he was summing it all up. "Phew. So now extrapolating from all this we have demands for a vaccine containing a DNA tracker invented, underwritten and manufactured by one of our own US hi tech firms with endorsement from our own potentially compromised medical fraternity. And this same lot are demanding a mandatory economic lockdown across the world plunging us towards a recession slash depression of epic proportions. And I am supposed to endorse this at a time when the greatest achievement of our administration has been the fastest economic growth rate in US history, the lowest black, female and Hispanic unemployment in modern times, the highest stock market records ever and an accelerating GDP which beggars the imagination. And, furthermore, I'm supposed to believe that this is a deliberately engineered virus sewn into the global fabric by the political and financial forces opposed to me playing their various compromised contributors like violins while the PRC are laughing all the way to the bank having failed to shut down their economy?"

The head of the NSA immaculate in his admiral's uniform nodded sagely. "It's actually worse than that Mr President. They tried to take you down with the Russia gate story, then the fake Ukraine allegations, then the botched impeachment and now this medical virus, which is the big one. Well, maybe, there again, maybe not.

"What do you mean by that?" The president seldom looked puzzled. "You mean there's something bigger than the bug? Like what? Civil war?"

It was the admiral's turn to look uncomfortable. "This infection is part hoax and part real. It actually comprises several viruses out there. The big one in Iran and taking off in Italy, and which we strongly suspect is now just making its first appearance amongst the Italian community in New Jersey, is the L strain. That means it's the lethal strain and it will kill many elderly people with previous collateral morbidity infections. Then there is the Wuhan strain. That came into the west coast before we could properly shut the door. The S strain from Wuhan is slightly less lethal but nonetheless very dangerous. Both strains carry an implanted HIV spike and at least one of them has two SARS injections as well. The hi tech and big pharma collaborators in this know full well that many will die but not the millions that have been projected by Imperial College in London. On that note my colleague from the NGA has some vital information for you." He glanced at his colleague, the hitherto largely silent vice admiral.

It was the Director of the National Geospatial Intelligence Agency who shifted miserably in his seat. His agency had successfully remained relatively low profile unlike the CIA and the NSA. His outfit was responsible for interagency mapping and satellite imagery. The NGA's technological powers were prodigiously secret. It had played a major part in the intelligence community's technology integration plan which travelled under the moniker of ICITE – the

Intelligence Community Integrated Technology Enterprise. ICITE married seventeen intelligence agencies and was the cornerstone of intelligence integration. The vice admiral hated giving the president bad information. "We are satisfied that there is a direct link between the PRC scientists and our own hi tech group here. In fact, we are very worried about one of your close allies. There may be an attempt to infect a leading European Prime Minister with the L strain to kill him. A revenge for his anti-globalist exit from the EU. We are also aware of the latest strategic military moves by the CCP to adopt a more aggressive global stance. 50 000 PRC troops on the Kashmir-Ladakh PRC border, naval deployments in the South China Sea, a 250 plus PRC fishing fleet preparing to head for the Galapagos islands and my NSA colleague is monitoring serious 'chatter' between the PRC and North Korea."

"Is that it?" the president asked suspecting there was worse to come.

The vice admiral knew his boss was smart but he had the uncomfortable impression that the president was always several steps ahead of him. "No, Sir. This is very preliminary intelligence which means we are still verifying it, but it looks like the PRC are smuggling weapons and money into the US to support an internal insurrection. There are also unverified reports that Kim Jong-un may have died or be seriously ill and his radical sister, Kim Ya Jong, is moving into the breach. It's all very fuzzy information at this point in time but it looks quite possible, in which case she will collaborate or advise him to collaborate on the arms smuggling operations into the US."

"Smuggling? On what grounds?" The president reckoned

he was nowhere near wrapping up the briefing.

"Frankly Sir, we don't know precisely but here's the drift." He glanced nervously as his colleagues.

They both nodded in agreement. "Tell him, even if it's unverified. Just tell him," the admiral from NSA said softly.

"Well, Sir, this is also unverified at this stage but…" he saw the president wince. A bad sign.

"It's OK, just tell me. Let me decide, ok?" He meant it reassuringly but that was not the way it came out from the big blond man in the dark suit behind the Resolute desk.

The vice admiral pulled himself together. The last thing he wanted was an argument with the most powerful man on earth. "There are suggestions that if the virus does not succeed in shutting down the world economy and destroying your presidency, then there will be a violently staged internal incident of some description. Designed to discredit law and order and the security forces. Might be racial, might be religious, could be both. There is evidence that at least 75 cities across the country will be involved in rioting and mass disruption before the elections. There will be liberated zones and occupied cities. People will be attacked and murdered. Statues will be torn down. Homes of prominent leaders will be harassed and attacked. There will be calls to defund the security forces when they respond. There will be chaos on the streets and near civil war. If you win the election despite all this, your opponents will say that you gerrymandered the outcome. They will take your opponent either to the west coast or the east coast and inaugurate him as the real POTUS. When you and your party reject this, they will demand that the military remove you."

"That's not going to happen. The JCS are loyal to me!" The president sounded very confident.

"Yes, Sir, the JCS are indeed loyal to you. But there are a hell of a lot of compromised senior commanders out there who are not. The odds are that the JCS will issue a public statement refusing to act. Your opponents are planning to call for UN intervention to overthrow your presidency because you will be seen to have usurped the presidency. That is the un-verified narrative that they are, allegedly, planning and they control the media sufficiently to make a persuasive case. Through the UN they plan to call on the PRC to assist in removing you. This is grade B2 intelligence at this time, meaning probably confirmed and probably reliable. It remains to be verified. But we thought it serious enough to tell you now." He glared at his colleagues. Providing unverified intelligence was like sharpening the knife to slit your throat.

The president was sitting back listening intently while he rubbed his middle finger against his upper lip. It was a character trait one of his predecessors had made famous. John Kennedy would often sit in his rocking chair in the Oval office and listen to his advisors in that pose. "Two questions. Have you any current assets inside the compromise operations and have you warned my colleague across the pond?"

The admiral glanced at his colleagues from CIA and NGA. "We have warned our allies and we hope that they are taking us seriously. We have several women who have come forward about the compromise operations but a number of assets have been murdered and we have no one on the inside currently. We are looking now."

"Get me the asset, protect him or her at all costs, and I mean at all costs, and lets blow this stinking rotten shithole wide open before the election. And I mean wide open! If we allow them to get away with it then we are in World War Three!"

The DCIA couldn't resist it. "Sir, in the Company we term the Cold War against the Soviets as World War Three. This is World War Four we are looking at."

The president looked at his DCIA grimly.

For a split second she reckoned she had gone too far. But then he did respect people who challenged him.

The president put the gold pen in his pocket. "Gina, I do recall that. Sometimes you sail close to the wind. But that's why you're DCIA isn't it!"

There was an almost collective sigh of relief as the three intelligence chiefs exited the Oval Office.

Stefanie sat opposite John Price and wondering how she could break the ice. He certainly did not match the profile of her customary clients. For a start he was most immaculately groomed and well dressed. His bland dark blue tie on a spotless white shirt was dead straight, his slacks immaculately pressed and his tweed jacket looked as if it had been tailored for him and hinted of Saville Row. But for the American accent he could have been a British army officer. She was willing to bet he was even wearing suede shoes. Not a hair out of place and courteous to a fault. When she walked into the interview room he had immediately stood up to shake hands with her. She was slightly taken aback. Due to viral threat the entire country was reduced to wearing surgical masks or the equivalent thereof. She was reluctant to break the rule, but if she was to see his facial expressions and establish a rapport with him both of these new social regulations needed to be violated. She instantly decided to discard the mask and to shake hands. He removed his mask with relief and unhesitatingly shook hands with her. She could see that he had rugged good looks and a strong face. Another government recommendation involving 1.5m social distancing ignored. But then the stakes were high enough she reckoned.

"Good day Mr Price," she said noting the firmness of his hand shake. "Dr Stefanie Westbroke assigned as the evaluator for the purposes of your sectioning. Please sit down and let's use this preliminary meeting to get to know each other."

Price did as he was invited and sat down. "It's a great pleasure to meet you Doctor, and thank you for your time and trouble on my behalf. Rest assured that I am determined to assist you as much as I possibly can and I look forward to co-operating with you."

Well, that was an unusual beginning Stefanie reckoned. Patients were usually hostile, aggressive and combative. They generally looked rather scruffy and bad language was a regular feature of the challenges she managed. She had dealt with the odd American before and they usually called her doc. This was man was courteous to a fault. Price carried all the hallmarks of a thorough going professional. He also seemed amazingly relaxed. She tried to ignore first impressions but she liked this man from first go and her intuition told her he was ok, but first impressions could be wrong. "Would you like a tea or coffee while we talk?"

He nodded. "A coffee would be very much appreciated.

Thank you." She was going to get up and order one from the male observer behind the two way mirror. This was standard procedure in first interviews where the staff member managing the enquiry might be in danger. Proceedings were filmed and taped and a large male orderly kept on stand-by just in case matters turned unpleasant. A sudden inspirational thought crossed her mind. Scrap the standard operational security procedures and take him out of this environment where they could talk without being monitored. It was unusual and might be risky but she reckoned she could get away with it and the canteen would prove far more congenial. She excused herself and walked out of the room shutting the door. She slipped into the observation room and assuring the orderly that all was well, thanked him for his time and trouble.

"It's going to be fine Stanley. I'm breaking all the rules but I just have the feeling in this case we are probably safer in this hospital with him around than without him. He is a solid officer and gentleman so we will go to the canteen and chat. Thanks for your help." Stanley thought Stefanie was breaking the protocols which she was. He decided to discretely go and have a coffee in the canteen himself not far from the two of them. Stefanie returned to the interview room.

"We usually hold these interviews here for specific reasons but this is a really cold and impersonal setting. Can I tempt you to accompany me to the canteen and we can sit and chat there?" She had never had fewer qualms about breaking a rule. They discretely slipped their masks back on and once comfortably seated in the canteen removed them again. During the walk they had made small talk and she reckoned that she had successfully broken the ice. She ordered tea and he had a coffee. But her confidence was momentarily shaken with his first question.

Peter Westbrooke wracked his brains. There had to be a way to get past the bureaucratic and political stone walling. He was driving home one evening when the realisation dawned. He pulled over to the side of the road and looked for Mohammed's contact details. The British mobile number probably would not work as he had helpfully explained that he would be returning to the US to tie up a few loose ends, finish his contractual obligations and then take up the post in Europe. A few calls and in minutes he had him on the line. The young man sounded very guarded. There was only one way to handle this and that was the blunt way. He was very sorry about the unpleasant detention and interrogation at Heathrow but it was all for the good. There had been some progress in the case he could not discuss on the phone. Would he agree to help Peter if it might contribute to locating Emma? It might even help to save her life. All his expenses would be covered and he could make a real contribution which the British security services would hugely appreciate. There might be some danger attached to it. Far from disenchanting Mohammed the thought of endangering his life to help Emma seemed to serve as a stimulus. The matter was so important that Peter would arrange to fly to New York to meet with him. There was protracted pregnant silence on the phone. Had he taken fright? Then to Westcott's relief he consented. It was almost as if the thought of danger acted as a stimulus. Did they need him in London? No, Peter would fly to NY to meet him. Say, day after tomorrow, only, of course, if that was convenient. But the best laid plans of mice and men....

"So, do you work for the British security services or are you really a medical practitioner?" John Price leaned forward and thoughtfully stirred his coffee. His blue eyes seemed to look through Stefanie. It was as if he was reading her soul.

The question almost threw her off balance. He had waited until they were comfortably seated before firing it and ensured that she was suitably relaxed. She would have to watch this one very carefully. "John, may I call you John?" He smiled and nodded. "John, I am employed by the British Government Health Services and paid by them. I have never in my life had anything to do with the military. And whilst I am about it let me be really up front. I have a brother in law who was in the Royal Navy and is now very high up in the British counter terrorism unit operating somewhere in a hazy relationship between MI5, our Security Service like your FBI in some ways, MI6 which as you well know is our version of your CIA and the Scotland Yard Metropolitan Police Counter Intelligence unit, or something like that." She watched his reactions closely. "I don't actually know what he does and he plays his cards very close to his chest as you guys all do, but I have enormous respect for, and trust in, him and nowhere more so than now." The moment she said it, she wished she hadn't. My God but she would have to be careful with this one.

His eyebrows shot up at the comment. "You mean because of me."

A monstrous look of pain crossed her face and she had a hard time keeping the tears back. He took it all in immediately. He reached out and touched her hand. "Oh my God, I'm so desperately sorry. It's something personal. Nothing to do with me at all. And you've been hurt, very badly hurt. God,

I am so sorry I raised the subject."

She put her hands up to her face and a tear welled out of her left eye. This was going horribly wrong. She had come into work to get her mind off the subject. Now instead of being the professional analyst her subject was inadvertently turning the tables. It was all falling apart before the assessment had even commenced. She took a deep breath and tried again to speak but choked. He seized the initiative in an astonishing way. "Listen Dr, er, Stefanie, I'm a specialist trained soldier which means I have to read people fast and accurately. Strangely enough in my line of business we try very hard not to kill people. We explore every avenue short of violence which means that some of us, well, we are trained in psychological evaluation just like you, but in a specialised different direction. If we can persuade our opponents to collaborate or co-operate with us rather than force us to kill them, we are under the strictest orders to do it. Of course," he added as an afterthought, "…if we have to kill them we do so as efficiently and effectively as possible, and we reckon we are very good at it. Trust me, we don't enjoy it, although some of the people we have to kill are very bad people indeed. And they have done very terrible things. But let me share this little secret with you at the outset. When you kill somebody, even a very bad person, you kill a little part of yourself too. A part of yourself dies as well. We don't admit it and we don't like to talk about it, but it's true. So persuasion and diplomacy even at the point of a bayonet, is preferable to killing. And by the way, much more rewarding and satisfying, both personally and from an information gathering perspective too. You have been appointed to assess me and I respect you for that and gave you my assurance in the interview room I would assist you in whatever way possible. Now you need to know all about me and I am going to give you my life history. I will answer all your questions directly and honestly unless they touch on issues of international security to my country and yours. But let me make you this offer right here and now. If you have been badly hurt, and I think you have, and you want to share that with me, no obligations, please do so."

He sat back and looked at her wiping the tears off her face. She sobbed and noticed his hand still rested on her hand. "Thank you. I'm so so sorry. It's really very unprofessional of me." Then she blurted it out. "My husband died some years ago. All I have is my 19 year old daughter Emma, a student at RADA. Or she was, a student at RADA. Now she is missing. I asked my brother in law to help and he is moving heaven and earth to assist but it's like she has vanished off the face of the earth. I feel like my life has been torn apart. First her dad, and now this." There was a long uncomfortable silence. She pulled herself together, "But we are here to talk about you. Let's start with your background."

He squeezed her hand and wouldn't let go. It seemed like an eternity but it was only a few seconds. Then he withdrew his hand and said, "Stefanie, please listen carefully now. Thank you for sharing that with me. It makes me feel far more trusting in sharing my details with you. If I can help you in any way whatsoever either now or when this is all over, whatever your recommendations, I am at your disposal. With a brother in law like yours it's highly unlikely but the offer is there. Now let me give you a short summary of my life to date and you can use that as a basis for going forward."

She nodded agreement and sipped her cold tea. And so

Stefanie entered a world beyond her wildest dreams. Of a privileged young man born into a rich American family with the world at his feet but with his father's determined independence and his mother's deep sensitivity. Of a keen, driven, fit and highly intelligent young man who loved the outdoor life and excelled at the opportunities offered by the military. He described his privileged life style which so contrasted with hers, his choice of universities and why he had changed to the military. He described with humility his affinity for languages and electronics, his volunteering for the SEALS and the brutal selection course. She was astounded at the awful stresses and strains of the selection course. The fire hoses, the log exercises, the route marches and the sleep deprivation in cold water for hours and hours after already being exhausted. He explained how they were bound hand and foot and thrown into a deep swimming pool, and the drop-out rate of those who had the disgrace of returning to unit. He touched on his training and the visits to different parts of the world, South and Central America, the Middle East and Africa as well as South East Asia. It was far too much for one session and so they met regularly and over protracted periods. Stefanie gave up making notes. She felt that much of what he was sharing with her, was dodgy security related information so she noted it and tried to forget it. In the process she assembled an amazing insight into how governments actually work. She learned about the secret world of covert operations, espionage, electronic intelligence, satellite spies and cyber warfare. The fact that warfare was merely an extension of diplomacy by another means had never crossed her mind. It was all compelling and fascinating. Some of it was quite incredible but she believed him. He was unemotional on most issues but loyal and patriotic to a fault.

Only once did he falter when describing how he had lost friends on a recent mission. That was when the psychological mask slipped. He started to explain and then stopped. She had taken him out to a little pub called the Rose and Crown in Rickmansworth which was popular with the residents of Harefield. He found the wisteria covered old 17th century pub with its undulating roof and interior lanterns utterly charming. It was the epitome of what life in England was all about. They had found a quiet corner and ordered a classic pub meal with a drink. She noticed he didn't touch alcohol. He loved traditional English fish and chips and it was while they were tucking in that she suggested to him that notwithstanding all the training there had to be times when the pressure was excessive. His answer intrigued her.

"You know, Stef, we are trained to cope with these things but sometimes, just once or twice, there are events which just seem overwhelming…. are you going to eat those chips?" He noticed she was carefully pushing her chips to one side.

She looked up and laughed. "John, I have got so many chips on so many shoulders …I don't need them round my waist too." They both laughed. "Go on then, take 'em."

He burst out laughing again, and relieved her of her chips. Then he suddenly looked very serious. "You know sometimes, once in a blue moon, things go wrong. Horribly wrong. I touched on this before in several of our conversations and I'm truly sorry to bring it up now, but we had a mission just before this incident in Northwood Hills. Things went terribly wrong and I am to blame. I will blame myself for the rest of my life. In fact, sitting talking with you, and all the other chats we have had, you know that has been a real treat, almost therapeutic in a weird way. But that operation went badly. It will haunt me for the rest of my life."

She watched his face intently. This was the real John Price. She put her knife and fork down. "Can you share it with me?" She reached out for a half pint of beer.

He looked at her long and hard. Then he inverted his fork in the British way and tried to squash the mushy peas on the top of the fork. They rolled round the plate. He smiled and caught her studying his face carefully. "Don't know how you Brits do it. In the States we use the fork shovel method." He reversed the fork and carefully packed the peas on board. "There, you see, much easier," he said triumphantly. They both laughed spontaneously. Their eyes met and then averted. For just a split second they felt that there was more to this experience. She knew he was avoiding the issue but felt he desperately wanted to talk about it.

"John, you have shared so much with me, already, I mean, it's really appreciated. Don't know if this helps but they made me sign the Official Secrets Act before this job so I can't tell if that makes it possible for you to be a little more forthcoming. I do know it means I go to prison for ten years if I reveal anything sensitive in this enquiry. Can you tell me about it? You see I think it was the trigger for what happened outside the hotel. You were just being loyal to your mate, really. You were on a short fuse as we say in England. The old chap just got in the wrong place at the wrong time. "You are fiercely loyal to your mates, aren't you."

It was his turn to get emotional. He stopped eating. She was a very attractive and highly intelligent woman. She was starting to read him like a book. That was her job. How much was real and how much was she role playing, he wondered. There was a loud crash at the bar as someone knocked an empty pint mug to the floor, followed by shouts of, "Oh Oh, drinks all round mate, drinks all round," and roars of commiserating laughter. He looked into her searching eyes. "Signed the Official Secrets Act, eh. You did mention that when we first met." It wasn't an accusation. More of a statement.

"Are you really surprised? Does that make a difference?"

He demurred. "No, I guess not." He cast another long look at her. What was that phrase the Brits loved, in for a penny, in for a pound, or something like that. He made the decision. "OK Stef, here's the short version of what happened."

CHAPTER 16

Emma was waiting to meet this anonymous VIP in the sunroom overlooking the pool garden. The door opened and she turned round. Her hands shot up to her face. She recognized him immediately. Anyone who had watched the international cable news networks would have known the anchor-man immediately. The tall good looking man with the immaculate head of hair walked over to her and shook hands. He had an amazing air of authority. The blue eyes did not smile with the rest of the face, she thought. His grip was hard and firm, dominating from the start. "You obviously weren't expecting me," he said.

"You were just about the last person in the world," she said and wished she hadn't. "They never told me...."

"Well, I hope it's not too much of a shock for you. But to meet someone so young and lovely you can rest assured the pleasure is mine."

Well, it's certainly going to be, she thought to herself. If I mess this up they will probably kill me.

Emma lay back on the bed exhausted. She had done everything asked of her but then following her uncle's advice she sought to engage with her so called lover. He was clearly not accustomed to this. His women were not there to engage with him but to satisfy him. Small talk was the limit of their involvement. To his amazement this young woman actually wanted to discuss the media and relations with the major political movers and shakers with him. As they were dressing she asked if he would mind – could they please take coffee together on the veranda in the sunroom. She was interested in his views on marriage and did they survive in the fish bowl that was Hollywood. No woman had ever asked him that before.

This was a first. He thought about it briefly and then agreed. It would be a novel experience to share some of his self-perceived wisdom with an intelligent young woman who also seemed to know instinctively how to satisfy him in bed. As he buttoned up his shirt he glanced at Emma's figure admiringly. "You know they've found life on Mars. I shouldn't tell you that but I mentioned it once in a Hong Kong TV interview and the roof didn't fall in." She looked up at him sharply. So there might be a chance to learn something new from all this. A chance to get her mind off what they had just done.

"That's amazing." She wondered how to address him. When he was anchoring, or reporting or making a documentary film he was always Mr ……. But he was not on set now and that seemed much too formal after what they had just shared in bed. That was something that Nikki had failed to brief her on. In fact, on reflection, there was quite a lot she had failed to share with her. And Nikki was so much in awe of him that she constantly ran round just calling him "the" VIP. But she thought to herself, what an opportunity this is. This is the man who talks to the world on the leading cable news network. This is the man who walks with presidents and talks to kings yet does not lose the common touch, as her father used to quote Rudyard Kipling to her. If anybody could give her keen insight into what was really happening in the world he most certainly could.

Where to begin and not let her overwhelming curiosity spoil it. She took a deep breath. How could she break the ice with a man whom the leading political figures of the world all too often asked him to interview them, and not the other way round. "Of all the interviews and topics you've covered in your media career, what has been the most pertinent?"

His eyebrows shot up in genuine surprise. He looked pensively at her. "Do you know, no one has ever asked me that!" Another tantalising pause. It was his turn to take a deep breath. "Space exploration, Emma, I mean serious space exploration, must top the list. It's the final frontier, the real unknown and astoundingly it has been almost entirely privatized. If you want to keep a secret in the US government, then outsource it. The general public have absolutely no idea what is going on out there."

Emma was intrigued. She understood instantly that this man was not only a brilliant top ranking media expert but unlike many journalists he had a very high level of discerning intelligence. Because of that he was the journalistic equivalent of a massive A listed movie star. This provided him with a unique overview and a vastly wider general knowledge than most. She had read a lot about him in magazines and the tabloid papers yet he came across as a very ordinary humble man. Yet what on earth was he doing in this cesspit? That might be a question for later. "Does that mean that man has gone beyond the moon?" It struck her as a naïve question in the light of what he had just said.

He swung round and stared at her. He might be old by her

standards but he was actually quite handsome when he did that. There was a long silence. He approached her and put both his hands on her shoulders. "Emma, rest assured on this score. If you have read it in the comic books or seen it in the sci-fi movies like Star Wars or Star Trek, then know not only that we can do it, but we are doing it. This country is doing things in space and elsewhere that are at least fifty years ahead of conventional technology and beyond your wildest dreams. And if you ever repeat that it would prove very unhealthy for you." She felt his fingers tighten on her neck then relax and a shiver of fear swept over her.

After the threat he slid his hands off her shoulders. She had no idea how to respond to information like that so she quietly said, "That's really awesome. I think I should forget this conversation."

He nodded, almost absent mindedly, and picked up the intercom phone by the bed, whilst fastening his special cufflinks. It was an open necked light blue shirt and she noted that it accentuated his sun tan. When the switchboard security operator answered he summoned Janet, the girl from Manila, who knew just enough English to get by. Would she deliver two coffees and some of those delicious muffins to the sunroom. He stroked Emma's hair and smiled at her. "Well now, where did you learn to take an interest in astronomy and foreign policy? Harry told me you are studying to be an actress and I gather he might be setting some Hollywood auditions up for you?"

She ignored the hint at the lure that had seduced her into this terrible mess. "I have always had an interest in world events thanks to my dad being English and my mother from Jamaica. My dad said it was important to know what is going on in the world as you never know how it might touch your life or your career."

He was intrigued. "Harry tells me that you lost your father some time back. Sorry to hear that. Your mother still alive?" He asked the question guardedly. Mothers missing their daughters could be very dangerous but he relaxed when she provided him with her carefully thought through answer.

"Mum and I don't really get on all that well." She watched him closely. The face relaxed which meant she effectively handled that issue for the moment. "She thinks actresses are flighty and unreliable. She says they are emotionally screwed up but that's just her psychological training."

His ears pricked up. "Psychological training? For what?"

Emma's intuition said to her this was a touchy subject with all sorts of possibly unwelcome ramifications. "Oh, she works as head of the Psychology Unit at Wexham hospital in England." A short silence to see how this went down but no reaction. The cufflinks were giving him trouble. They were really very beautiful with the gold embossed name and his famous signature on the back. "Here, let me help you." Her fingers deftly attached the cuff links. He noticed they were long and slender. She really was very attractive. Waxman had done him proud this time. But then Harry had never let him down yet. "She deals with people who have problems, you know, drink, depression, wife beating, hard drugs, soft drugs and that sort of thing."

He seemed disinterested in the answer as she rolled out the details. Her senses suggested that she had got that one right. Emma took him by the hand as they walked down the long hallway to the staircase. The mansion was built in a gigantic square with an inner courtyard. The façade looked out over the long driveway which disappeared into the forest on the front of the property and the rear comprised a glassed in sunroom with rolling lawns, a large heated swimming pool and tennis courts. Off to one side some distance away was the helicopter landing pad.

They took up the recliners and moved them slightly closer together. She wanted to draw him out. How do you feel being regarded as one of the most powerful men in media? I'm sorry that's a bit trite. Sounds like it's a line I pinched from the movie Air Force One. But it's true isn't it? I mean power is kind of addictive." She wondered if she had gone too far.

He laughed cynically. "You know Emma, that's what they say. And when you are first in the big time, it takes some time to realise and appreciate the power at your disposal. And you learn it in the oddest ways. I mean people will read books because you mention that you are reading the books. Or they find out what after shave you use and then the sales go through the roof. And at first it's all quite novel, exciting and you suddenly realise that the world is watching your every sniff, twitch and comment. And then it becomes a bit bizarre. In fact, to be brutally frank, it becomes quite irritating. And you know why? Because there really is no privacy, nothing for yourself and hardly any quiet moments."

She was fascinated. "So how do you cope with that?"

He laughed again. "You really are your mother's child, aren't you? I bet she asks her patients those questions."

She felt a bit awkward now. More awkward than making love to him in bed the way he wanted it. "Oh, no, I didn't mean it like that. No, not at all. I meant, well, you are regarded as one of the most powerful men on the goggle box."

He looked serious for a moment, and put his arm round her shoulders. This girl was very unusual. Bright, intelligent, curious and inquisitive. His senses tried to warn him to be careful with this one but he was on a bit of a roll now. "You know a lot for a 19 year old wanna-be Hollywood star." He looked into her eyes and saw the alarm or was it hurt. He gave a kiss. "Sorry, that sounded wrong. I didn't mean it in an insulting way. But it's nice to talk like this."

Trying to get out of this awkward situation Emma changed tack and asked, "If the stories you report on are controversial, does the buck stop with you or the media company?"

His answer surprised her. "No, not at all. In fact, all media companies may make money or waste money, as they are judged by the public who pay money to obtain their news from them. I am just one part in the whole thing. At this moment I am happy that my reportage responses have been on the plus side."

He paused and sniffed, like a panther smelling the morning air. Then reassured, he carried on. "The job obviously carries power. Well, it carries influence, really, more than power, in an unexpected way. But Truman got it wrong, too. The buck does in fact stop with the president, so to that extent the sign on his Oval office desk was right. But there is always someone or something above you calling the ultimate shots." He stopped walking and looked at her again. An enigmatic grin creased his face. "But you see Emma, even influence has its limitations, and in point of fact it really means nothing unless it brings you money, which in turn attracts more influential power, until it becomes a sort of self-fulfilling prophecy."

She reckoned this was the way kings used to live in the old days. And she was, after all, talking to a sort of modern king, who had influenced the nations of the world. It all seemed a bit unreal. Could there really be a Hollywood career after this, or would she be discarded and thrown out on the trash heap of ex-lovers, or would they just kill her. Uncle Peter had always said that she must play the game and stay focused on escape.

They sat down on the recliners and he took up the theme. "And yet, you know something, Emma, it's not real power. Former journalists, correspondents, anchor-men and even other leaders will never tell you this but the real power is in the shadows behind you. Oh yes, you have the …," he paused as the maid servant delivered the coffee and muffins. He dismissed her with a wave and continued. "As I was saying take our President. You have the guy with the football who follows him around everywhere….," he raised an eyebrow but she shot back.

"The nuclear launch codes, yes! My dad talked about that once."

"Hmm, you were well taught. Well, this guy is his shadow and it is true that you have the power to start wars and even end them too, I suppose. But the real power lies in your constituency."

"The listeners or the voters?" It was her turn to raise an eyebrow. "Surely not." She said it defiantly.

He sniggered. "Voters, viewers, listeners….. much the same most of the time." He warmed to his theme. "My girl, a high up friend in the government once told me that the voters

203

are irrelevant once they have cast their vote. Democracy only lasts in the split second that you pull the lever on the voting machine, many of which are pre-tabulated by the way. Or if you make your tick in the box." He paused to sip his coffee reflectively. "Then the voters are more of an irritation than a relevance. The real power lies in the forces and powerful vested interests that catapult you to the forefront in the electoral system of your party, the hidden interest groups with the hidden agendas, the powerful industrial and financial magnates, the military and the banking groups all over the world. It lies with the allies that you keep or dismiss and the alliances that you are locked into." He took a bite out of a muffin. And then he added reflectively, "And make no error, my girl, you can get very, very rich from power. Unbelievably rich from power and that is where these alliances are really important."

She wasn't sure that this was the right reason for being a top man. But perhaps it was not the time to say so. "What are the spin offs of interviewing the president in a bombshell report? Do you actually get to rub shoulders with the real deal?" She thought that was a much safer line of questioning and he warmed to the theme.

"Emma, there is sometimes a lot of spare time between interview takes, camera angles, wardrobe, sound, you yourself know this. The rich, famous and powerful politicians do come to see how it is all contrived. And they even share some of their secrets. In my spare time I read up on current politics which interests me immensely."

She wanted to know more. "Does America really get locked into alliances? How does that work?"

"Well, take the Five Eyes. We have an agreement between

five countries. We call them the Five Eyes." He explored in his pockets and found a cigar. Now surely there was a lighter in that right hand coat pocket. He fumbled round and located the lighter. "You see, we share almost all the information that we gather round the world with our allies, your country, Canada, New Zealand and Australia." He carefully unwrapped the cigar and applied the lighter without putting the cigar in his mouth. Eventually it started to ignite and he gave it a gentle exploratory suck. It reminded her of the way he made love. Gently at first and then as his confidence grew, more forcefully. A large cloud of smoke rolled lazily into the air above his recliner. He noticed Emma watching him with fascination. There was nothing better than a drink, a cigar and a good conversation after a satisfying physical union with a beautiful and intelligent woman. A chance now to share conversation that interested him instead of the usual nonsense. He reckoned this was a young woman who could go places.

"But surely there are huge dangers in sharing such information. I mean in the acting profession if we get a lead for a stage or film role, we tend to shut up about it or just share with our closest buddies who might benefit? Can't your allies use your information against you and anyway where does this all come from – spies, eyes in the sky, satellites?"

He laughed and blew a large smoke ring. He looked at her with new eyes. "Emma, you are far too clever to be an actress. No insult intended. We have spooks, or spies, or assets as we call them yes, but the bulk of our information comes from a network of satellite and listening stations round the world which scoop up every electronic communication on this globe and beyond." He warmed to his theme. "Emma, stop and think for just a moment. Imagine the power you have when you can read every electronic communication across the world, the innermost secrets of commerce, business, finance, politics, the military and other intelligence services. Think for a split second of what you can do if you control the very sources of information on which corporate chiefs and political leaders base their decisions. We can control, manipulate and pulse markets, investments, countries and entire continents. Think of what it means when you can hack into the innermost sanctums of the leading merchant banks, powerful governments and finance houses, take out information and insert other information. Then take it further beyond your wildest dreams, where you can actually invent the narrative communicated by the media and your targets react as you desire. You can not only buy and sell journalists as you wish, but at whim or will you can invent the narrative, create the cyber data base and feed it into the global media machine in such a slick way that no one is the wiser. Why, we are so smart we even begin to believe our own narratives. And if we can believe our own rubbish, then the public stands no chance."

He saw her eyes light up with genuine interest. "It's not like James Bond. He wouldn't last five minutes in the real world. We vacuum up every single electronic communication on the planet and some that would surprise you from places further afield but that's another matter. We keep this information for 72 hours and outsource it to various private companies in Canada, your country and even our old enemy Germany."

Emma was hooked. This man should give up anchoring and go into politics, amazed at his depth of knowledge on world events "Why? Who runs these private firms?" She used the British word firm rather than company. Ironic he thought to himself. The CIA was known as "the Company" and the British called their spooks "the Firm". He knew he had to be careful here. "Well, you see Emma, in terms of the American Constitutional provisions which control our government there are things other governments can do for us, and even private companies, which we are not supposed to do for ourselves."

"What, like spying on your own people and manipulating them? But if you can do that, you can influence elections as well." This conversation reminded her of discussions with her uncle Peter. Better not to mention him at all she thought. Where was Uncle Peter now she wondered? Did he even know about her? Must do.

She was a fast learner this one. "You sure you don't have any connections with the intelligence world?" He said it as a joke but her swift reply was just a little too quick.

"Pure as the driven snow," she retorted and instantly regretted it. Uncle Peter would have clipped her ear for answering so fast. He always said play dumb but not too dumb. Play along but in a challenging way. Never admit to knowing me or what I do. And know that if anything ever happens to you or your mother, I shall move Heaven and Earth to help you.

That conversation was happening at just about the same time Peter Westbrooke was trying to cadge a lift on a USAF flight to Washington DC but his usually friendly US Embassy liaison officer would have none of it. Colonel Lyn Hansen was adamant. "The president has sealed the border. No one, and I mean no one, gets in there. Not even your Prime Minister, even if he could go. And Pete, if you don't mind me saying so, old Boris is looking a little peaked himself."

So that door was well and truly shut. How on God's earth could he soar over the authorities blocking him? And who could he go to? It would have to be someone high up. Very high up. The answer came surprisingly. He was due to meet a contact at the Imperial War Museum on another matter and had taken an underground train to get there. The meeting was to take place under the massive 14 inch guns of the battleship King George V mounted in front of the museum. On his way to the meeting Peter had picked up an abandoned newspaper off the seat of the train. He was not in the habit of reading discarded cheap tabloid newspapers. It was the headline on the second page of the folded paper which caught his eye. It made a reference to the arrest of paedophile rings in the US at the instigation of the American president. He glanced through the article. The White House had established a special task force to shut down over 1 200 such rings with the arrest of over 11 000 paedophiles. All of these had either been charged or tried and sentenced, usually to long gaol terms. Some were being investigated for murder. Many of these were linked to the well-known Epstein case. The rings were clearly a target for the president. It was rumoured that he was even having some of his predecessors investigated on the quiet. He became so intrigued with the article that he nearly forgot to disembark at the Lambeth North underground. Pity there was no way he could reach the president. The thought came and went.

On his way to the museum he passed the house where the notorious Captain Bligh had stayed, commemorated with a traditional circular Blue London tourist marker. What a bastard that man had been, he thought to himself. No wonder the men on the Bounty had mutinied. Denied food and particularly water to feed a bunch of plants. Beaten if they complained, tortured if they remonstrated and constantly victimised in petty ways it was unsurprising that they had taken the law into their own hands. In a sense he was doing the same thing, by trying to go above his boss. Plants were not the issue here, but a young woman's life was, and a relative at that. But Bligh had surprised the mutineers. Cast off from HMS Bounty in a small boat amidst the mighty Pacific Ocean with a few reluctant loyalists for company, Bligh had achieved the impossible. With his brilliant mathematical prowess he had navigated their way to survival. The reckoning when it came had been terrible. But for a few desperate exiles on Pitcairn Island there had been no retribution. So the moral of the story was that occasionally the gamble paid off. But to avoid the Bligh syndrome of retribution it was essential to reach the top. Almost on cue it began to rain. Up went the umbrellas and so did Peter's reflection. As he reached the museum and stood under the massive guns waiting for his contact, a diplomatic Mercedes Benz car with a UAE pennant and diplomatic plates swept up to drop some Arab VIPS at the entrance. It was then that the thought struck him. Young Mohammed hailed from the UAE. During his intensive interrogation he had explained that his father had just returned from serving as UAE Ambassador to Washington. What if, but at that moment his contact arrived and after shaking hands they joined the queue to enter the building.

Peter knew that all calls were monitored but perhaps he could connect with Mohammed via another method. He went back to his house and retrieved his wife's cell phone.

She was playing tennis and never took it near the courts. He walked from their semi-detached house in the charming Guildford suburb of Burpham through the winding side streets, across a stream to a small wooded park outside Sainsbury's. As shoppers came and went, he stood near the adjacent wood and placed his call. Mohammed answered cautiously on the second ring. It was obviously not a number that he recognized. But it had the British 0044 area code so he decided to take the call. There was no time for felicitations.

"Hi M, no names, you know my voice?"

Mohammed was sharp as a razor. "Yes, sss…", he was going to say Sir, and then thought better of it.

"Listen once, and once only. Are you alone?"

"I am," came the cautious reply.

He noticed an attractive young mother decant her child and try to head for Sainsbury's. "Can you talk freely?"

"I can," he said, sounding puzzled.

The child was not co-operating with the attractive mother, kicking legs to prevent being safely put in the stroller. Normally he would have offered assistance but this was not the time. Focus, he thought to himself. "Listen, there's a problem. I can't get over to you. Need your help. I think I know where your female friend is! Make no comment." He let that sink in. Mohammed had not gone to Harvard for nothing. He knew exactly what was going on. His heart beat at a rate of knots. He started sweating. He could actually feel the droplets of perspiration rolling down inside his Brooks brother shirt. He wanted to shout out loud and demand more information. But all his instincts told him to shut up and do as he was told. Allah be praised, so she was still alive. Who would have dreamed it.

Having set the bait, Westbrooke continued. "Your dad was envoy to where you are, as I recall?"

"Yes," answered Mohammed cryptically. His heart was beating so hard he was scared Westbrooke could hear it down the phone.

"Did he know the big blond man in the pale house in DC on the avenue named after William Penn?"

Mohammed had to work this out. There was a long silence. Westbrooke expected this. He kept quiet. Two young boys came out of the Sainsbury's parking lot and took the trail into the wood to the suburban homes across the stream. Once out of sight they produced a box of Dunhill cigarettes and lit up. Well, at least they were just smoking fags and not something else, Peter thought. Expensive tastes kids had these days. Funny how convenient these woods were. He wondered what else went on in the woods. But he was willing to place money on it that no one had ever tried to achieve what he was attempting.

Mohammed's brain was working in overdrive. Obviously these calls were monitored and the eavesdropping system worked on the basis of trigger words. So an anodyne conversation was the safest and least likely to attract unwelcome attention. What the hell was the Englishman on about? DC was Washington, William Penn? Ah, Penn must refer to Pennsylvania Avenue, and the big pale house ah,,,,,1600 Pennsylvania Avenue, the White House, got it. Obtuse damn Englishman, of course he was referring to the American president. "Yes," he answered cryptically. This was an annoying conversation but also rather fun. Like the movies. Then he added, "Met him several times. Knew him from before. On first name terms. So, what about it?"

Westbrooke continued. "I said keep it short. Need your dad to get hold of the man. Tell him about your female friend. She is in the same country. I am sure she is being held on an estate. Now listen carefully. Only once, ok. The name of the estate owner is a notorious and very well-known human trafficker from Hollywood. I said trafficker, got it. He is male, preceded by the stuff candles are made of. Got it? Think."

Another long silence. Mohammed thought quickly to himself. A male is a man, candles are made of wax, holy moly, Hollywood mogul Harry Waxman. The whole fucking world knew about Harry Waxman. Allah be praised. What on earth was Emma doing with Harry Waxman, the guy Hollywood actresses publicly and unashamedly called God at the Oscars. He wanted to shout out the name but pulled himself together just in time. There was a protracted silence and then he said, "Gotcha."

So far, so good, thought Peter. "I am being blocked on both sides of the pond. The blond man has a keen interest in wrapping up human trafficking. He will help us. Ask your dad to please call the blond man and ask him personally to intervene. He can use names when they talk." He was going to add that using names would not matter because it would take at least 24 hours for the satellites and cyber systems to log in and to analyse the dialogue and then probably dismiss it. So there could be no leaks. Well, he thought to himself, there could be no leaks that would actually matter once the blond man was involved. Then another thought crossed his mind.

"You still there?"

"Yes."

"Got all that?"

"Yes."

"One more thing. After you contact your dad, he, that is your dad, MUST place the call ASAP. Same reason this call is the way it is. Got all that?"

Mohammed was shaking. "I understand."

Great kid, thought Peter. "Good. Will text you another number to contact me. Good luck….oh and thank you."

There was another long silence. "Thanks," and the phone went dead.

Mohammed phoned his dad who was on the golf course at the time. Cell phones were forbidden on the golf course in Dubai but former Ambassadors could pull rank. In the Middle East it was natural to take advantage of one's enhanced status and close relations with the ruling royal family. Mohammed's father certainly did. When he had heard his son out, he smiled with satisfaction. It was actually very convenient. There was another not so small matter he wished to raise with the president involving Israel, the UAE and the world.

The president was a very hard worker. Unlike Churchill who had a habit of working his staff to death, the president was very considerate of his staff. He worked long and late and when he retired he did not like to be disturbed unless it was a matter of serious urgency. The problem was that just about every issue was a matter of serious urgency by the time it reached his level. The White House switchboard knew this. The switchboard system worked on a series of filters linked to computers. Callers were voice checked by computer as soon as they identified themselves. Simultaneously the switchboard computers could check the source of the call. Once the voice check confirmed the caller it was at the discretion of the operator and a senior White House staff supervisor to determine whether or not to disturb the president based on the information about the caller and his reason for calling. The president had friends. Personal friends seldom called after hours. Then there were official personal friends. They did not call after hours unless it was really important. If the issue was one of national security then the president was willing to be woken up by an official personal friend. The caller from Dubai hit all the right buttons, his voice tallied, his record on the computer was flawless and he had played a critical role in trying to cement ties between Israel and the UAE at the behest of the President.

But it was after two in the morning and the president was probably just drifting off. It was said that Margaret Thatcher could get by on 15 minutes sleep a night although she preferred more. Her late working habits had saved her life in the Brighton Hotel bombing. Had she gone to bed when the IRA expected her to, she would have been killed in the ensuing blast. The president was rumoured to survive quite easily on four hours a night but he, too, preferred more. The switchboard operator and the senior staff supervisor listened carefully to the caller from Dubai. The glamorous blond supervisor knew he was in regular contact with the president and the diplomatic consequences for the entire Middle East if such an exchange of envoys could occur would be of monumental significance. There was also something that was so sensitive he only wished to share it with the president. She approved the call. The phone rang twice. That was a good start. It meant he may not have been asleep. The president answered the phone. His staff were under the strictest instructions never to apologise for waking him up. All calls were monitored by a supervisor and recorded.

"K A here Sir, it's the former UAE Ambassador on the line from Dubai. It's not personal."

"Put him on," the president sounded alert. What the hell could have gone wrong. They were so damn close to a rapprochement with the Israelis. Dammit.

"Yousef, you old devil. I take it this is not about your golfing handicap. It had better be good?"

"Mr President. My apologies for disturbing. Two minutes please?"

"Go ahead." The president was a man of brusque manner and few words which made many dislike him for the wrong reasons. He was, above all else, a really good listener.

"I'm speaking in clear. No scrambler."

"Go for it."

"Mr President, my new friends, the Red Sea Pedestrians, …." he hesitated. The Ambassador used the British term for the Israelis… "you with me, Mr President?"

"Go for it," came the laconic reply.

"They say, unverified at this stage of course, that there is another bug on the way after the China bug. It is being conveyed via the Middle East and is now in a Beirut warehouse. It is allegedly much more lethal. A real killer. To be released just before the election."

There was silence on the other end. Then a slight cough. "Understood. That took less than one minute. Anything else?" A small bead of perspiration broke out on the president's forehead.

"Yes. My son, from Harvard has an English girlfriend, Emma Westbrooke a 19 year old RADA acting student, who was kidnapped in London two months ago and he is certain like others, has been trafficked to a certain Harry Waxman in your country. Waxman has close links to a rich Russian in London and this has been going on for some time. The girls are moved regularly so it is hard to get a bust on them. Any sign of a bust and they are tipped off, the girls threatened and moved to a safe house. A top British counter intelligence officer related to her, called Peter Westbrooke, has tried to extract her but is being blocked by his superiors and your Agency people. Her US kidnapper is also apparently being protected by your Agency people. This British officer believes she is being used for entrapment and compromise operations involving your swamp opponents and was unwillingly lured into this on the false promise of a Hollywood career. Can you please help?"

There was a protracted silence whilst the president took it all in. Many times in his life the right opportunity had magically appeared at just the right time. God truly worked in mysterious ways. The silence worried the former UAE Ambassador. "Mr President, Donald, are you still there?" He said it hesitatingly. They were good friends but one could sometimes take liberties. It was a miracle the switchboard had put him through.

"Yousef, you are the answer to a prayer. Truly, God is great. Leave it to me. I owe you one. Thank you. Anything else."

"Just to let you know my handicap is getting better." Had he gone too far? The timing was just right. A wonderful stress releaser.

A short silence then a chuckle. "Well done you. Two minutes up. Oh, and Yousef?"

"Yes, Mr President."

"Much appreciated and thank you on all counts. Good night." The line went click.

The president hung up the phone and switched on the bedside light. He thought for a moment and then pushed the intercom button. His glamorous wife rolled over and hid her supermodel features under a shock of dark hair. He squeezed her shoulder gently. An alert voice answered on the intercom.

"Yes, Sir."

"K A you did very well. Thank you. Call Gina and ask her if she would please be kind enough to come through here now. Well, say in an hour will do. A cup of coffee wouldn't go down too badly either. Oh, and Mike too, please."

"Which Mike Sir, the Admiral or Secretary of State?"

"Ah, both Mikes now that I think of it." There was a pause and then he added, "That was a critical call. You did well. Really appreciate it." Despite the hour of the night K A positively glowed. "Oh, and K, bring me up the tape as soon as you can, please?"

The Director of Central Intelligence was accustomed to being summoned to the White House in the middle of the night. What surprised her was to find the Director of the National Security Agency and the Secretary of State also present. Despite the hour the president was impeccably dressed, suit, white shirt, matching red tie and clean shaven. It was going to be a long day.

The president looked at his DCIA like a cat with a bowl of cream. "Gina, how would you like a gift-wrapped agent inside the paedophile network?"

She looked perplexed. "We are working on it, Sir!"

"The Brits have come up to the plate."

"Sir?" she said puzzled. The president sometimes spoke in riddles.

"There's no extra charge for this," he said with a smile. The president explained that they appeared to have a ready-made asset within the Waxman household. Since the arrest of Epstein and his apparent suicide the focus on the compromise and control operations had shifted to Waxman. The problem was that the girl was British, and had a relation in the British counter intelligence field who was being blocked on both sides of the Atlantic. The mission was to unblock him, liaise with the girl, run her as an asset and smash the compromise ring without risking her life. The Secretary of State would have to clear it with the Brits but carefully because there were problems on that side of the Pond as well. That was the first mission. The second mission was even more important.

"I'm saving the best to last." He paused for effect. They leaned forward. "We have another bug on the way!"

All three intelligence officers shifted slightly in their seats. The Secretary of State felt deep sympathy for the DCIA as he had been her predecessor. And the president was good at this. He loved being ahead of his thirty billion dollar intelligence agencies. He pressed the play button on the tape of the earlier dialogue with the UAE envoy. They listened in rapt silence. The conversation stopped. The Director of the NSA made a note to have that satellite telephone intercept removed immediately. He was the first one to speak. "Well, I'm glad his handicap's improving." They all smiled nervously. He continued. "Damn, we are just contending with one bug and they have another lined up and ready to go."

"It's to be neutralised," the president said. "Timing is everything. We just about have the UAE-Israel link sewn up. Watch Beirut like a hawk and if it looks like they are going to move it out then we have to act." He peered inquisitively at the DCIA. "Gina, how do you think they plan to infiltrate it into the West?"

The DCIA shifted uncomfortably in her seat. She coughed to give herself a momentary reflection. Time for some quick thinking. "Well, Sir, the UK and other countries still have open borders with the PRC. That could be the route. Shift the bug to an infection point and distribute from there."

The president switched his gaze to the portrait of Andrew Jackson. "So, who takes it out?"

The Secretary of State smiled. "Sir, maybe it's better if they all act."

The president stared at him fixedly. "Elaborate."

"Well, Sir, what if it's us, Israel and the UAE. Make it a team effort a few months down the line. Best bet is to have UAE start a deliberate conventional fire, one of our subs puts a conventional cruise missile in to heat it up and the Israeli's deliver a small tactical 1 to 2 kt nuke to finish off the job. That way we are all committed, no one blows the lid on anyone else and good faith is shown all round." He sat back in his chair. His two colleagues were stunned. Then he added. "What better way to start a collaborative relationship and do a service to the entire world simultaneously."

The president looked thoughtful. "Mike, you really are a Machiavellian in foreign policy. I hope it doesn't go that way but we have enough trouble already with this China virus. Another one would be globally catastrophic. Let's leave that there for the moment with contingency plans at the ready."

The DCIA made a note of the name "Westbrooke." She would contact him immediately. The former Ambassador's son would be the best contact. The girl would trust him. They could fly Westbrooke in to work on the COIN operation. There were swamp elements protecting the rings inside the intelligence services, of that they were sure. This would have to be handled at the highest levels.

She had been right. It was to be a long day.

Harry Waxman was delighted with the "VIP" response to Emma. He introduced her to other financial, film and media executives. The feedback was terrific. Emma had brains, beauty, charm and exceptional talent in bed. It was all working like a dream. And then came the mistake. He had introduced Emma to a cyber billionaire, William Felgate by name. Felgate was married, and fabulously wealthy. He, like the former "VIP" enjoyed talking to his lovers. He was arguably one of the most successful of Silicon Valley entrepreneurs. His firm was producing technology that was sold round the world in every cyber market imaginable. The world was at his feet, he had it all, and he knew it.

He also knew, or strongly suspected that, they were being filmed and taped, but it strangely did not worry him. He had interests all over the world, his wife frankly bored him, and he was looking for something more than mere physical satisfaction. Emma was still not allowed off the estate. Accordingly the meetings were arranged in the mansion. It was before the sex that a most curious conversation had taken place in the vast library along one side of the house. Felgate liked to get to know his women. He also enjoyed displaying his inside knowledge. She had been asked all the usual questions about where she came from, her family background, what she wanted to do with her career and so on. It was when she had revealed her passion for the stage and film that Felgate had slightly opened the door to freedom.

"I think we need to get you an audition somewhere. Harry is so busy these days backing the Democratic Party and helping them financially for this coming election I get the feeling he is neglecting your own aspirations. Let me set up an advertising shoot for you which is due on a site not far from here. One of Harry's firms must have a product they are keen to launch. That gives him the incentive. And they can't object if I take good care of you whilst you're off the estate," he said with a broad wink. Her heart leapt into her mouth. But to show any emotion other than excitement at the prospect of a real video shoot would have been disaster on the spot.

"Would you, could you, do that, please." She jumped up and gave him a big hug. It was a serious hug too. In the back of her mind it struck her that the whole thing might be yet another hopeless hoax. But if she could just get off the estate for a few hours, there was a chance, a very small chance, but nonetheless not to be dismissed, that she might get a message out.

He added quickly. "Of course. It may only be a small part but it's a chance to show your worth. Leave the arrangements to me," And so saying they went up to the bedrooms.

The door to freedom had opened fractionally.

The CIA Station Chief in London was not accustomed to receiving calls from the DCIA in Langley. He was summoned to the sound proof bug free encryption room. There, on an encrypted line direct from Langley, he was told in no uncertain terms to provide every assistance to a certain Mr Peter Westbrooke who had to be conducted to the US on a private jet aircraft with immediate effect. What about Covid-19 precautions? The president had waived them for the purposes of national security. If learning that the DCIA wanted to speak with him personally was not enough, the fact that the president of the United States had personally waived any COVID19 restrictions meant that this man was exceptional. He emerged from the room shaken. A number of phone calls were placed and arrangements were made for an unmarked aircraft to collect Mr Westbrooke at a local air base within twenty four hours for immediate delivery to Andrews Air Force base outside Washington DC. It was made clear that this was a matter for the eyes of the Station Chief only.

Meanwhile just as the Chief of the British Secret Intelligence Service was obtaining a phone call from his American counterpart. The British Foreign Secretary was receiving a call from his American colleague in the US State Department. The US Secretary of State sought the full backing and support of his British counterpart in assisting with the expediting of critical assistance from a British intelligence officer involving a British national under criminal coercive detention in the US. The British national was a young girl uniquely placed to provide crucial information in the interests of the national security of the United States. Providing that he was kept up to speed with developments would the British Foreign Secretary allow the US government to do whatever they could within their power to protect and rescue the young woman in question. The Foreign Secretary reckoned that it would do wonders for Anglo-US relations if such assurances were provided at a time when it seemed to him that the British economy was heading for a serious challenge due to the Covid-19 virus and in the midst of complex negotiations to accomplish Brexit. It looked to him as if the world was plunging into economic chaos and the United States would be the first country to recover. Therefore, he reasoned, if Britain could hook her economic coat tails to the recovering US economy the outlook might prove much rosier than if Britain had remained plugged into a moribund and struggling Europe. He assured the Americans of his full co-operation.

Looking out over the Thames from his Secret Intelligence Service rooftop office near Vauxhall Bridge, Sir John, as he was known to his colleague at Langley, tried to explain that Peter Westbrooke was actually a senior counter intelligence officer liaising between the British Special Branch and MI5 or the Security Service and that he was only tangentially involved with the SIS. His mind was actually focused on reports that there were sound reasons to believe that his Prime Minister, now fighting for his life in a London hospital, might well have been deliberately infected with a particularly lethal strain of the Covid-19 virus. He actually wanted to ask his American counterpart about research reports emanating from the UK Porton Down Biological Warfare Centre that there were actually 11 strains of the disease. But perhaps this was not the time.

The CIA Director explained patiently, courteously and counter intuitively that she was well aware of Mr Westbrooke's career, probably more so than Sir John or even Mr Westbrooke himself. She knew full well of his covert operations in the Middle East and in Ireland and his exceptional talents and skills in the intelligence field. The work in which he would be engaged on behalf of the United States as well as his own country would inevitably have ramifications for the Secret Intelligence Service and it was therefore in everyone's interests that his transfer be facilitated with the greatest possible alacrity. She then added that there was another not so small matter involving her colleague in the NSA and herself, concerning Britain's gigantic electronic monitoring post on Cyprus. Would Sir John be kind enough to warn his colleague in GCHQ that the Americans had a particular special interest in any and all materiel involving the port of Beirut and the movement of goods, people or services from a certain warehouse the details of which were on their way to him now by special courier. Sir John agreed to this with alacrity and wondered in the same breath if it might not be appropriate for the Admiral in charge of the NSA to speak with his counterpart at GCHQ. That, said the DCIA, was happening at this very moment. Sir John put the phone down and stared out the window at the sluggish Thames River. He pondered for a moment just how big this whole affair might be when the entire world was reeling from a Chinese sourced viral infection that was causing more damage to the global economy than even a direct war with the PRC might inflict. He was thinking of the Russian term, asymmetric warfare, when his scrambler phone rang and his political boss the Foreign Secretary politely asked for sixty seconds of his time.

In the UK the control of espionage operations overseas falls under the Foreign and Commonwealth Office. The role of counter espionage is shared between the Security Service, MI5, and the British Special Branch and its Counter Terrorism division, all of which report to the Home Secretary. Consequently, it was only natural that the request for assistance from the British involving a British national overseas, albeit kidnapped and illegally abroad, should be directed to the Foreign Secretary. There were no pleasantries in this short conversation. The Foreign Secretary explained that he had just been contacted by his American contemporary and it would be very much appreciated if the British security and intelligence services would kindly render every assistance they could to their US allies. No, he was not aware of the problem or problems in detail, or indeed even in general, but he was well aware of the importance of the request from Washington, particularly after the embarrassing efforts by a former MI6 man and a colleague at GCHQ to discredit the president before he had even taken office. The time had come to make amends. Sir John got the message loud and clear.

As for Peter Westbrooke, he reckoned that he had now played his ace in opening up to Mohammed. Assuming the young man did as he was asked, and his father complied, there might be some rapid follow up action. Accordingly, he contacted Stefanie and invited her to come down and dine with the family at his home in Burpham, a suburb of Guildford. She could stay the night in their house and return the following morning. It was likely that Stefanie would be almost beside herself worrying about Emma and a reassuring dinner with the family plus encouraging insights to the effect that there was some movement on the case might be helpful. Stefanie was only too well aware that Emma could be in serious trouble. But he knew she had bravely taken on some sort of professional case at the hospital with important overtones to keep her busy and distract her mind. They both appreciated that the new lockdown regulations made travel extremely difficult. However, being essential medical personnel gave her a luxurious freedom of movement to which most citizens were not privileged. For his part, Peter Westbrooke, being in a security related position, enjoyed almost total freedom of movement and association.

Stefanie found the drive down to Surrey quite therapeutic in some ways.

Spring was in the air and the welcome empty highways, though slightly odd in some respects, made the trip much less stressful. She had successfully developed a close working relationship with John Price. In doing so she had come to admire him and respect him. There was a sense of honour and integrity there that she had always associated with her late husband. She actually found herself looking forward to the little excursions they had undertaken together, wandering down charming canals, exploring little villages and visiting quaint English pubs. With the lockdown these excursions had become more difficult but when challenged she was always able to produce her medical documentation substantiating the right to be outside and escorting a patient. This had become something of a joke between them. As he had pointed out on one occasion, in most other countries where he had been operational, he would have been escorting her as a single vulnerable woman, not the other way round.

The narrative of his experience in Iraq had left her deeply disturbed. It had also served to cement the degree of mutual trust and respect between them. When he had described the reasoning behind the assassination of al-Sadr it had given her a whole new insight and understanding as to what was going on in the world. In some ways it raised more questions than answers but she was reluctant to go down avenues and rabbit holes unrelated to her immediate medical mission. She could also keenly understand and identify with his enormous personal distress and unjustified self-condemnation. She had devoted much of her time to helping him overcome the irrational guilt. They had discussed it on several occasions. After a while her counselling initiatives had started to pay off. It would have been helpful to discuss that with Peter but she was forbidden from discussing it with anyone.

As if that was not sufficiently frustrating there was one other aspect of the case that she would have liked to have explored with Peter and Sandra, his devoted wife, had not fate intervened. She had noticed that she was developing a deep and abiding affection for the younger man. At first, she had been too distressed herself, to pay much attention to it. But the thoughts kept creeping in. Then she put it down to having a shoulder to cry on after losing Emma. But the conversations and their emotional overtones began intruding into her mind with increasing frequency. There was nothing motherly about it. He found her compellingly attractive and she was both fascinated and intrigued by him. There was an old world charm and courtesy about him, plus his strong reassuring presence that she found utterly enchanting. Her therapy was restoring his self-confidence and the result was a tall, good looking and compellingly attractive man. This was awkward. The first rule of therapy was to never, ever, under any circumstances, become personally involved with the clients. When the door shut and they were out of the office environment, they were also out of your life. That was the first law of professional therapy. But it wasn't working out like that at all. It was so frustrating. Perhaps she could hint at it in a distant sort of way. In any case, Peter and Sandra were super bright and they would understand if she made a vague reference to it.

She arrived at the red brick semi-detached house well in time and admired his new roll-on artificial lawn by the front door. She noticed a very out of place large plastic Coca-Cola bottle full of water lying prominently on the lawn which puzzled her. "It's for the dogs," he laughingly explained. "They were defecating on the plastic grass but now avoid the place like the plague," he said and then winked. "Not perhaps the right term these days, is it." A quick drink in the garden and in they went to the dining room at the back of the house for a delicious home cooked roast leg of lamb.

The dining area was conveniently adjacent to the kitchen and overlooked the walled in back garden. The roast had been expertly carved with Peter's customary surgical dexterity and they were just sitting down to eat while Sandra poured small glasses of the most excellent red South African wine when Stefanie thought she heard cars pulling up outside. Peter was preoccupied explaining to her that Emma whilst probably still alive appeared to be in an extremely awkward and dangerous position when the doorbell rang. He walked to the bay window and glanced outside. A large official looking black American Chrysler car was parked in the driveway and behind it a dark blue Jaguar. Each car had a driver in it. There were two men in suits standing at the door. He briefly wondered if they were being investigated for breaking lockdown regulations when the doorbell rang again followed by a hard knock. Before he could intervene his wife answered the door.

Even before she could open her mouth she was met with, "Good evening, Mrs Westbrooke?" from a short balding man in a rather crumpled black suit. Behind him stood a tall grey haired man with a crew cut.

"Good evening," she replied. "I had no idea Peter had invited other guests this evening?" As she said it she knew it sounded very hollow.

"No, we were not invited. My name is Langdon and I am from London in an office related to Peter's work. Mr Richards here is from the US Embassy." He gestured towards crew cut who silently nodded unsmilingly. "We need to have an urgent discussion with Peter please."

"Just a moment," she replied taken aback. "Please come in," but before she could finish her husband had walked into the hallway.

"Darling, keep Stefanie company for a moment. It's obviously important." He waived her away. "Come in please gentlemen."

The two men glanced at one another and stepped through the doorway into the small hall. They turned right into the living room and without asking permission drew the curtains over the bay window. Without being invited both men sat down on the leather couch as Peter closed the door. When he turned to take a chair they already had cards to give him. Richard's card simply read James Richards, Cultural Affairs Officer, Embassy of the United States of America. Langdon's card read Terence Langdon, Army and Navy Club, St James, London. Peter glanced at them and handed the cards back. They were as good as useless but he knew exactly what they meant.

Langdon spoke first. "Mr Westbrooke, we understand you are investigating a missing girl, related to you, who is now illegally resident in the US."

Peter nodded. "That is correct. Her mother is dining with us tonight. How can I help you?"

He continued, "Yes, we know that. She is not to be told about this. Mr Richards will explain." He gestured towards the American.

"I am instructed by the White House via the Director of Central Intelligence to ask you to accompany me to the US air base at RAF Alconbury where you will board a special flight to the United States to assist in further enquiries concerning Miss Emma Westbrooke. You have thirty minutes to get ready and pack a suitcase. Just pack essentials and any other clothing you require can be purchased in the US at the cost of the US government, within reason of course." He managed to crack a smile which Peter thought must have been a painful experience.

He had been expecting a reaction but not quite this. He looked at the two men in amazement. "What on earth was Emma mixed up in?"

"I'm afraid I cannot tell you that without the permission of my own government agency and of course….."

Langdon unsmilingly interrupted. "The British Government has assured the United States Government of your full co-operation. The Foreign Secretary discussed the matter yesterday with the US Secretary of State."

Sweet Jesus, he thought to himself. How high does this go? It was Peter's turn to interrupt. "What about the Covid 19 travel restrictions?"

"The White House has waived the restrictions and cleared your access to the US. It would be appreciated if you would use the remaining twenty nine minutes….," he glanced at his watch meaningfully, "…. to pack that bag, retrieve your passport and any other documents you deem essential to international travel. I have two thousand US dollars in cash for your wallet and a government credit card in your name, obviously for official purposes only. I don't exactly know who you are or what you do, Mr….ah… Westbrooke, but at this precise point in time you are arguably one of the most important people on the planet and your presence is required in Washington post haste. We will wait in the cars." With that the two men got up and walked to the front door.

Peter walked into the dining room. Both women looked up at his white face. "Got to go now. I mean right now. Won't be back for a while. So sorry about this. Something has come up."

His wife looked as white as he did. She had known it the moment she opened the door. Stefanie started softly sobbing. "It's to do with Emma, isn't it. And you're not allowed to say….." He stared at her and a tear formed. In the small garden outside it was starting to rain again.

"Part of the job. Just goes with the job." And then she knew.

CHAPTER 17

Their destination was not the United States Air Force base at RAF Alconbury as it turned out. That had been for the benefit of any unwanted listeners. They lifted off from a UK airbase in Oxfordshire closer to London called RAF Brize Norton. Curiously named, RAF Brize Norton is home to the RAF's Strategic and Tactical Air Transport Command and Britain's Air to Air Refueling forces. The commander of the base is, surprisingly, an extremely good looking and highly intelligent woman – Group Captain Emily Hutchinson OBE ADC MA MENG CENG FIET. She was not there to greet them but she was aware of the operation. As they drove in the gates and identities were being checked, first by the omnipresent police officers and then by the immaculate clad, but heavily armed, members of the RAF Regiment, Peter noticed that the motto of the base was 'Move with Confidence'. Well, that's encouraging he mused.

The start of the journey had been less so. Sandra and Stefanie had been in tears but for different reasons. A quick firm hug and they were off. Richard's driver followed the Jaguar with Richards seated in the front next to Langdon's driver. Langdon sat in the back next to Peter. He lifted the rear seat arm rest and placed his battered leather briefcase with its travel documents on the seat between them. As the rain drops idly creased down the windows Peter glanced at

Langdon and then at the American car behind. Both drivers seemed to be wearing ear pieces and both wore clear wrap round glasses. As they slipped onto the M25 motorway and accelerated up behind a dark green Land Rover, Peter said, "May I ask, was it really necessary to send two cars?"

Langdon laughed. "There are actually several vehicles, Mr Westbrooke." He paused and thoughtfully rubbed his chin. "The dark green Land Rover in front of us with the standard armed VIP Protection Unit officers belongs to our convoy. The Land Rover is also equipped with a CATL system. As you may know that stands for computerised anticipatory traffic light controller which will enable us to change the traffic flow to accommodate the convoy as we approach the lights. If you glance back over your right shoulder you may note a grey Range Rover accelerating to close the gap with the Chrysler behind us. In front of the Land Rover are two uniformed police motor cycle outriders to stop any unwanted traffic and although you cannot see them there are two non-descript scruffy looking motor cycle outriders well behind the Range Rover. All of them are armed and in radio communication with each other as well as with HQ for instant cyber number plate identification. If you glance out the window you might occasionally spot a small low flying helicopter above the highway. The pilot is in touch with the convoy and keeping Brize Norton apprised of our progress. And in case you're wondering, there is an SAS section on standby should we encounter any unexpected serious problems." He rubbed his chin again as if it was a nervous habit.

Peter shrugged his shoulders and glanced back. Sure enough, they were all there and he could feel the Jaguar vibrating as they accelerated well beyond the speed limit, the weather notwithstanding. "That's a bit of overkill, isn't it. I mean we're just catching a plane?"

There was a short silence and Langdon turned to look him straight in the eye. "Our job, Mr Westbrooke, is to get you to Washington as swiftly, safely and as comfortably, as humanly possible and we intend to do that. Now I'd be grateful if you would keep your thoughts to yourself and allow the drivers to concentrate."

Peter sat back in the seat stunned. The convoy moved at incredible speed. Whenever a courageous if incautious motorist sought to cut in, the convoy closed up automatically like a concertina cutting off the irritated driver. As soon as the intruder fell back the convoy opened up again. The drivers were constantly talking to each other, identifying other cars, trucks and even the occasional pedestrians. At intersections the police motorcyclists blocked the roads and waved them through then accelerated past the rear guard motor bikes, the Range Rover, the Chrysler, their car and the green Land Rover to resume station in front. It was an extremely impressive and well-rehearsed highly professional routine.

Peter couldn't resist one final question. He glanced nervously at Langdon, not sure of the response he might get. "Forgive me, last time and then I'll shut up. Who do these guys look after when it's not a non-entity like me?"

Langdon stared ahead and there was an embarrassing silence to the point where Peter feared he might have gone too far. Then Langdon replied curtly without taking his eyes off the road ahead, "The Prime Minister or Buckingham Palace."

The convoy swept through the second set of gates accessing the actual airfield and drove across the tarmac to an isolated building. He noted with relief that the vehicle and motor cycle escorts seemed to melt away as they pulled up. The helicopter hovered near a plain white A318 aircraft. It remained airborne, he noticed, watching the proceedings. No sooner had they cruised to a halt than two uniformed female RAF personnel opened his door and stood back. The boot was already automatically open and he saw his luggage disappearing up the gangway. Langdon walked with him to the steps as Richards jogged lithely up into the interior of the aircraft. "Well, Mr ..ah…Westbrooke. Here is where I say cheerio and wish you a pleasant flight."

He didn't offer to shake hands but Peter thought bugger that to himself and extended his hand instead. "Thank you. I've done some strange things in my time but this is in a league of its own. Thanks for your help."

There was a moment's hesitation and then Langdon gripped Peter's hand firmly. "I don't know why but I get the impression that you have absolutely no idea what you have got yourself into. Best of British luck, old man." He squeezed Peter's hand so hard it hurt, and then briskly turned back to the cars. An RAF non-commissioned officer offered to help him with his briefcase but Peter waived him away. The officer stood back, clicked his heels to attention, saluted and spun round to march away towards the cars. Peter walked up the gangway into the yellow welcoming glow of the cabin. The engines were already beginning to whine, the chocks were being pulled away and the rain continued in its dismal half drizzle. Cheerio England, he thought.

Emma was looking forward to her acting debut even if it was only for a commercial. She reckoned that this might be the opportunity to get a message out. Her hopes were dashed when she was told that they would be flying her on a helicopter to a landing stage and from there onto a yacht on Lake Michigan. The advert was for the launch of a new perfume range in the Clandestine Couple mode which made up part of the Waxman cosmetics empire. Emma would be sailing the yacht attracting a good- looking man in another yacht. The scene as Nikki explained it to her was quite complicated. The other yacht sailed by a handsome young man would approach Emma head on. Attracted by the pretty girl he would swing round past the stern of Emma's craft and in catching a whiff of the perfume the youthful sailor would swing his vessel hard in again alongside her boat. Enchanted by her perfume he would abandon his yacht and leap across the intervening railings to become romantically involved with the fair Emma. It was agreed the shoot might last for three days and during that time Emma would stay aboard the yacht. There would be no chances to go ashore. Filmed only in profile, her face would be largely obscured, but her long hair and dashing figure at the helm of the yacht would so entrance him that this perfume guaranteed love at first sight. Well, that was the narrative, anyway. Emma was excited and disappointed. But at least it offered her the chance to get off the estate and who knew what might eventuate. Little was she to know that in the meantime there was another client to entertain. A political flunky from Washington was due to arrive in the next few days. This was to prove a surprise on several counts.

A very attractive blond stewardess dressed in a smart light

blue but meaningless outfit greeted Peter Westbrooke in an American accent. Peter noted with approval that every hair was in place and her legs looked stunning. He was missing Sandra already. "Can I please use the loo before we lift off," he asked plaintively. "It was a fast departure," he added in a lame justification.

"Loo, Sir?" she said with a raised eyebrow.

"Sorry, toilet," he explained. Same people, different language.

"Oh," a look of flustered panic set in. "Well, we are moving in a minute." She gestured meaningfully towards his seat but he refused to surrender. She really was very pretty but obviously under orders to get them seated immediately.

"Just a second, promise, won't be long," he smiled. She caved in and pointed to the toilet. He handed her the briefcase and shot into the toilet like a frightened rabbit. The plane was already moving. Good Lord Almighty, he thought to himself. They were not wasting any time. He did what he had to do as the aircraft was moving towards the runway and exited just in time as they lined up. The pilot was waiting for the toilet occupied light to go out. Before he had even fastened the seat belts in the seat next to Richards, they were hurtling down the runway. Take-off and landing slots in Europe are normally strictly rationed. But with the onset of the virus the flight schedules had drastically shrunk. Still, the pilots were keen to get away. He earned an unhappy glance from the stewardess and settled back in the seat available for him.

He noticed Richards reading a copy of the International Herald Tribune. The headline reported that the Prime

Minister appeared to be recovering from his brush with the virus. He wondered if it was true. He had looked pretty grim before going into hospital. The distressing thought crossed his mind that there might be long term after-effects. The aircraft was comfortable and yet he was puzzled. It carried no identification at all. They climbed steeply through the clouds and headed west. He wondered if he could try and engage with Richards. The stewardess came back and offered them drinks. He asked for a fruit juice. Richards ordered a martini. "Sure, you don't want a real drink, Mr … ah…Westbrooke?" It's a long flight.

"I might later. Thank you for your assistance in getting me here, well, back there." Richards nodded. "Do you think that they might have the kindness to feed us? I didn't get much of that roast back in Burpham."

Richards stretched his long legs out and folded the IHT. "Sheila will take good care of us, have no fear," he said laconically. "First time you ever done this, huh?"

Peter nodded. "Everyone keeps asking me that. Is it that obvious?"

Richards laughed. "Well, it's none of my business why the Brits are lending you to us, but it's a first for me too. Somebody high up in DC wants you and wants you pretty bad."

"But you have done this before, surely?"

Richards snorted. "Flown like this, yeah, many times, but not at the order of the man at the very top. That's definitely a first."

"But this is not an American aircraft. I'm surprised it's got the range? I would have thought a Gulfstream would have been more appropriate?"

Richards shook his head. "Too obvious, though we do use them for rendition operations. This is actually on loan from another government. Just to confuse people. It's a cash carrier with extra-long range tanks and you happened along at the right time."

"A cash carrier?" Peter sounded puzzled.

"Yeah, in fact we have a full load. US dollars four hundred million in cash being transferred back to Uncle Sam."

"Good grief," Peter was astonished. "Four hundred million US dollars in cash? So this flight is not specially for me after all."

"Well, yes and no," Richards added enigmatically. "Yes, in the sense that you conveniently need to be urgently conveyed to DC but no in the sense that this aircraft would have been going anyway, without us, of course. You may notice a guy sitting right at the back." Peter in his urgency had not in fact. "Well, he is escorting this load, which weighs about 4 tons by the way. There would be more but they cannot carry insurance for more than $400 million so that's the limit. Governments and the private sector do it all the time but in the case of private sector international transfers they need the government of the currency in question to be notified. No need to look so anxious. It's all perfectly legal."

"What on earth do they use the money for?" Peter was intrigued.

"Embassies, banks, finance houses, African leaders, sheikhs, sultans and other private sector interests, even Russian billionaires ....they all do it. In the good old days before the present administration it was apparently a reasonably straightforward exercise. A great deal of the money goes to Dubai from various parts of Asia and Africa. In the early days it was a pretty straightforward operation with a simple notification to the government concerned. When the new president came in he insisted that the system be cleaned up. He wanted to know where every single banknote outside of, and inside, the US was at any one time. So now they have to fill in a multiple sheet questionnaire asking all sorts of awkward questions like where did it come from, how was it earned, why is it being transferred and so on." He looked reflective for a moment as if he had said too much. Then he added. "But you know, on second thoughts, this president is determined to clean up the swamp and that means that there are a quite a few international swamps that require cleaning too. So maybe it's a good thing."

"And this aircraft is designed for that? What about airport security?" He still found the whole idea slightly incredible. Criminal syndicates would definitely seek to transfer enormous sums of cash. So would corrupt African governments and leaders of unstable East European governments, but he had never encountered such legitimate transfers.

"Well you might ask. There are certain places in the Middle East, not to mention Central and South America where we are extremely cautious. But most airports are very secure with their own specified areas, or even allocated landing zones like RAF Brize Norton. Geneva airport, Dubai etc… they all have designated secure sectors. If you knew how much cash, I mean in hard-core banknotes, most of it American dollars but also other currencies too, was flying round the world at any one time, well, it would put your hair on end." The stewardess approached with the dinner trays. Richards rubbed his hands together in anticipation.

"Sorry Mr Westbrooke, no menus here, but the food is still damn good". They started eating.

A thought suddenly crossed Peter's mind. "I trust that we are still heading for Washington and not somewhere else?"

Richards smiled. "It's Andrews Air Force Base outside Washington DC and from there to the company HQ at Langley. Somebody at the top wants to meet you."

Stefanie and John Price had almost become an item. The end of the four week sojourn at Wexham was coming into sight and both of them knew that this could mark the end of a mutually happy and rewarding emotional experience. As they had become close to each other she had no doubt that she would give him a clean bill of health and short of any other unexpected issues arising it was likely that the court would abandon any further interest in the case. Then he would disappear back into the world of smoke and mirrors and they would never see or hear of one another again. On the other hand, the thought had crossed her mind, that with the growing implications of the international lockdown, the alarming deaths from CD19 in Iran and Italy, and the growing global paranoid atmosphere with all the conflicting information on what was now being termed a pandemic rather than an epidemic, John Price might stay on longer in England. It also depended on the medical progress of the retired Colonel Cartwright still languishing in a coma under constant nursing care. She was finding it increasingly difficult to locate venues where they could legitimately go. Britain was in a Stalinist form of lockdown. Restaurants, pubs, and cafeterias were all closed. Even walking outside was only permitted for one hour a day. Police were arresting people in parks for sitting on the grass and also people sitting on the beach. Stefanie reckoned that she had never seen the world changed so fast. Stock markets were plummeting, and tourism had virtually come to a halt. People on cruise liners found themselves as popular as skunks in a suburb, as John had observed, and it was becoming difficult for luxury liners to find harbours prepared to take them. The international airline industry was starting to lay off employees in their thousands. Even jobs for pilots were in short supply. Those were the main problems on a macro scale. On a micro scale in the third world developing countries millions were contemplating starvation. One evening over dinner at her home, John Price explained the implications of the global lockdown to Stefanie.

"You know Stef, if we had gone to war with the PRC I very much doubt that we could have inflicted as much economic and social damage on our societies as we have suffered with these travel bans and lock downs. Europe had its economic problems before this nonsense started. Now it will be brought to its knees. In my country the president has done everything in his power to limit the economic damage but his political opponents are determined to exploit the entire exercise for maximum political gain, this being an election year. The great achievement of the president has been the fastest economic growth rate in the nation's history, the highest employment and the highest GDP. Now it's all under dire threat."

She hoped she didn't look too worried but it was hard to concentrate on what he was saying when all she could think of was what Peter had told her about Emma. He noticed that she was not really concentrating. "I'm so sorry, dearest John. I know and understand the importance and the relevance of it all, and yet it all fades into insignificance when I think of Emma."

He could sense that she wanted to talk but felt professionally constrained not to do so. "Come on, out with it. We know each other well enough now. You've heard something haven't you?"

Stefanie stared at him long and hard. She took the plunge. "About a week ago I went down to my brother-in-law. He has enjoyed a long and distinguished career as I mentioned to you obliquely before, and he put the whole thing on the line about Emma. The plan was to have dinner, and he would fill me in on a few details and then I would drive back the next morning. We had just sat down for dinner when two men arrived in chauffeur driven cars and he was immediately taken away. One of the men looked and sounded like an American and the other was a Brit. They chatted very briefly and then Peter came into the dining room and told Sandra and I that he was departing immediately."

John looked up sharply. "Departing for where, exactly?"

Her face darkened. "He was not allowed to say. But when I saw his expression I knew it had to do with Emma. I already knew she was probably still alive, but he suggested there was evidence pointing to the fact that he had information proving she was outside of the country."

John sucked in his breath. She looked even more worried. He smiled and took her hands in his. "Listen, Stef, if your intuition is right then you ought to be reassured. The mere fact that he has been whisked away means that he has managed to get official help. If you are right then the cavalry are on the way. If I can give you some advice, it is my experience that in our darkest hours is when the tide turns.

Did you ever watch the movie The Lion King?!

She looked at his quizzically. "Why, yes. But what has…"

He cut her short. "Don't you recall that when the king has been assassinated and the kingdom had been plunged into hopeless ruin, a line crops up halfway through the film…… But time changes everything."

She gripped his hands with such surprising strength he thought his fingers might break. "You mean…."

He let himself go. He pulled her to her feet and threw his arms round her. "I mean what has happened is a good omen…there is hope for her, my darling. Now you must stay strong for her. As an Irish friend of mine says, keep the faith!"

She melted into his arms as he kissed her and squeezed her into him. They would not be returning to Wexham that evening.

The aircraft landed at Andrews AFB dead on schedule on time. It seemed that they had hardly finished taxiing to the enormous secure hangar before the gantry was in place, the door opened and an attractive young woman came striding into the cabin. He had hardly had time to say farewell to Richards when she approached him. "Mr Westbrooke," she said with a slight smile. "On behalf of the Director Central Intelligence welcome to the United States. Forgive me for not shaking hands but it's a curse of the times. Slip your passport into this plastic bag and permit me to take your temperature." She handed him a mask. "Would you be kind enough to put this on please."

He fumbled in his jacket, produced the passport and slid

it unerringly into the bag. The mask was a plain surgical job. He loathed them. She aimed what looked like a small plastic pistol at his forehead but he ducked instinctively. "My wrist if you don't mind. I have an aversion to gun like objects being aimed at my head." He slipped his cuffs back and she fired the thermometer at his wrist. She glanced at the reading and made a note on her phone.

"Please follow me." His suitcase was already in the back of the yellow taxi with the engaged sign switched on at the bottom of the gangway and his precious briefcase lay on the back seat. She sat in front next to the driver. The car swung round off the tarmac and only halted at the gate for the driver to flash his pass. She got out, removed her mask, and showed a document to the guard, then opened the back door and slid into the seat beside him. It seemed a strange vehicle for an official pick up. He glanced across at her and said, "I see under the new president you've taken outsourcing to extremes?"

She didn't crack a smile. "This is an official car Mr West-brooke, and it's not for public hire." Looking mildly irritated she straightened an invisible hair and stared ahead.

He wondered what Emma would say if she could witness this happening. He considered what she might be doing at this time. It mattered not. He assumed they were heading to Langley. Sure enough, eventually the famous building came into sight. Clearing security they drove down a vast ramp into the basement. He was ushered through a metal detector and his brief case slid through a bomb detector. Then it was down a brightly illuminated corridor to the lift. She punched some codes into the wall, the doors slid open, she preceded him and held the door. For the first time he had the chance to inspect her up and down. Short dark hair impeccably cut. No jewellery. He put her at about 35 but it was hard to tell these days. The mask didn't help. No name, no uniform but a very smart beige skirt and jacket emphasizing a good figure with high heeled shoes and eyes that said mess with me at your peril. The silence was eerie as the lift hummed upwards. The doors opened and she led the way into a large waiting room and reception area. A substantial American flag was hanging in one corner and photographs of previous CIA Directors decorated the walls. As they walked into the reception area she gestured to an armchair. He had hardly been seated and nodded to the exceedingly fit young man he took to be the PA to the DCIA when the door opened and he was shown into a large office with a spectacular view over the greenbelt of Washington. A dark haired authoritative looking woman with dark rimmed glasses stood up and hurried round the vast desk to greet him. "Welcome to the CIA Mr Westbrooke. I think we can be of mutual assistance to each other."

Emma's "guest" from Washington, arranged at Waxman's behest, was, to her astonishment, not a man, but an overweight woman from the US Congress. This was not to Emma's liking at all. She had never had any predilections in that direction. Now what? They were introduced by the swimming pool after the inevitable helicopter had come clattering in. She took a deep breath and tried to keep calm. Uncle Peter had always said to her play along, but surely there were limits. Emma pulled herself together and tried to make out as if she did this sort of thing every day. Elizabeth Slatzky hailed from New York but represented a constituency in the mid-West. She had an intriguing background. A former CIA employee and an administration appointee under the Obama administration she had specialized in the Middle East and Africa. She had a gift for languages and apparently spoke Swahili and Arabic fluently. She had been an analyst with the Company before working for the Pentagon and then gravitating into politics. But it was obvious from the start that she was determined to make her mark in the political world and nowhere more so than in the forthcoming election. That was to become clear after the physical entertainment.

Having sex with a woman, Emma decided, was not all that different to having sex with a man. She was astounded later to learn that Liz was married with several kids, but got her kicks through less customary methods of physical stimulation and entertainment. There were more toys involved and all sorts of curious preferences which she sought to fulfil to the best of her ability. But it was afterwards when they were just laying in the bed together that Liz, as her constituents called her, started to talk quite frankly. Emma was grateful for her parent's training in watching various news bulletins and reading the papers. Her mother had favoured The Guardian whilst her father preferred The Daily Mail. Her mother had always said, "My girl if you want to play any meaningful role in an international movie, you had better know what is going on in the world or you won't have a clue how to spark the role." Emma ruefully looked back on those days that now seemed to belong to another lifetime and wondered what had happened to her mother and how she was coping. Just as the thought crossed her mind, Liz Slatzky asked, "So what brought you to America?"

It was a long session with the DCIA and several of her staff members. When it was over, even Peter, with his years of experience, felt as if he might be in a state of shock. It had been intimated to him over seemingly endless cups of tea and coffee, that the CIA knew far more about himself, the men who had kidnapped Emma in London and her present circumstances than even he might have dared to imagine. It was made clear to him that the president himself was taking a keen interest in the Waxman operation not just due to its shocking human trafficking and paedophile connections which stretched well beyond the United States to Britain, Russia and Germany but because it linked to the ease with which the leading politicians were compromised, not to mention scientists, academics, Hollywood, the media and the security forces. It was courteously explained to him that Emma might well have intimate access to plans being formulated involving the PRC, the international criminal cartels and the internal unrest that involved a wealthy multi-billionaire American businessman of Eastern European extraction sponsoring radical activist movements and the promotion of general mayhem as the elections approached. Details were sketchy but if Emma could just be persuaded to stay a little longer in the Waxman operation before being rescued, she could provide vital information to the US intelligence community which might confirm intelligence from other sources warning of serious impending trouble.

Peter had agreed with all this in principle but when advised of the security precautions surrounding Emma and the Waxman operations, he could see no way in which to provide Emma with a heads up. Finally, as the problem grew larger and larger in his mind he could not restrain himself any longer. Addressing the DCIA directly he said, "This is all good and fine but how can we contact her. The weakest link in any intelligence chain is the method of communication. I just don't see how…"

The DCIA laughed for the first time in the conversation. "Peter, if I may call you that as we are going to be working together, rest assured we think we have a way in but this is where your personal assistance is required."

"I'm all ears," he said curiously.

"Well, you see we have done our homework on this very carefully indeed and….," but at that point an aide entered the room and they were offered a light meal.

Liz Slatzky was genuinely fascinated to find herself enjoying the favours of an extremely attractive half English and half Jamaican girl with a brain to boot. Emma had explained her background and conveniently left out the more sordid details regarding her abduction in the UK. Anyway, if Liz wanted the details she had only to ask Waxman and he would provide chapter and verse. Instead she thought she would reverse the situation. "So, what does it take to be a member of the most powerful parliamentary body in the world?"

"Well, it's not as easy as you might think," she observed swinging a fat naked leg experimentally round in the air. "In fact, it's a bit like going back to school. You can have all the extra parliamentary experience in the world but they will still treat you like a school kid and God help you if you open your mouth too soon. I am a pretty strong willed woman and I can tell you I made some comment on the floor of the House about a bill to do with foreign aid funding and a congressman behind me immediately sneered, "Not here five minutes and you just had to get your two cents worth in!"

"Not an encouraging start," Emma remarked trying to sound sympathetic.

"Oh, I don't allow these things to worry me. I just made a careful note of who he is and we will deal with him when the time comes."

Emma was taken aback. "You mean you will nail him in the House on another issue when the time is right?"

"Oh, fuck no," Liz shot back. "I mean we know where he lives, where his family lives and every time he takes a shit. When we take over the country people like him will have their day of reckoning. Let me explain, but before that, how about some more nookie?"

Here we go again thought Emma. She wasn't sure how long she could keep this up.

Mohammed thought his role in the Emma affair was over. He actually couldn't get her out of his mind but he reckoned it unlikely he would hear more any time soon. He continued with his preparations to move to Europe. He was wrong. To his surprise his cell phone rang early one morning. It was an American number which he did not recognise. He answered anyway. The voice was instantly recognizable. He would have known that crisp UK accent anywhere.

"My old Middle Eastern buddy you came up tops! Well done. How are you?"

A short pause and Mohammed collected his thoughts. "Very well indeed now that you are here. I won't ask how that happened?"

Peter laughed. "There are more things in Heaven and Earth, my dear fella. But I need your help. Or more to the point a young English woman needs you to help her. Are you up to it?"

This time there was no long silence. "Of course. But what can I do? Travel is restricted, and the world is in lockdown."

"That's true, but from where I am sitting anything is possible. Your company Halford and Yates have an office in DC, do they not?"

No hesitation this time. "Yeah, so what?"

"A travel authorization will be sent to this phone in a few minutes, well, seconds really. I want to see you in DC tonight."

"Allah be praised," Mohammed sounded incredulous. "Are you serious, tonight." He heard his phone going ching as it received an incoming email. He took the phone from his ear and sure enough he was invited to a very swish hotel on outskirts of Washington DC. He put the phone to his ear but Peter had gone.

Emma's experience with Elizabeth Slatzky had led to some astonishing revelations. Invariably the talk had turned to politics. What did Liz think would happen in the elections?

She seemed unphased by the question but was curious. Had Emma studied international relations? No, but she came from a politically aware family where her mother voted for the British Labour party and her father voted Conservative. So surely there were families in the US in the same league?

Oh, there most certainly were, Liz told her and one of them worked in the White House. A lady close and loyal to the president had a husband who loathed her politics. In fact, he was not backward about being forward on what he thought of his wife's political views. Emma was amazed.

"Surely that leads to personal difficulties?" she asked naively.

"I'm sure it does, but some families can manage the crisis. What about your folks in the UK? How did they manage their contrasting political views?"

Emma sniffed. "We had civilized debates and discussions round the dining table. It was all very polite. I was brought up in a more tolerant and less passionate household. But it seems to me that political views in this country are much more polarised and people take things personally. Imagine if this president wins a second term. Will the opposition accept the result?"

Liz sat straight up in bed. "You've got to be kidding me, right? He will never win a second term and even if we can't manipulate the polls which we are very good at doing with the cyber systems at our command, I can assure you that he still won't be allowed to win a second term." She glared defiantly at Emma and pulled the sheet up over her pendulous breasts, getting into her ideological stride.

Emma felt maybe this was the wrong subject to be discussing under these circumstances but her curiosity got the better of her. Liz was also corroborating what the VIP guest had shared with her in an equally unguarded moment. It was surprising what people shared before and after sex. "You mean the manipulation of the much vaunted opinion polls? But they really got it wrong last time, and in Britain with our Prime Minister too."

Liz laughed uproariously. "Rest assured it's not just the opinion polls we control. We can manipulate the voting systems too. Our Chinese allies own the company which makes the voting machines. We tested the system in Venezuela so we know it works. Why do you think the Venezuelan electorate cannot vote their communist government out of power. Postal ballots are ready made for manipulation. We have poured millions into that operation. This time we can invent up to 80 million fake votes. Our problem last time was that we didn't manipulate enough and we were too confident."

Emma was fascinated. "So, you lost to the incumbent. But what if you believe your own propaganda and your own contrived polls? Isn't that what really happened in 2016? Surely there is a real risk that this will happen again, this time round? And even if you can manipulate the voting surely there is a risk attached to that?"

Liz was really getting into it now. "Yes, we did make that mistake, but it won't happen this time. As for getting caught, we have so many 'stay behind' groups in the government, in the intelligence services, and in the Department of Justice that they will take care of any problems arising. Why, we even had sympathetic sleeper cells operating in the president's office but he seems to have sadly rooted most of them out. So, what do you think of that?"

Emma tried to forget what she had just been forced to do by concentrating on the political discussion. "I think it sounds as though you have it all sewn up.

Liz took a deep breath and started dressing. Emma slipped out of bed and started dressing too. "Hold off on that. I just love that beautiful shapely body of yours." Emma leaned back against the mirror of the built-in cupboard and folded her arms across her breasts. Liz continued pulling on her clothes whilst casting admiring eyes in her direction. "Mark my words, in a short time, all hell will break loose in this country. If what the president calls the China Virus does not do the essential job of collapsing the economy and make him look a complete fool and unfit to govern the USA, other plans will be put in place. We reckon we can cause mayhem in close to 80 cities. We might even occupy a few and shut others down from a commercial point of view." There was a long silence. Emma wondered why she was being told all this. To show off, she thought ruefully. Liz had almost finished dressing. "Just step aside from that mirror if you don't mind?" She straightened her clothes and tidied her hair. What she would give to have a body like Emma's.

Emma took this as a signal to start dressing. She wanted to get this ghastly woman out of her life, but she was keen to learn more. "So it's as simple as that. Cause mayhem, hijack the presidency and then what? What if the presidency can't be hijacked? What about the police?"

Liz had her hand on the door handle. "My helicopter awaits me, my love. But I'll tell you this much. CalExit like your dumb Brexit, is on the cards. If the voters are too stupid to support us in the ballot, we shall simply start causing civil unrest left, right and centre. As for the police, watch us launch calls to have them castrated, defunded and nationally detested and despised. The police will be easy meat and the president cannot deploy the National Guard to the rescue without the approval of the mayors or the state governors. So in the states we control, well, you can rest assured that just ain't gonna happen." Emma's eyes widened at the very thought. "Don't believe me? What do you think the Las

Vegas massacre in Trump territory was all about? That was just a dry run for what's lurking round the corner. There will come a time when every household, every apartment block, every isolated farm or remote small holding will be a target. Why do you think we keep hammering the gun control and confiscation laws? You want to know where this is all going – take a look at what we accomplished in overthrowing the democratically elected government in the Ukraine when I was in the CIA or what happened in Bosnia. We'll have our street snipers, propagandists and racially inspired violent protestors and killers just like they did and do."

She pushed the door handle down and stopped. One last look at that delicious little body. She walked over and kissed Emma on the mouth. "Take care of yourself my darling. It's a dangerous world out there! Accidents can happen so easily."

It was about a week later and well into late April after the tortuous and sickening session with Congressman Liz Slatzky, that Emma had been told to prepare for the film shoot. At last a chance to go back to "normal" for a short time. Emma had handled her situation so well, thanks to the advice from her uncle coupled with a very strong will to play along and hope for a chance to escape from this nightmare.

She was told not to worry about a wardrobe for the advertising promotion. All the requisite kit would be provided on the yacht. They lifted off from the helipad in a Bell Jet Ranger and swung north. It was her first trip in a helicopter. The vibration and the noise were devastating. She buckled her seat belt as tight as she dared and the G-forces as they swung away from the massive estate left an uneasy feeling in the pit of her stomach. The countryside was lush, rich and green and for the first time Emma began to get a feel for the size of the property on which she was effectively a prisoner. They flew for over three hours and then landed on a floating dock. She was ushered off the helicopter and into a magnificent teak decked waiting speedboat with a deep throated engine roar that could only be described as immensely sexy. The craft throbbed out to a luxury yacht wallowing in glorious weather. Seeing the camera crew and the drones was reassuring. The shoot would take place from several angles. It had crossed her mind that they might be going to do something terrible to her but even Nikki had reassured her and explained that Mr Waxman would never allow anything untoward to happen to her as he would have to reckon with Mr Strelnikov in London. Not even Waxman wanted to get on the wrong side of Strelnikov.

If the yacht from the air was magnificent it was awesome close up. Emma noticed that from the moment she jumped off the helicopter one of Waxman's ugly thugs kept a close eye on her. They went on board the yacht and Emma was taken to a cabin suite specially arranged for her. A beautiful wardrobe had been laid out on the bed and the producer carefully ran through again what was expected of her. One shoot would be done in a tightly fitting yachting outfit, another one in a bikini and a third in high class office gear. Emma was taken on deck and shown how to steer the yacht. It was carefully explained to her how the angles had been worked out and the way in which the handsome sun tanned young male model on the other yacht, actually being controlled for him, would sail past, whip round the back of the yacht, smell the perfume and adroitly swing alongside her yacht. He would then appear to have abandoned the wheel of his yacht and dashingly leap over the rails onto the deck of hers. In the distance she could see the other yacht.

Could they please do a rehearsal, she pleaded. No, that would not be necessary as the actual sailing techniques had been well rehearsed prior to her arrival. Emma was escorted downstairs into the luxurious interior of the yacht and heard the cabin door lock behind her. They were taking no chances. She changed into the yachting outfit, knocked on the door to signify that she was ready and came up on deck. The makeup artist worked on her features diligently for about ten minutes, making the encouraging remark that it was hard to improve on perfect! A number of admiring wolf whistles emanated from the support staff which added to her confidence. The director again ran through the instructions. The mahogany speed boat with its cameras and sound teams took up position. The drones were carefully launched and set off into the crystal blue sky. She noticed with relief that the thug had disappeared onto the mahogany speed boat to assist with the filming.

Emma took the wheel of the yacht and felt the craft respond to her touch. It was amazing, almost intoxicating. She watched the other smaller craft approach from the bow and sweep down the port side but concentrated on keeping her craft in a straight line. She caught a glimpse from the corner of her eye of the slightly unshaven young man with the Ray Ban sunglasses in the white slacks and sailors cap at a jaunty angle as he swept his yacht round her stern through the wake behind her. Nonetheless she worked hard on keeping the yacht on course. Something struck her as vaguely familiar about him but she stared straight ahead. The two craft were now sailing almost side by side and the motor boat was filming on the starboard side with the drones in front and above. Special fenders were in place should the yachts actually crunch together. The figure on her right suddenly threw his hands off the wheel, took a running jump, swept in dashing debonair fashion over both railings and with a gallant sweep of his cap threw his arms round her in a crushing embrace. She had been told not to let go of the wheel. As the male model hugged her so tightly she had to release the wheel and a familiar voice nestled into her neck, quietly muttering, "My darling Emma. Don't React. Your uncle sent me for you. We will get you out of here but it's a process. You don't know me. Hug me back hard and then release me. Our lives depend on this. No recognition. I love, you, oh God, I love you so much….."

"CUT CUT CUT", the director was shouting. "God almighty, Mohammed, just give the girl a God damned hug and then stand back to admire her fucking perfume. It's a seduction scene not a rape!"

CHAPTER 18

They were sitting in a secure conference room at an undisclosed location in Ohio. Peter had been flown into the area via a flight to Wright Patterson USAF base. The meeting was designed to determine how to proceed once Mohammed had made contact with Emma. The insertion had been arranged by the Company on Canadian based GCHQ electronic intercepts passed to the NSA in which they had learned of the model shoot for the perfume. A convenient former employee of the Company involved in the advertising world had been mobilised as an asset. He engaged Bill Felgate and Harry Waxman. The latter was reluctant to allow Emma to be filmed but Felgate persuaded him to allow the shoot. Michael Metcalfe had been in the advertising business for years and thanks to his Company contacts had successfully built up a respectable international operation allowing him access to an extraordinary range of American and international business, political and financial figures. Mohammed had been brought down to Washington where he readily agreed to play the role of the male model. A short course of instruction by a genuine professional modelling agent and a covering legend that he did this sort of thing for the fun of it and to meet good looking women, which he swiftly memorised, and he was ready. Peter was astonished at how easily he had slipped into the role. Within forty-eight hours Mohammed had a cover story that was so close to his real life history that it was almost impermeable.

They had carefully briefed him that he was to make contact with the girl and assure her that all was well in arranging her extraction. Contact was the challenging part of the counter intelligence operation but it was hoped that once she had successfully accomplished one film shoot, others would follow. It was left up to Mohammed how he would sustain the link over the shoot which was expected to last for at least two days. The director was instructed to drag it out as long as he could. The longer the shoot, the more it would cost Waxman, so it was in his interests to save money by keeping the process short. Directors in the advertising industry generally understand that the longer they can drag it out, the better would be the financial rewards. In fact, the longer the shoot, the better for Emma to understand what was expected of her.

Mohammed had been equipped with a miniature cell phone to pass to Emma. It was no ordinary phone. Emma had to keep the phone concealed at all costs and every 24 hours she merely had to press a button to confirm that she was ok. Another button transmitted an emergency signal for help. In that event rigorous efforts would be made to extract Emma by force if necessary. Peter was impressed by the efficiency of the Americans running the operation and the alacrity with which the essential measures were put in place.

Emma sagged to her knees in shock and relief. Mohammed held his arm round her waist and waved acknowledgement to the director. Seeing Emma's apparent weakness, the director asked if she was all right. "I'm fine, just a bit frazzled from concentrating on steering the yacht and then focusing on something else." She tried not to stare at Mohammed. Her head was swimming with what he had just told her. So, Uncle Peter had found her after all. But now there was a catch. How could they both get off the yacht? Mohammed had let her recognize him and his confession of loving her was almost as much of a shock as her seeing him.

The director was unimpressed with the first take. "Well, we are just going to have to repeat that." They did. In fact, there were probably ten takes that day and not once did Mohammed have the opportunity to talk with Emma. It was over dinner in the evening that they were allowed to relax on the yacht and have a conversation. Mohammed entered the dining area on the luxury yacht carrying a dark blue jacket. Sewn into the lining of the jacket was a concealed pocket with the phone. He took his place next to Emma and placed the jacket between them. As the evening wore on the others put on their jackets. He offered his to Emma with a wink. The crew spoke about sailing, the weather and other shoots they had accomplished in remote and exotic parts of the world. No one noticed or cared that Mohammed had loaned Emma his jacket. When he helped her on with it, he patted the phone pocket gently against her body.

"That should warm you up." She looked at him sharply. "Hang on to it for the moment."

"Oh, thank you," she said. "Won't you be cold without it?"

"No," he murmured gently. "Keep it if you like, as I have another one in the cabin." She noticed that the jacket did not look new and even had a few light stains on it.

"That's really very kind of you and thank you." She said it

so softly and with a smile that would have melted butter. She snuggled the jacket against her torso. She could feel the slight lump. Now the dinner took on a new frustrating atmosphere for her. She could not leave the table fast enough. Mohammed made small talk with her and asked her about her background. She answered guardedly noting the security guard watching them from another table. He didn't seem suspicious but he was on the alert. She asked Mohammed about his studies and how he had entered the modelling world. His answers were so slick and smooth she almost believed them herself. He had been well groomed. There were no further references to the jacket but she was very anxious to take a closer look at it.

They politely said good night and Mohammed took an inflatable across to the other yacht. She could hardly wait to get back to the cabin but the director wanted to prolong the plans for the morning. Eventually she dragged herself away. She got back to the cabin and locked herself in the bathroom. It was a standard blue yachting jacket with a dark red interior. She could feel the phone but struggled a bit to find the access zip to the interior of the jacket. Eventually she succeeded in opening the panel to the interior and extracted the instrument. She unwrapped a small piece of rice paper wrapped tightly round the phone. The first sentence warned her that within five minutes of exposure to the light the script would vanish. It instructed Emma on what to do in order to activate the phone. At the end of it was written "Eat Me". She wonders why she should eat it if the print would disappear. She waited for a minute and read the instructions several times. Then to her amazement the print faded completely. She popped it into her mouth and it tasted slightly of lemon.

It was a tiny instrument unlike anything she had ever seen before. She pushed the identified button according to the instructions and activated the phone and Uncle Peter's cool, calm dulcet English tones came through loud and clear. She listened very carefully and put the phone as instructed in her cosmetics bag. The essence of the recorded message was pure and simple. She must take it all in on the first hearing as it would automatically vanish after playing. As long as she kept the device with her they could track her anywhere in the world via satellite. She had landed in the middle of a revolution. She was close to the centre of the web. The information she might come across was vitally important. She was to keep a voice report of the conversations that were taking place within her ambit and pass on the information using a burst transmission system peculiar to the phone. She could also call out on the phone at any time to contact Uncle Peter but that would be a short call on an encrypted system. The phone could also make ordinary calls which were inadvisable. She was in a dangerous but critical position and her status was being watched at the highest levels. The phone contained a small incendiary self-destruct device. If the right procedure was not followed in turning it on, it would burn out. Then it was as good as useless. If apprehended with the phone she was to tell them she had found it on the yacht. There followed a list of items she was to look out for. Details on child and human trafficking, who was involved, where they came from and what they were about. How far and how high did it go?

On the afternoon of the third day, when the shoot was completed, she hardly had time to say goodbye to Mohammed before they were heading back to the floating dock and the waiting helicopter. He had given her a hug and a kiss closely monitored by the security thug. His parting words had been reassuring. "We will keep in touch and I look forward to seeing you again." A tight squeeze and he was gone. The flight back to the estate seemed to go faster than the outward journey. She had much to occupy her mind. There were so many questions. How had they traced her? What was Uncle Peter's role in the operation? Why was he involved at all? Why couldn't they just raid the place and take her back home to the UK? She decided that as soon as she had a quiet moment she must file the first of two reports. In her head she was already formulating how she could convey the essence of the conversations, particularly the extraordinary information from the congresswoman.

Nikki met her on the landing strip and asked her how it had gone. She said it had been hard work but very enjoyable. They had been nice people to work with. Nikki looked at her sharply as if this was intended as a rebuke. "Mr Waxman is not here at the moment but he is returning later in the week and would like a personal report from you once he has seen the edited version."

It was roughly a month later that Igor Strelnikov was sitting in the ornate study of his country home, after a splendid evening dinner, smoking a sizable Havana cigar with a small circle of friends. They were celebrating his wisdom in having sold off his oil interests and invested in platinum group metals, known as PGMs. In the corner of his large book lined room with its smell of leather, deep plush Persian carpets and various collector's items from the Middle East he was regaling them with a story from the early days of the Putin revolution. In the corner a small television set monitored the international news channels. Strelnikov was just getting into his stride on an event that had happened shortly after the oligarchs had brought Putin to power.

"I tell you, Anatoly, the setting was unreal. Eighteen of us summoned to a meeting with the new man in, of all places, Stalin's dacha. It must have been the largest collection of wealth in the world at one time. None of us knew what he was really all about or even why we had been ordered to meet with him."

Anatoly Suvarov came from a long line of distinguished Russian military. He was not in the military but of the military and headed Russia's version of what had been the old Soviet military industrial complex. He was not supposed to be dining with Igor, but the oligarchs were a law unto themselves even in England. He took a sip of his port and watched Igor's cigar smoke spiralling into the air over the wood panelled fireplace. "How did you all get there?"

Igor snorted. "Some arrived by car, others by helicopter and one or two travelled together. The security round the place was monumental. We were made to walk through a bomb detection machine, searched and then checked again before entering the conference room. We were all mystified as why this venue had been chosen. Some of us reckoned he was our man as we had helped him to power so we were even more perplexed by the nature of the gathering. The time for the meeting came and went and nobody appeared. Then just as we had started to make jokes about how the Chechens would curse themselves having missed this opportunity to take us all out, it happened." He pulled on his cigar and took a sip of brandy. "The doors crashed open and an unsmiling Vladimirovich entered the room. We all noticed his curious walk. The doors crashed shut behind him. We were all sitting down but everyone simultaneously rose to their feet. He walked up to the first man and then with a broad smile shook his hand and bade him sit down and then he worked his way right round all eighteen of us. He has an odd habit of keeping his right hand by his side. Some say that is to draw a gun and derives from his days in the KGB. Who knows? And he is not a tall man, but by God, does he carry an air of authority."

Anatoly studied his port glass against the fire in the grate. The light shimmered through. "But surely you all knew him? I mean that is why some of you chose him?"

Igor laughed. "I tell you, Anatoly, I laugh now, but I didn't laugh then. He sat down at the head of the table and some of us were thinking, why this meeting here in Stalin's dacha and what is the purpose behind it. And then he clasped his hands together and looked round the table at each one of us directly in the eye. His eyes are gimlet blue grey and they look through you more than at you. There was a silence and then he smiled and welcomed us. Next moment his face turned to granite. His ensuing words left several of us ice cold. He said that some of us had supported him. And some of us had not. Another pregnant silence. The tension was palpable. I could see Golitzin squirming. Then he smiled a sort of curious non-smile, if you know what I mean, and said not to worry as that was now all in the past. It mattered no longer. Truth be told, we were not so sure of the veracity of that comment. He observed that we had all become extremely rich. Some by fair means and others less conventionally. He looked right round the room at us and this time those eyes were like lasers. He said that was good for us. It was also good for the country. Industry and commerce were important. We could carry on. But he added that from now on we were to stay in business only. Politics was his affair."

"Dramatic stuff," observed Anatoly.

"You better believe it. And that's not all. Then the doors crashed open and in walked 18 armed FSB officers in uniform and they took up position behind each one of us. We wondered who was going to be escorted out or even dealt with right there. But it didn't happen. Instead, the doors crashed open a third time and in walked junior staff with tea trays which they handed to the FSB officers who set them down in front of each one of us. The message was loud and clear. And quite a few of us realized that we had seriously miscalculated. This was not another Yeltsin flunky, or even a Gorbachev. This was a Stalin type character and we had better play the game or……, Strelnikov stopped in mid-sentence and stared at the television. "What, what the hell is that…..?" he almost shouted spilling his brandy.

Both men now stared at the television. Strelnikov, white with sudden anger and Suvorov, in perplexity. It was an advert for a perfume. An American perfume called Clandestine Couple and the girl in profile on the screen steering the magnificent luxury yacht bore a striking resemblance to Emma, the girl he had trafficked to Waxman.

"Do you know the product?" asked a puzzled Anatoly.

"Fuck no," shouted a distraught Strelnikov. "It's the girl steering the damn boat. She belongs to me and I loaned her to Waxman and now he's put her in the public eye. Has he gone mad?"

He stared at the screen for several seconds then reached for the phone. Sanity prevailed briefly and in a split second he threw the phone down. No, never act in anger. He had learnt that lesson the hard way as a child. Waxman had broken the unspoken rules of engagement. So now what should he do. Think it over and eventually when in a calm rational state of mind do what had to be done. Emma was now a liability. If Strelnikov had learned one thing in his life it was that one never gambled with liabilities. Liabilities had to be removed. He would consider carefully his next move.

Emma's last useful meeting was quite by chance with a senior man from a prominent corporate aerospace agency. He did not work directly for NASA, which he regarded more as a military intelligence organisation than a space agency, but dealt with a substantial amount of data assimilated by NASA. He was keen on underage girls but had been told how "special" Emma was and he always sought relaxation through stimulating discussion afterwards. Nikki had fulfilled this role until the arrival of Emma. Although Emma did not know it, this was to be her last information gathering operation before being hauled out of the US back to the UK. She had already transmitted accounts of her earlier liaisons. The reports had been carried direct to Langley and it was said that those at the top who were looking for confirmation of what was coming had been mightily impressed. It was ironic that at the very same time Peter and his friends in the CIA were working out how to extract Emma, Strelnikov in London, was saving them the trouble.

Hyman Meade had come to the aerospace business through his college in Boston. He was bright but lonely. Waxman provided light relief and some exotic entertainment which suited his more animalistic predilections with minors. Meade, like the British spy who worked for the Russians,

Geoffrey Prime, at GCHQ in the early 1980s, was obsessed by young girls. Prime had been sexually abused in his youth, much like Meade by his stepfather. This is a common trait. The products of such abuse have a tenuous sense of their own masculinity and a low sense of self-esteem. Meade, like Prime, had led a lonely life and was distrustful of adults. But whereas Meade had been talent spotted by the deep state, which could feed his aspirations, Prime had been forced to find his own victims and this had led to his downfall. Meade, on the other hand, had reached a stage in his life where he knew that he needed medical help but also understood that his deviancy had led to his promotion to one of the most extraordinary and secret appointments in the strange relationship between private enterprise and the state. Emma was to enter his life at the moment critique which is perhaps why he opened up to her the way he did.

He had already showered and was sitting in the garden overlooking the forest near the helicopter landing pad.

Nikki brought her through for the introductions. It was rare that Emma only had to talk to one of Waxman's clients this time rather than physically satisfy them too. She often wondered what happened to the young girls who came as mysteriously as they went. She had a more than sneaking suspicion that some of them at least were violently dealt with and the bodies never found. Secrecy was everything on the estate. She knew better than to ask awkward questions of Nikki or even Waxman himself. Now that she knew Uncle Peter was aware of her existence and keen to extract her when the timing was right, she threw herself into the role with renewed passion and commitment. It was her avenue to putting right the wrongs that had been so flagrantly and violently inflicted on her. If she could but save just one girl from experiencing the trauma she had been subjected to, then it might all have been worth it. If the information she was providing to the intelligence community meant that other such rings were shut down then her pain, suffering and sacrifice would not have been in vain.

Meade saw her arriving and remained seated to greet her. He at least was gracious enough to offer her a drink. At nineteen, although an incredibly attractive young woman, she was too old for his interest. Nonetheless he had been assured that she was an interesting and intelligent girl and if he could spend a stimulating hour in her company, so much the better.

"So, Nikki tells me you are from England." He made it a statement rather than a question. She nodded and smiled. He looked back at her over the top of his half-moon glasses without smiling back. He had square set rugged features, blue grey eyes and was tall with short curly grey hair. For a scientist he seemed extremely fit and was quite good looking in a lizard like way. He appeared languid and very much in control of himself. It conveyed the impression that he had supreme self-confidence and knew more than the person he was talking to. Emma reckoned he was the sort of man who would walk with a slight swagger. She pondered idly what it might take to bring him down a peg or two.

My dad was British and my mother Jamaican. I was born in England, so I used to say that I have a part of each country and their culture in me. She took the chair next to him. "And yourself?"

He laughed. "From California but then studied on the east coast and gravitated into the rocket business…." He watched her face but she emulated a Mona Lisa smilingly unsmiling response. That gave him a bit of a kick. He had taken an instant liking to her which surprised him. The more they spoke the more he was impressed by what he saw. "They tell me you are an aspiring actress. With those stunning features I am not surprised." He looked her up and down admiringly as if he was a connoisseur appraising a good vintage. She had the feeling that she was more of a marketable commodity than a cherished human being. And yet there was a curious empathy almost from the start. She had the feeling he was drawn to her even though she was not in his sphere of interest. Her head inclined slightly. Not a sign of submission but more of agreement. "Well, if anyone can fix you up in Hollywood then our boy, Harry can." It was as if he was reassuring her. Not very well, either, and he sensed it.

Emma was not reassured but she appreciated the effort. "Mr Meade, may I ask…," but she got no further.

"Call me Hyman, sweetie," he interjected. "You were going to ask what I do for a living?" She laughed and nodded.

"I am the link between the government and the private sector. And in case you are wondering – I am the side of the private sector link, but let's talk about you?" He was genuinely intrigued. Her accent, her own self- possession in what must have been an unsettling situation, where she must have been wondering if and when they would allow her to go after she had served her purpose. Nikki had warned him that she was, in every way, vastly above the intelligence, looks and charm of the average girl they had come across. Emma for her part was just relieved that her only task was to entertain him verbally before the inevitable helicopter arrived to whisk him away and the next one would fly in.

"I've just shot a scene for an advert which actually went well, and in due course I hope for further auditions with a small firm in Hollywood." As she said it she realised the falsity of her words. Thank God for Mohammed, and Peter Westbrooke and the little cell phone now in her possession.

"You'll do well," he said quietly. "You know honey, there is a dark side to this business. You think you've seen some bad things? You ain't seen nuthin, as they say. Remember this. There is always a cost to becoming a star. Sleeping with the director, or his friends, that's just the start. There are the drugs, the satanic cults, even the ritual murders and it gets worse and worse. You have to play the full game if you want to climb the greasy pole to the top. They don't all do it, but most do and once they are suckered in, that's it." He leaned forward. "And it's not just here in this fake celluloid business you are so keen to get involved with." He stopped and looked round the estate with the rolling forests in the background. Should he try and do something good for once in his life instead of his suicidal self-serving power grabbing customary way of looking at the world. "It's just about all over the place. Take my advice honey, you are a really good looking kid and they haven't damaged you too much here so there is still time to make a plan and get out of this. Try and get back to England."

"Didn't you try to escape?" Another naïve question she thought.

He was unfazed. "Me, I'm trapped in this garbage already. The people who run and organise this trash know my weaknesses and I'm hooked into the trap already." He paused and reflected on where he was going with this dialogue. "I'm at the top of that greasy pole and enjoy all the privileges. It's only once you seriously start climbing that you learn about the haunting horrors. But you, you still have a chance. What do you think your long-term chances are? Do you really think they will let you out to become a super screen star after the people you've been meeting and servicing here – sorry that's the polite term for it – I somehow doubt it." He looked at her intently. "And so you should."

"But others have done it," she said defiantly. "Haven't they?" The latter a little less confidently.

Emma was very perplexed. She wondered if this was a set up and he was checking her out for Waxman. There was only one way to find out. Her little voice said ask him.

"Why are you telling me this?" The question sounded so naïve.

He put his drink down. "Because Emma, it is Emma, yes?" She nodded. "Emma, the moment I saw you walk across the lawn with Nikki I could see why they had offered you to me for a conversation piece. You are different and you don't belong here. Me, I sold my soul to the devil a long time ago. I got all the way to the top because of it. Hell, I'm so close to the top, it sometimes frightens even me. I mean the real top, the outermost limits of the 'corptocracy'. Now I deal with a different world literally – on items, matters and issues beyond your wildest dreams. But let me tell you this, that when you do get to the top, assuming you ignore my advice and they don't do to you what they have done to so many other innocent young girls like you, and I don't want to go into that. But believe me I've seen them come and go, when you are at the pinnacle of your career and you look back, you will realise that it wasn't worth it." He stopped and looked round. "I sure hope they don't use directional microphones here. I doubt it. All the rooms in this place are bugged. Yours too for that matter. Even the toilets are bugged. They have CCTV cameras throughout the estate. That's how they got me. Years ago I was a budding young aerospace engineer with tons and tons of ambition. Someone talent spotted me. I was invited to the island."

Emma held up her hand. "You mean Little St James Island – Jeffery's Epstein's retreat in the Caribbean?"

"The very same. Now that's a mighty strange place. Jeffery had a separate building there built in blue and white stripes. He called it the temple. It was modelled on an ancient temple site in Aleppo, Syria. It's called Hammam Yalbugha."

Again she interrupted. "I know that they performed rites there in a temple setting on the island." He nodded. "It was some sort of cult arrangement. They have a place here like that." She glanced over her shoulder nervously. "It's a gigantic room on a screw mounted lift accessed via the tunnel between the guest lodge and the mansion. I was forbidden to go there."

"And rightly so," he added quickly. "If they try to drag you there run like hell. But listen to this." He leaned forward conspiratorially. "Yalbugha was a massage parlour of the Mamluk era, a sort of public bath built in 1491 for slaves, located next to the citadel of Aleppo. The citadel was where they celebrated their god, Hadad. Ever heard of him?" He was staring at her intently now and answered his own question. "No, I bet you haven't. Hadad is another name for Baal. Moloch. In other words Satan. These guys are Satan worshippers. Do you get it?"

Emma inclined her head fractionally, but she couldn't take her eyes off his eyes. The conversation was almost hypnotic. She felt a chill of real fear surge through her body. It started at the base of her spine and swept up to the back of her neck and she could feel all the little hairs on her neck stand up involuntarily. Satan worshippers. What was she mixed up in? "I'm pretty much with you, but who were the Mamluks?"

"The Mamluks were Turkic or Caucasian Christian slave soldiers for the Muslims. Between 1250 and 1332 AD and from 1382 to 1570 AD they served the various sheikhs and sultans who raised them. These were the elite troops of the Turkish army. They played a pivotal role in the great siege of Malta but the Knights of St John and the Maltese people repelled them. Their daughters were used and traded by the sultans as female slave concubines. These people were obsessed by the sun. And what do you also find on the island – a gigantic occult painting of the sun embedded in the ground disguised as a sun dial. Don't believe me? Check out the aerial photographs of the island."

"So what is the meaning behind the Temple and the recessed chamber here?" She asked in a sibilant whisper.

"The temple is an ode to the Mamluk era when captured children were taken as slaves to do the bidding of the elite ruling class. Young boys would be trained as child soldiers and the young girls were taken and groomed to be the personal concubines of their masters. See the parallel between the Mamluks and Jeffery?"

He went on. "Jeffery brought lots and lots of girls, much younger than you, and some slightly older to his island. They were little better than modern slaves. I had a field day. Little boys were available too. I thought I was normal, whatever that means, but I was as deviant as anyone else. In my case I like younger girls. They fed me, filmed me, and then I noticed my career was taking off. But all along my corporate promoters impressed on me that I must play the game. Do as you are told, and your career is assured. That's what they will tell you. And it's fatal – because you cease to become your own person. Once they've really got you its literal suicide to try and escape. And It's not just me. They do it with everyone who takes their bait. CIA, FBl the judiciary, politicians and industrialists, academics and even as high as Supreme Court justices and foreign royalty. The entire establishment is corrupted. So, my advice to you, is play the game and make the break when you can, and until then be as compliant and careful as it's possible to be. Anyway, you're an aspirant actress so it might not be too challenging for you. Acting comes naturally." He stopped for a drink. She noticed he wasn't watching her closely. It was as if he was trying to atone for something. He glanced at her and flicked an imaginary speck of dust off his pants. "Sorry, I didn't mean that in an arrogant or hurtful way."

Emma was in half a mind to tell him that this was precisely what she had planned, but it seemed that perhaps discretion was the better part of the other thing, as her father used to say. She was still trying to fathom him out. There were so many things he had said which she wished he might amplify upon. Where to start. "What would Mr Waxman say to your comments?"

He stopped drinking abruptly. "He would make life for both of us very lethal. Heard the term CLA? Well, what I am doing is a severely Career Limiting Action. But you know something Emma? You have to live with yourself. I sat there watching you walk across the lawn with Nikki and I thought to myself, my God, here comes another lamb to the slaughter. Talking of which how the hell did you end up here?"

She was wary. "I was abducted."

"In this country or abroad?"

She looked at him sharply. "In England. They offered me a …." But he held up his hand.

"Don't tell me. They offered you a modelling or acting role." She nodded. "It's a favourite trick. They use it on East European women too. A young girl, usually from a troubled family background is offered a modelling assignment and told to come to a local airport with her passport and a suitcase. A jet plane arrives, all very impressive and off they go. At the outset the treatment is impressive and so are the settings. Then the hell begins. Drugs, booze, beatings and sex. So, Emma, take any opportunity you can and get out. You are cut out for something far superior to this."

She was itching to share with him her plans. Instead she looked very thoughtful and serious. "Can I ask, what is that you actually do?"

He took a long breath and looked round the estate. It was a magnificent afternoon with a slight chill in the air. "If I told you honestly what I do, I doubt that you would believe me!"

"Try me," she said with an impish smile.

"Do you have any idea how many people go missing on this planet every day?"

The question took her aback. He saw the expression on her face and the momentary fear. "I don't see the …."

"The relevance? Let me tell you the relevance of the fact that 607 adults go missing on this planet every day. That makes just under a quarter of a million. In your age category it's vastly higher. Nearly 22 000 kids vanish off the planet every day. That is roughly 8 million in a year. Most of them never to be seen again. Many of them are kidnapped just like you were for child sex rings and cult rituals. Some of them end up in Eastern Europe or Mexico and others in India. Once there it is almost impossible to get them back. Then they are disposed of. But many of them disappear as if they had just vanished off the planet. The final frontier you might call it."

Emma was not sure what he was trying to tell her. "You mean they were murdered?" She felt it was a bit naïve but it was the best that she could do.

"No. Not in that sense, although they might just as well have been. What is the final frontier?" She tossed her head back as she asked the question which made her feel very naïve although she was intensely curious.

Emma was bemused. "The final frontier, you mean space," she said hesitantly. "Like they say in Star Trek?'

"Exactly so, and where is humankind's future destiny?" He watched her closely.

"Exploration?" Emma wondered where on earth this was going. Perhaps it was not on earth.

"Precisely. But 'why' is the question you ought to be asking yourself. The old petrol-based technologies will be replaced by an alternative which will make our present technologies look like child's play. One of the many reasons we have seen Space Force introduced is to mine items like Helium 3 from the lunar surface. It is not easily found on the Earth but is plentiful up there." He gestured towards the sky and drew a deep breath. "A pound of Helium 3 is worth over a billion dollars. Any idea why it is so valuable? Because it is used in nuclear fusion as opposed to nuclear fission. Fission is employed in the splitting of atoms to generate steam which powers turbines and they create electricity. But this is dangerous in that it produces tons of toxic and lethal nuclear waste. If we use fusion with Helium 3 the cast off is organic and non-toxic. Do you think that the international space station is the limit of our exploration of space after all these years?" He was impressed that she needed little or no prompting.

"Well, it's as far as we have been told about. Are you suggesting we have gone further?"

"Very much so. You have put your finger on it, when you say as far as we have been told. We have gone so much further already we are building space hotels, so what else is out there kept secret from the rest of humanity, for very obvious reasons."

Emma felt a chill. "And they will need people, like you, to do the same thing as you are doing down here. Evil has no boundaries and can reach to the stars that you look at each night. The realisation had dawned on her like an electric shock. Up to this point she had reckoned that what had happened to her was about as bad as it could get. It seemed that she was still hovering on the tip of a terrible and evil iceberg.

He had got to his final point. "Yes, my dear, so what I am trying to tell you in an oblique way is that they have two options where you are concerned – you risk playing the game and making it to the top or you are disposed of.

Emma was silent for a long time. It was a salutary conversation. She was trying to get her head round what he had just said. "Who does this? Governments, big companies, rich individuals….? How do they pay for it? What have they got out there?

He sat up and turned towards her. "You have trouble believing me? Who does this? Let's call it the corptocracy – a combination of the technology rich private sector and certain very deep state agencies. Eisenhower called it the military industrial complex back in the 1950s and that's pretty much what it is today." There was that word again, the "deep" state. She had heard it before. Where was he going with all this? He watched her very closely now. It was like he was trying to get something off his shoulders. "When you have a chance look up Solar Warden. It will explain a bit more than I can, sitting here now. But that is the tip of the iceberg. Will you remember that?"

"Solar Warden," she repeated it several times. "I'm not likely to forget. But why are they doing this, and in secret? And who pays for this?"

He shuffled uncomfortably in his chair. "It is man's destiny to explore. From the stars we came and to the stars we shall return. Not my words, but someone else who was famous, or rather, notorious. If I told you, you wouldn't believe me. In space we can mine minerals and riches beyond measure. But you seem surprised? Why?"

An insect landed on her leg and she instinctively flicked it off. "Impossible," she muttered. He was opening up new worlds and avenues of thought for her.

She picked up his thread. "Assuming what you say is true, what is in it for us? I mean, the sky is literally the limit." She was hooked now.

He laughed. "Why Emma, what is in it for us indeed. But first you must ask where did the money come from for such a secret massive space project. It came from the military industrial complex and input from others. There are twenty one trillion dollars missing off the US budget as we sit here now. It is skimmed from budgets and redirected to the cause. Emma, my dear, twenty one trillion dollars is more than a King's ransom and quite sufficient to create a new civilization. It's before your time, but the day before 911, the US Defence Secretary, Donald Rumsfeld, announced that several trillion dollars were missing and unaccounted for in the US defence budget alone. Add that to the skimmed amounts from so many other sources, the international drugs trade and other criminal type syndicates and the money all adds up."

Emma felt a bit faint. "So where are these Solar Warden craft located?"

There was long silence. She felt quite awkward. He looked thoughtfully at his finger nails. How far could he go? How much would she believe? Did it matter anyway?

"Off planet space stations, the size of aircraft carriers, known as the Orion Class, quite a few of them in fact, linked with space craft capable of travelling at phenomenal speeds, some of which are known as *Aurora*. Much of this is Tesla technology involving the exploitation of wormholes. Although the information is in the public domain, people conveniently forget that the president's uncle, Professor John Trump, an electrical engineer and physicist, inherited the Tesla papers. So what does this president know that the others did not. There are off planet bases too. Ask yourself Emma why all the talk now of colonising Mars and the Moon. Because the public must be psychologically programmed for what is coming. They must be prepared for the time when these things are revealed. Imagine if the planet becomes uninhabitable. If too many people continue to drain its resources on all fronts. The population needs to be reduced. Drastically."

He said it as if trying to convince himself. "This current president is a serious obstacle to our work but he will not be there forever. That's why the current election is an extremely important, nay, a pivotal one. We have all sorts of plans to remove him. Even before he reached the Oval office there were at least 24 attempts to take him down. They all failed. He seems to enjoy uncanny protection.

He paused but noted her intense curiosity. Reassured he continued. "Now the forces aligned with us are working to make this country ungovernable. Our plan is titled 'Preventing a Disrupted Presidential election and transition' and later this year it will be widely and secretly distributed. We have hundreds of thousands of faked ballot papers. The voting machines have been loaded with algorithms to tip the vote in our favour."

Her gaze had drifted down but now she looked up at him sharply. "That's incredibly dishonest. Anyway, how do you know that they work?"

He allowed himself a thin smile. "We tested them in Venezuela, the Chinese provided the money, and the cyber systems, the Italians have allowed us the use of one of their encrypted Leonardo satellites to forward the data to Europe and the processing will be done in Germany. So you see…" But she interrupted him again. Visions of her conversations with Liz Slatzky floated before her.

"Surely the CIA can intercept these transmissions? That is what they are there to do, aren't they?"

He paused for a long time. A slow grimace crossed his face. "To tell you the truth, we could not accomplish all this without the help of certain elements in the CIA. And the FBI for that matter. In fact it is already arranged for the vote manipulation to be conducted in the CIA station at the US consulate in Frankfort. There are cadres of individuals in those organisations as keen as we are to bring these changes about. This president does not stand a chance."

It was her turn to make a face. "But surely the president knowns all this? Doesn't he?"

He looked away into the distance. "Do you know something? In all probability he likely does know it. Or he strongly suspects it. But what can he do about it? We control the courts, we have compromised and intimidated judges on our side, even in the highest court in the land, and about 70 per cent of the politicians are compromised. They will do what we tell them to do. He is one man standing alone, well, almost alone, against the world. Stalin allegedly said that he did not give a fig for the voters. It is who counts the votes that really matters. And that is the case here. As for the current bug and the international lock downs, well, that is a chimera. You think Covid 19 is a health threat?"

She stared at him in blank amazement. "But it must be. The governments of the world have shut their countries down, Surely….?" She felt seriously out of her depth now. A bit like a child told that Santa Clause was all a ruse.

"It's largely rubbish, a dry run, for what's coming. Oh, some strains of the bug are lethal, sure, but in general it's akin to a bad dose of influenza. For the elderly it's a killer too, or those with predisposed medical issues. But for healthy people it's an irritation rather than a hazard. There are three real primary aims to this ongoing world-wide lockdown exercise. The first one is to launch a global economic reset and introduce the cashless society. That enhances the process of global control. The second one is to accelerate the transition process through Artificial Intelligence to Transhumanism, linking technology to the human brain. It will make us less human and vastly more technologically adept. At some point we will cease to be human and AI only. The human mind will be connected to a technological grid controlled from a central point. The essential issue will focus on who actually controls that grid."

Before he could continue, she said it for him. "And the third is the global eugenics movement to slash the world population like you just said. The vaccine will weaken the immune systems of the global population and the 5G will determine who lives and who dies. My dad spoke about this last one. When he learned that he was going to die, he started doing the research and what he told us was every bit as fantastic as what you are telling me now. In fact, in some ways you remind me of my dad."

He stared at her. "Harry was right. You are much too beautiful and brainy to hang round here. Your dad knew all this?"

She felt very unsettled. Had she said too much? "My dad died from 5G involving his work in England. He said it was a form of weapon, directed energy weapon, I think, was the term he used, but being adapted in a communication mode."

Meade was impressed. "Yes, that is absolutely right. I'm sorry to hear about your dad. The good news for you is that 5G is already obsolete. We are already on 6G. Your dad did not die in vain."

"6G?" She repeated it again. "But, my God, they are still deploying 5G?"

"The Russians and the Americans are preparing to unveil 6G. Our concern is that this president will beat the world to it. He is working with that South African billionaire, Elon Musk. Musk's Starlink satellite system is being deployed in collaboration with a secret technology company called CIALabs. The name will probably be announced later in the year. They will benefit from the patents and licenses for the intellectual property they create. Musk's Space X company is putting up the 6G satellites at the rate of one launch every 14 days per Falcon 9 flight. 12 000 are due to be launched with a grand total of 42 000 planned. Over 700 are already up. Why, he's so close to the CIA, he just weirdly named his baby after the CIA spy plane X AE A-12. The satellites will link to up to a million small antennas the president has already authorized for deployment across the US."

"But why?" she asked even more bewildered. Now he had her personal interest.

"Why? Because a linkage between these satellites and antennas can be accomplished by super high frequency transmissions based upon the development of a common global 6G standard where science fiction becomes reality. The applications are mind blowing. I dare not extrapolate any further." He knew he had said far too much already.

Emma was transfixed. Her head was spinning.

He thought it better to change the subject. "Rest assured that this exponential population growth is a serious problem although 5G is but one of many avenues open to us to curtail the earth's population. Escape back to England if you can.

Discuss this with Harry, or Nikki or indeed anyone else and you're as good as dead." He sat and stared out over the forest and then suddenly started to rise as the sound of the helicopter pricked his ears. They stood up simultaneously. "It's been nice visiting with you. Think about what I said." He reached into his pocket. "Here take this." He handed her a slip of paper. "It's got my number. If you can reach a phone and need help call me. Don't waste too much time. Once you have outlived your usefulness here......"

They shook hands. She thanked him as he walked away. He didn't look back.

Later that evening she sent a message on her special phone. She outlined as much as she could remember but she was so shocked by what she had witnessed that she forgot the elementary precaution of turning on the television in her room. It was Bruno who listened to the monitors and wondered why she was talking to herself, or had she somehow managed to get a phone from someone. He would capitalise on that later.

The NSA team monitoring the Strelnikov corporate and personal communications in the UK and round the world were riveted by a conversation their system intercepted involving a dialogue between Strelnikov himself and Harry Waxman. It was passed to GCHQ without delay and Peter Westbrooke was immediately notified. The NSA monitoring system operates on the basis of Artificial Intelligence scans of key words in the ether. It is said, not without a sense of pride, that the NSA monitors every single electronic communication in the world. That is not exactly true but its close enough. There are four basic aspects of signals intelligence – collection, storage, analysis and distribution. One might add storage again after distribution but they amount to the same thing. In the old days all data went to Sigint City, the NSA's vast complex halfway between Baltimore and Washington. But Sigint City with its thousands of employees has been largely expanded, duplicated and replaced in part by the NSA Data Centre in Bluffdale, Utah. There are those at the top of the NSA who reckon that an Extinction Level Event, or ELE, is on the cards. Such an extraordinary event might involve pole shifts and tidal tsunamis of epic proportions. So the NSA moved their major facility deep inland of the continental United States. It was here that Strelnikov's landlines and mobile phones were all placed on a watch list monitored from the NSA listening post at Menwith Hill in Yorkshire. Usually conversations are monitored and assessed by a complex system of algorithms looking for key words such as terrorist, assassinate or nuclear amongst an entire lexicon watch-list. Once the conversation is kicked out for further inspection the Artificial Intelligence directs it to a more sophisticated filter. If the dialogue is still worthy of note it is made cyber accessible sometimes with a notification and sometimes not, to an analyst. The system was later adapted for censorship or curating on popular social web sites such as Facebook, Twitter and Watts App. So important was

Strelnikov now that he had his own dedicated analyst.

Lisa Hopkins had been a British army trained Russian language expert before emigrating to the United States and being attracted by a better salary with the prospects of a more exciting career than training British army officers to speak passable Russian. She had worked in Sigint City with a good reputation and lived nearby. Her assignment to the team made sense thanks to her British background. Subtle innuendos which might escape American officers would never escape her. It was a quiet Wednesday afternoon when her computer screen blinked and a dialogue came up between Igor Strelnikov and Harry Waxman. She was unfamiliar with the degree of significance attached to the 'chatter' intercept other than that it was very important. What she heard had her sitting on the edge of her chair.

Strelnikov's PA spoke to Waxman's private secretary. There was a short delay and the dialogue exploded. Waxman was berated by Strelnikov for having placed them all in jeopardy allowing Emma to make what appeared to be a film shoot at sea.

"Harry, I sent her to you as a gift because I knew you could use her obvious physical talents. I did not send her to you so you could put her on the television screens of the world, it was meant to be just the USA."

Waxman rebutted the accusation. "Igor, she's my property to do with as I wish. Personally, I think that she has done very well here, as she did for you. The advert was not clever I agree, but it was a reward for her services."

Strelnikov bristled. "Harry, the deal was no publicity. You know that."

"It was implied Igor, never spelt out."

"The hell it was. She is now a terminal case."

Waxman made a ruthless offer. "Come on Igor, give me a break. You want her taken out?"

"Just send her back to me, because the fat is in the fire and the advert is showing in the UK now. This is a wet one, but frankly I don't trust you to get it right. I'll arrange it."

Waxman saw his chance. "Can't do that Harry. We are under stringent lockdown. Not unless you can make a plan.

Strelnikov played his ace. "Harry, send her back or life will get really challenging for you and all your operations both in the UK and in Europe. She knows too much about all of us. I will make the arrangements. Just isolate her and wait for my arrangements."

The line went dead. Lisa Hopkins marked it urgent and sent it to the Q Group supervising the Westbroke case. Within hours Peter and his team had listened to the conversation. An animated discussion followed on the merits of getting Emma out of the US and back to the UK. It was clear that Strelnikov wanted to see her before removing her. Emma was in grave danger. Her reports had confirmed the game plan for the destabilisation of the US and much else besides. Perhaps it would be a convenient time to bring her in. All eyes focused on Strelnikov's plans.

CHAPTER 19

Under an international lockdown certain essential services have to remain open. These include municipal services and the distribution of medical requirements, food and technology support systems. Of these, medical requirements are the most crucial. In the Covid-19 crisis of 2020 the leading lights in the medical fraternity reckoned that ventilators were critical in combatting the virus in its later stages of infection. At first this was the accepted treatment but gradually it became clear that only 3% of patients on the ventilators were surviving the ordeal. Thus began at the outset of the infection a mad global scramble for ventilators. With the inevitable politicization of the issue, certain states in the US were trying to show up the White House by claiming that they could not access sufficient ventilators. An appeal was made for international assistance.

There was one term in the conversation which placed everyone's hair on end. The term 'Wet One' was a KGB term for a murder. It had been adopted by the oligarchs in order for them to settle scores, and in the settling of scores they most certainly had indulged, with a dedicated brutality and ruthlessness. Its use in respect of Emma was clear. The experts put their heads together and had a comprehensive discussion. The idea crossed Peter Westbrooke's mind that it would be helpful if he could assist Strelnikov in extracting Emma back to England. After consultation with his colleagues and enlisting the collaboration of the higher levels of the British government, a plan was hatched.

For Emma life on the estate suddenly changed. She was confined to her quarters and forbidden to leave the immediate environs. Nikki became cold and distant. The security manager visited her to underscore the importance of obeying the new restrictions placed on her. She could not help wondering if he had been ordered to kill her. The hostility and contempt he expressed was almost tangible. Her quarters were searched and then searched again. She had hidden the cell in a watertight plastic bag inside the cistern of the toilet. They missed it. Something had gone wrong very quickly and she could not find out what or why. Had Hyman Meade reported back to Waxman? She could not understand what was happening to her. One night she cobbled together a verbal report requesting extraction. The answer came back quickly. "Keep your cool. Timing is everything."

Stefanie found John Price an inspiring source of comfort and solace. She had cleared him completely and the court had accepted her findings without reservation. Colonel Garth Cartwright had thankfully come out of the coma and been returned home to make room in the hospital for an expected deluge of COVID-19 victims. Stefanie suggested that they contact him and pay a visit. Initially John had expressed understandable reluctance but she pointed out that it could improve the colonel's chances of a full recovery if he was put in the picture as to exactly what had happened. The colonel lived in a respectably sized cottage on the Isle of Wight. Getting there under ordinary circumstances would have been a mission. Travelling there during the lockdown was both a breeze and a challenge. Stefanie was able to write herself an official authorisation for Price and herself to make the drive down to Portsmouth. The motorways were all but deserted. Only when they had reached the ferry terminal did they encounter the first checkpoint and after approval, were allowed to cross onto the Isle of Wight. A short drive and they were in the hamlet of Arreton comprising a splendid rural country seat, a school, an hotel, an ancient church and a few cottages, one of which belonged to the colonel.

It was raining quite heavily when they arrived mid-morning. Colonel Cartwright's niece came down the driveway and opened the gate to let them in. An attractive down to earth girl with shoulder length blond hair and crystal blue eyes, dressed in shiny flat heeled shoes with a red sweater and knee length hounds-tooth skirt. She showed them in through the back door. A large black Labrador took an undue interest in Price's tweed jacket and suede shoes before allowing them into the drawing room.

"I'm sorry about Ebony. He checks everybody before letting them near the old man." She gently pulled the dog by the collar and made way.

The colonel was seated in an ancient and rather well-worn leather armchair in a lamp lit corner of a small but cosy well-appointed room. The door into the garden was open and once the rain had eased off they were serenaded by bird calls from the heavily flowered plants. In addition to the customary regimental memorabilia of unit badges, distant exotic places and regimental parades, Price was surprised to see an impressive model yacht called Gladeye in the recessed bookshelves of the house. The colonel made an effort to stand up and shook hands with them.

"I'm deeply appreciative of your visit. So sorry I was in the wrong place at the wrong time. Damned inconvenient." He gestured for them to sit down.

Price noticed that he was still very pale but the bandage round his head had been removed. "On the contrary Sir, it was our, well, really, my fault. We've just come down to pay our respects and apologise in person."

The colonel must have been in his late 80s, but he looked remarkably fit. "Nothing to apologise for. In fact I rather hoped you dealt the fella a good crack. If my own experience was anything to go by it must have been a damn good crack. Can I offer you a sherry?" They nodded gratefully. "Lynda," he called to his niece. "Two sherries for our friends, please. So, are you Canadian or American? Never can tell these days until you pronounce the word out or about. Canadians delightfully say "oot" or "aboot". That's always a dead giveaway." He laughed at his own joke and accepted the sherry gratefully.

"American, Sir."

"Stationed in the UK or just visiting us?" He took another generous swig of the sherry.

That was an awkward question. Price decided to admit to just visiting, hoping the conversation might be re-directed.

"Ah, good to have you." He put his glass down and looked at Stefanie. "And you my dear, also in the service?"

Price was determined to change the dialogue. Stefanie smiled at Lynda. "In a manner of speaking Colonel Cartwright. I am attached to the Wexham psychological evaluation unit. There was a concern…"

The colonel held up his hand. "I know, I know. Lynda here told me part of the story. I'm glad it's had a happy outcome. And the young man here is part of the Special Forces, I gather." He gestured towards Price. "Just glance inside the annexe there, would you."

Price got up and looked through the doorway. The wall was covered in various small arms weapons behind bullet proof glass. They ranged from a 1917 Webley to a 1943 British army Colt 45. Price leaned forward and read the inscription. 'Major H Gordon, Gordon Highlanders. Government Model' He was astonished.

"I see you're a collector Sir. I wanted to ask you about the yacht?" He pointed at the Gladeye.

"If it hadn't been family tradition to join the Household Division, I think that I would have joined the RN, but there was a compensation in that we had a regimental yacht and the name stuck down the generations. Thousands of guardsmen enjoyed sailing her and quite a few marriages resulted." He winked at his niece. Never too old, thought Price. That was an encouraging discovery.

They chatted for another half an hour, but Price could see that the old man was tiring. He told them with relish of his early days in Northern Ireland. Of how they had run out on sporadic foot patrols watching their feet for trip wires and the locals for secret signals. How he had climbed Kilimanjaro with a regimental climbing team and saved the life of a young guardsman battling altitude sickness. He described exercises in Oman and jungle warfare in Belize.

It all sounded so familiar. They stood up, shook hands and took their leave. They had packed a picnic luncheon to eat in the car on the way back. The trip had done all of them a power of good. Price felt better, Stefanie got her mind off Emma, the colonel was at peace with what had happened and the weather had cleared. Overhead they caught the glint of the sun off the wings of an incoming airliner.

Despite the draconian travel bans aircraft belonging to the International Committee of the Red Cross were still flying. They transported Personal Protective Equipment, ventilators, testing kits and even medical and administrative World Health Organization authorized personnel between countries. Strelnikov had arranged for the oligarch whose aircraft was on rental to the ICRC to give his 'niece' a ride home for emergency surgery.

It was a glorious English evening as they swept in off the Atlantic. The Isle of Wight was unmistakeable, just as it appeared on the map, surrounded by a glittering sea. She could see Portsmouth with the familiar shape of Nelson's two hundred year old flagship HMS Victory, and not far away the first iron clad armoured ship HMS Warrior, the Black Snake as Napoleon III had called her, and the huge shed containing the remnants of the Mary Rose. They all looked like toys from up above. It reminded her of the time she had visited Portsmouth with her father. How much had changed since those halcyon days. Then the motorway to London and the railway snaking alongside it through the emerald countryside. Emma looked down at the green fields of England. She caught the flash of light from the windscreen of a solitary car heading towards the capital, so conspicuous by its isolation.

Her past few days had been utterly traumatizing. It had all started when Bruno, Waxman's chief of security, had visited her in her rooms. He had always struck her as a sinister character. The incident with the roving Dobermans had done nothing to disillusion her. He intimated that Mr Waxman had decided to terminate her services with immediate effect. She would be returning to England as soon as possible. Mr Strelnikov wanted her back. In the mean time she must confine herself to her rooms and on no account stray into the grounds or enter the mansion. They would be coming to fetch her shortly. The orders peremptorily conveyed. He then lingered. "I guess your usefulness is over," he sneered. "Time has arrived to cash in the chips," he added ominously. She looked at him. Was this how they were all dismissed she wondered. Did he perhaps think that she was now fair game?

She glanced at him nervously. "I think you should leave."

"Leave?" he said contemptuously. "I was just enjoying getting to know you. Do you know you talk in your sleep?"

It hit her like an avalanche. Meade's warnings about the bugged rooms had come back to haunt her. How much had he heard. "I don't know what you mean?"

He laughed. She was reminded of the witch in the Wizard of Oz. "Oh yes you do. You had quite a little dialogue going the other night. Rehearsing your lines were you, for when you leave? I have it all on tape you know. We can enhance it. But I have something else in mind for the moment." He advanced towards her.

She backed away one step as if retreating before an advancing leopard.

A snide little smirk crossed his face. "Why don't you entertain me? We have at least an hour before the helicopter arrives."

She was instantly flustered. So that was it after all. Something had happened, the pretence was over. Now that she was being dismissed, her usefulness at an end, she could service the staff. She was expendable. He advanced towards her. She backed away. "Mr Bruno, please leave."

He laughed. "No one here to help you now, bitch. You're all mine. Take off your clothes and let's get into that posh bedroom they've given you." It was an order not a request.

She said a little prayer. As she turned to enter the bedroom she saw on a side table a beautiful Italian pink rose quartz figurine of a glass bird. Uncle Peter had taught her that even a diminutive person with a small wooden paddle can immobilise a far bigger and more powerful man providing the blow was delivered in the right spot. Surprise was the answer. He had made her train on him to the point where she could see that, with surprisingly little effort or force, she could seriously hurt her uncle. But she must have a weapon.

As she approached the small round circular table with the glass ornament she stripped off her top and threw it on the floor. Behind her Bruno relaxed. "That's how I like my women," he snarled. She put her hands down as if to remove her skirt and whipped up the glass ornament. She swung round and slammed it onto the side of his head. Poleaxed, Bruno crashed to the floor but though he was down he was far from out. He lay there stunned and groaning with blood pouring down his face. She looked round frantically. A medium sized heavy Stewart crystal cut glass jug with glasses lay under a muslin cloth covering the table at the foot of the bed. She put her hand over the top of the jug and slammed it again with all her force on the original entry wound. She might as well have used a hammer. The jug astoundingly refused to break. Water mixed with blood formed great red pools on the marble floor. He went white and stopped breathing. She felt his carotid artery as her mother had taught her to do. She had killed him.

Panic. Think. Her hands were shaking uncontrollably and she was drenched in perspiration. She dragged his body into the bathroom. Towels cleaned up the mess on the floor. She threw them into the bath. Her underclothes were stained from the blood splashes. She stripped them off and showered trying to ignore him on the floor. A quick change of clothing and she was packed using the bag they had provided for the film shoot, and ready to leave. She locked him in the bathroom and went downstairs. They would surely kill her now unless she could leave before they discovered his body. She thought of phoning the police but the girl from the Philippines had told her of a girl who had stolen a cell phone to call the cops. The 911 lady had answered and said that she would call back. The victim had waited for ten minutes. She then called 911 again. The operator had unbelievably said to her, "The Sheriff is at the gate honey, and there is no way you are getting off Mr Waxman's property." That girl had never been seen again.

Sure enough after half an hour she heard the helicopter arrive. She decided to seize the initiative. Hoping that the Dobermans had already been confined before Bruno had approached her, she left the lodge. Carefully locking the door behind her she walked over to the landing pad. The pilot was stretching on the lawn next to the big concrete circle with the yellow H. It was a Bell Jet Ranger again. She hoped that she didn't look too flustered. "Hi there," he said with a broad smile. She waited for the enquiry about Bruno but it never came. "I take it you're the only passenger today. Pop the bag in the bay, hop in and belt up."

Then came the awkward question – "Is Mr Bruno round?"

She shuddered, slipped her bag into the little compartment and turned round. "I haven't seen him", she lied so convincingly it surprised even her, although her hands were still shaking.

"I wonder if I shouldn't wait for him to sign you out."

Oh my God, she thought to herself. I have killed the one man who could sign my release off the estate. "Mr Waxman said to go ahead. I think he had something important for Mr Bruno to do."

The pilot was keen to leave. "Ok, well, that's kind of irregular, but let's go." He strapped himself into the cockpit and the rotors whined into action. She was like the proverbial cat on a hot roof. Any moment they might come running. He signalled to her to put the headphones on with the microphone. "I'm instructed to drop you at the ICRC depot at John Glenn International Airport in Columbus. By the way, do you have a mask?" She had forgotten it in the tumult. No one on the estate wore them anyway.

"I left it behind by mistake," she confessed.

"No problem." He fumbled in his pocket and produced a blue and white medical mask. She took it gratefully. "You must just slip it on when we disembark. They're kinda paranoid at John Glenn." Not half as paranoid as they would be when they discovered Bruno she thought ruefully to herself.

The flight was uneventful. She could not help but wonder what was happening back at the estate. Then she dismissed the thought. The thug's body was their problem not hers. Her mother had taught her never to make other's problems, your own.

At the airport they landed next to a large nondescript cargo aircraft with a prominent red cross painted on its tail. True to form they were all wearing masks. A small Russian pilot approached her and escorted her onto the jet. His English was terrible and his sign language not that much better. She understood that she must make herself comfortable for the flight to the UK. He hoped that she had eaten. There was only bottled water on board.

In the Q Group monitoring the communications the plan had been for Emma to be collected at Stanstead airport by Strelnikov but midway over the Atlantic the Ohio task force monitoring the estate had learned of Bruno's murder. The hand held two way walkie-talkie radios carried by Waxman's security staff had hummed red hot. Then the phone calls had been made for a trusted medic. It was obvious what had happened. Peter reckoned he would have to organize Emma's extraction sooner rather than later. There was some vigorous discussion. Peter insisted that she be extracted with immediate effect. Strelnikov would not waste any time exacting revenge on behalf of Waxman. Emma was a confirmed liability and liabilities in Igor's mind were there to be dispensed with.

The phone call from Waxman when it came through to Strelnikov at his luxurious Moor Park mansion caused a sensation. Rage hardly did justice to Strelnikov as he listened to the way in which Bruno's body had been found. Waxman demanded that Emma be returned but that was far too late. Strelnikov had power, extraordinary power coupled with influence to boot, but even a calculated oligarch like Igor could not reroute an official ICRC aircraft. They would have to collect her at Stanstead. No sooner had he put the phone down on an apoplectic Waxman than he was calling for his trusted hatchet man. This was to be a particularly brutal revenge killing. Making an example of Emma was paramount in the gangster's mind.

Chapter 20

They swung in over London from the south and crossed the Thames valley, passing St Albans before lining up on short finals. Just peering out of the corner of her eye she could see Bishops Stortford. The M11 to London, almost entirely devoid of traffic, passed under their wings. It was as if all the people were dead, like a scene from a lousy Hollywood B grade movie. She reckoned the news of Bruno's murder must have reached Strelnikov by now and he would be looking for blood. The plane touched down to a perfect landing. They taxied to the makeshift ICRC processing centre. A gangway was brought to the aircraft and Emma slipped on the mask that she had been given by the American helicopter pilot. She was just reaching up for her little suitcase when two men in black jackets wearing black masks entered the aircraft. She knew straight away. An Irish voice as smooth as silk and sinister as hell said, "You won't be needing that, my girl. Just come with us." Resistance was futile. She just had time to snatch her bag.

The thugs took her hand luggage and grabbed her by the wrists to escort her down the gangway. The larger man with the Irish accent twisted her wrist so hard she cried out in pain. "One word, love, just one word and I'll break it." A waiting WHO official and representatives of the ICRC all wearing their anonymous masks watched her silently whisked into a waiting black Jaguar. The large thug climbed in on one side after she got in, and the other walked round to the other side. The driver ignored her. Once the doors were shut he pulled off his mask and looked back. It was her little friend, Melvin, alias Martin Peters, the gas man who had come to the house all those months ago. It seemed like another age. He smiled, almost with sadness on his face, because he knew what was coming. "That's her all right. I'll get out once we're clear of the gate." She thought of asking for help but realised the moment she saw the reception committee at the bottom of the stairs, any request for help from anybody would be superfluous. They had been well rewarded to ignore the formalities. The Jaguar accelerated towards the apron exit as the two thugs fastened her hands tightly behind her back with cable ties.

The car swung round the curious half traffic circle at the airport security gates and turned hard left. Emma felt herself crushed against the larger man. It was a repulsive feeling. Melvin accelerated the car to the first mini circle heading for the M11. He drove straight through and pulled over. A small Hyundai was parked in the tree line. He got out and walked to the Hyundai. The two thugs gagged and bound her and pulled a pillow case over her head and left her in the boot of the Hyundai.

Returning to the Jaguar they started the car and drove off. As the car entered the second larger traffic circle a Land Rover and two motor cyclists accelerated round the circle coming in from the right. They closed up behind the car. As the vehicles moved towards the M11 motorway onramp the driver failed to see men in police uniform moving orange road beacons onto the highway behind him to redirect future traffic down the road to the left. The driver vaguely noticed the Land Rover although the motorbikes were obscured behind the bigger vehicle.

It was the maroon Range Rover in front that caught his attention. It came out of the tree line on the left accelerating into his path. Suddenly the Range Rover was braking hard and as it did so there was a terrific bang on the right rear bumper. The Jaguar swivelled but to his credit the driver didn't entirely lose control. As he swung to correct the Jag, the Range Rover, being expertly driven, slewed to an abrupt stop in his path. The Land Rover slammed into the side of the broadsiding Jaguar and crushed it up against the maroon Range Rover. The last thing the driver saw was a motor cyclist at his driver's window.

The police radio crackled. "Girl not in car, repeat girl not in car."

It had been a pleasant evening. They had watched a bit of television, played scrabble and enjoyed a good bottle of Italian wine. Stefanie turned on the BBC television news, but switched the volume down. She was making coffee and glancing at the screen. Price was reading the Daily Telegraph. The news reader gave the latest Covid-19 figures in the UK as compared with the previous day, the same time the previous month and the month before that. There were signs that the infection was levelling off. Stefanie ground the coffee beans which drowned out the news reader's commentary and glanced at the picture. She stopped and then screamed. Price watched transfixed as a young woman's body was pulled out of the Grand Union Canal. As the body emerged the camera cut away but not fast enough to show that the head, and hands were missing. But this was not the cause of Stefanie's alarm. It was the dress that the corpse was wearing. It was the same expensive dress that Emma had taken from her cupboard for the ill-fated meeting with Melvin. Price rushed round the kitchen counter and grabbed Stefanie before she collapsed.

"Take it easy, Love," he said as she sagged into his arms. "It looks the same but it probably isn't." He helped her to the sofa and grabbed the remote. They listened to the remainder of the commentary accompanying the report. Price went into the kitchen and finished making the coffee.

"The body was spotted by a local resident walking his dog along the canal. Police are seeking anyone in the area of the Grand Union Canal who can help them with their enquiries. It is believed that the body may be that of a 19 year old woman abducted at the beginning of the year. The number to call is…..," but neither of them were listening.

She picked up the phone and dialled Peter's private number. There was an agonising delay and the recorded message began, "This is Peter Westbrooke. I am momentarily away but if you leave your name and number I shall revert to you as soon as possible." She slammed the phone on the settee. There was a short silence before the onset of the storm. Price could see it coming. She buried her head in his arms and sobbed. They missed the report about a burnt out Jaguar with two bodies in it found near the M11 Stansted Airport junction.

"He promised John, he promised! He said she would be protected. He lied. It's her, I know it's her." If there was any doubt it didn't last very long. The phone rang an hour later. It was the Thames Valley Division police. An Inspector Monroe asked to speak with her. Could he come up and see her immediately. There were two of them. Courteous, coldly official and unconsoling. They were deeply sorry to have to inform her that they had reason to believe that Emma's body had been found in the Grand Union Canal. Identification was difficult as the killers had mutilated the body but could she identify the contents of a handbag found near the scene of the crime. He produced a very unofficial looking large brown paper bag. Stefanie took one look at the contents and sank to the floor in a dead faint. Price told them to go and they left. The bag went with them. Half an hour later when she had somewhat recovered he took her in his arms. "Are you sure it was hers?" he asked trying to find an out.

"No doubt at all. She carried her father's signet ring in a small gold clasped carry bag in her handbag. It went with her everywhere. She said once she was married she would wear it with pride but not until. I might mistake other things but not that. It was her all right. I think I want to be sick. Again."

He waited until she had finished in the bathroom and while she was there retching her heart out, he had an idea. "You know my love, the US government spent a truck load of money training me. I've been thinking. Let me find out who did this to her and there will be justice for Emma. I cannot bring her back but I can give the murderer a terminal return on his investment."

She looked up at him. "You know, John, I was brought up to believe that vengeance is mine, saith the Lord." There was a long pause. "But I think in this case he might make an exception!"

"I take it that's a yes, then?"

She nodded. "But how will you find the killer?"

He managed a weak smile. "That's my business. You just keep trying to get hold of Peter."

Major Nigel Herrington had been expecting the call when it came. Indeed, he was surprised that it had taken so long. He was well aware of the relationship between Stefanie and John, and actually took quite a secret delight in it. He listened carefully to the request from John Price. There was a long silence. Between men in the special forces there is a unique bond. They are a true band of brothers and they will gladly sacrifice their lives for each other, both on the battlefield and off. He clearly said the one word "Strelnikov" and put the phone down. Sometimes in the spook world it was necessary to waste an asset in order to protect another asset. He poured himself a gentle scotch and looked out the window at the rain sweeping down in sheets whilst reflecting on the inanities of life.

At that precise moment Peter Westbrooke was flying back to Britain himself on an official American government aircraft. It was imperative that Emma be debriefed thoroughly and the Strelnikov network unwound for the operation to be a success. The Americans for their part, had been superb. Their systems worked brilliantly, their actions swift and decisive and the ramifications of the information they had obtained far reaching. Child trafficking networks across the US, the Far East and Europe were being wrapped up with breath taking alacrity. Compromised politicians, lawyers, businessmen, academics and even scientists were being identified and dealt with. The president reckoned his Director, of Central Intelligence, was the flavour of the month. Little did he know. Emma's information confirmed the alternative intelligence suggesting that the other side would cause murder, mayhem and bloodshed involving over 12 000 incidents in over 200 US cities of which over 600 were unashamedly violent. All of it at a cost of nearly two billion dollars. In Portland, Oregon, an entire city block was taken over with disastrous consequences for the residents and local businesses. Within a month half a million taxpayers fled New York. In California and other western states massive conflagrations were deliberately set off by left wing arsonists. The FBI obtained a copy of the proposed blueprint for disrupting the elections, unsurprisingly titled "Preventing a Disrupted Presidential Election and Transition". On the president's orders it was carefully released to the American people. On the basis of her confirmatory intelligence more than 2 500 documents were released from the FinCen files of the US Financial Crimes Enforcement Network, a US government supervisory centre at the US Treasury revealing some of the international banking system's most lurid and shocking secrets. They revealed gigantic money laundering operations on what could only be described as a cosmic scale involving the dirty money proceeds of crimes such as drug dealing, corruption, fraud, racketeering and human trafficking. The documents involved over two trillion dollars worth of illegal transactions and proved how criminals could transfer their ill-gotten gains around the world. Of special interest to Peter was the fact that the many Russian oligarchs in London had manipulated a surprising number of prestigious City banks to avoid the very sanctions that were supposed to inhibit them from smuggling their loot into the West. The ramifications were deadly and far reaching. Despite the best efforts of the cabal, the Covid-19 crisis started to plateau with the help of the vaccines. Normality started to settle in, with sporadic ongoing interruptions, as the opposition sought to crash the value of the US dollar and collapse the NYSE. The president was running a strong election campaign for a return to power and the markets gradually recovered. Normality as it had been known might not return for a while, but it was, most assuredly, on the way.

Strelnikov was delighted when he heard the news of Emma's death. What should have worried him was what had subsequently happened to the Irish hit gang he had paid to do the job. It was not in Strelnikov's make up to worry about other people. He was a classic narcissist 'I, me and myself' were the mottos he lived by. He was proud of his ability to be ahead of the game and one up on the rest. He carried on with his life much as he had before until he learned that even his own intelligence contacts in the UK could not save him from the wrath of the free world. Two weeks after Emma's death he began to wind up his affairs in Britain. Thanks to the lockdown procedures he was forced to work from home. In the mornings he would venture out for a stroll on the prestigious Moor Park golf course adjacent to the Moor Park residential complex.

Early one morning just as the Prime Minister had announced the possible intensification of the lockdown procedures Igor was strolling on the Moor Park golf course near the tennis courts. It was a foggy morning, made slightly thicker, with the ground mist swirling over the immaculate fairways and greens. As he came up the deserted fairway a gentleman and his lady immaculately dressed in slacks and a tailored tweed jacket approached. The woman was dark and very attractive. She was holding a dog lead in her hand

and staring at the shrubbery. The man looked fit, even in his hounds-tooth jacket and cap. Almost too fit. Neither of them could be identified through their masked faces. Yet, Igor Strelnikov thought the woman looked vaguely familiar as if he had seen her somewhere before. The man nodded politely and passed by him. The woman stopped in front of Strelnikov and muttered something about a dog. He leaned forward to hear what she had to say. Without warning he felt a hand round his chest and felt blood oozing from his throat. The world went black, his knees buckled and John Price laid him gently on the ground under a bush in the copse. He wiped the commando knife on the lawn and slid it back up his sleeve.

"Vengeance is not necessarily always mine," he remarked to Stefanie as they walked off the course. "But in this case, the Lord has indeed made an exception."

She squeezed his hand tightly. "Thank you, darling. I had to see it myself." The two of them adjusted their masks over their faces and quietly left the fairway.

With his demise the Strelnikov Empire disintegrated like the morning mist before the sunshine on the Moor Park golf course.

CHAPTER 21

Roughly a week after the body of a prominent London-based Russian oligarch had been found on a leading local golf course, a quiet funeral took place in an obscure graveyard. He had been buried with few regrets.

Stefanie was making breakfast and John was packing for a return to the United States. He planned to resign from the Special Forces. Stefanie was still badly shaken by what had happened but she took strength from John's devotion and incredible support. Their marriage was a certainty. The landline telephone rang.

"Can you grab it darling, I'm struggling with these damned locks," he called.

Stefanie walked round the kitchen counter and lifted the phone off the hook.

"Westbrooke, hello?" There was a brief silence.

A distant tinny voice said, "Hello, is that you mum?"

Stefanie watched the room go round and round. A numbness shot from the base of her stomach to her neck and head. She croaked out, "Emma". She said it again in disbelief. Her imagination must be playing tricks with her mind. "Emma, is that really you?" She knew it couldn't be. Her stomach wanted to heave into her throat. She croaked out, "Please who is this?"

Another silence then, "It is me, mum, its Emma. Really and truly. I'm back, alive and safe. Can I come home? Please?"

John hearing Emma's name, shouted from the bedroom. "Who is it?"

"Sweet Jesus, it's Emma!" Stefanie choked out through tears. "I can't believe it."

"Good God, but how?" he said rushing through.

"We thought you were dead. I identified your things!"

"It's a long story mum. But they had to pretend I was dead to wrap up the human trafficking network and a lot more besides. I'll tell you when I see you. The girl you identified was a body double who died from a drug overdose. Oh, by the way two things, I was rescued at the gates where I was held, the gas man will get old in prison and do you remember Mohammed?"

"Yes....," Stefanie managed to choke out as she sank to her knees. Price put his arms around her and brought her back to her feet.

"He helped rescue me. He's here now. Can he bring me home, please?"

"Of course, my darling girl, of course."

"Thanks mum. See you in half an hour!"

Stefanie made to hang up.

A distant little voice added, "I love you." The line went dead.

GLOSSARY

AI	– Artificial Intelligence
ATC	– Air Traffic Control
BBC	– British Broadcasting Corporation
BSL	– Bio Safety Laboratory
CCTV	– Closed Circuit Television
CIA	– Central Intelligence Agency
CLA	– Career Limiting Action
CO	– Commanding Officer
DCIA	– Director Central Intelligence Agency
Deep State	– a covert cabal of state and non state actors playing a clandestine role in the democratic process
DNA	– hereditary genetic materiel in human beings and other living organisms
ELE	– Extinction Level Event
EW	– Electronic Warfare
GCHQ	– Government Communication Headquarters
GPMG	– General Purpose Machine Gun
HMG	– Her Majesty's Government
IED	– Improvised Explosive Device
IHT	– International Herald Tribune
IO	– Intelligence Officer
IRS	– Internal Revenue Service

KGB	– Committee for State Security in the former USSR
LSRV	– Landing Site Rendezvous
LUP	– Lie Up Point
MERS	– Middle Eastern Respiratory Syndrome
MOSSAD	– Israeli Secret Intelligence Service
NATO	– North Atlantic Treaty Organization
NBC	– Nuclear Chemical and Biological Warfare
NGA	– National Geospatial Agency
POTUS	– President of the United States
PRC	– People's Republic of China
RADA	– Royal Academy of Dramatic Art
R & D	– Research and Development
RAF	– Royal Air Force (UK)
ROTC	– Reserve Officer Training Corps
SARS	– Severe Acute Respiratory Syndrome
SAS	– Special Air Service (UK)
SATNAV	– Satellite Navigation
SEALS	– United States Navy Sea Air Land Teams special operations
UAE	– United Arab Emirates
UNESCO	– United Nations Educational Scientific and Cultural Organization
USN	– United States Navy
WHO	– World Health Organization

Printed in Great Britain
by Amazon